HARBOR

—————

BEARDS & BONDAGE

REBEKAH WEATHERSPOON

REBEKAH WEATHERSPOON PRESENTS

BOOKS BY REBEKAH

BEARDS & BONDAGE
Haven
Sanctuary
Harbor

COWBOYS OF CALIFORNIA
A Cowboy To Remember

LOOSE ENDS
Rafe: A Buff Male Nanny
Xeni: A Marriage of Inconvenience

THE FIT TRILOGY (And Friends)
Fit
Tamed
Sated
Wrapped

SUGAR BABY NOVELLAS
So Sweet
So Right
So For Real

VAMPIRE SORORITY SISTERS
Better Off Red
Blacker Than Blue
Soul To Keep

STAND ALONE TITLES
The Fling
At Her Feet
Treasure

PRAISE FOR REBEKAH'S WORK

A COWBOY TO REMEMBER

"In an anxious time, *A Cowboy to Remember* is a weighted blanket of a book." - Maureen Lee Lanker, Entertainment Weekly

RAFE

"'Rafe' is a breeze and a delight, a perfect book to read over and over again."- Jaime Green, The New York Times Review of Books

HAVEN

"...the perfect balance of sexiness, action and angst." - Alexa Martin, author of INTERCEPTED

SATED

"...I LOVED IT. The book was respectful of geeks, people with disabilities, people of color, and the BDSM community, and it was informative and entertaining, and it was funny." - Carrie S, *Smart Bitches Trashy Books*

TREASURE

"This story is rich yet beguiling, magnificent yet down to earth, and intriguing yet heartwarmingly human." – J.J., *Rainbow Book Reviews*

ABOUT THIS BOOK

Betrayed and set adrift...

Months before she's set to walk down the aisle, assistant district attorney Brooklyn Lewis suffers an unthinkable loss. It's bad enough her fiancé is violently taken from her, but along with her grief she must also process the fact that the man of her dreams was unfaithful. Friends and family want to see her heal, but Brooklyn doesn't know how to move on from the trauma and deception until she discovers she's not the only one broken by this tragedy.

A light in the storm...

Attorney Vaughn Coleman and his partner Chris Shaw have also lost the love of their lives, who was found lifeless in the same bed as Brooklyn's fiancé, taken from them by the same killer.

Unmoored by grief, Brooklyn, Chris, and Vaughn fall into a relationship that both fulfills them and threatens to pull them under the waves of guilt, but they soon realize it may take the love of three people to bring their battered ships back to shore.

This romance features a polyamorous relationship between two men and a woman, with BDSM overtones

While this is a stand-alone novel, I do recommend reading the previous books, Haven and Sanctuary, to provide more context for the supporting characters and Silas and Liz's farm.

CONTENT WARNING

Below you'll find just a few notes about the goings-on of this story. If you consider such warnings to be spoilers, please do skip ahead. xoxo - Rebekah

- Death of romantic partners before the start of the story
- Graphic Sex Scenes with BDSM elements
- Discussions of death.
- A sexually fluid adult with unsupportive parents.
- Conversations with the police.

DEDICATION

To everyone who had big plans for 2020. HA! Amirite?

ONE

Vaughn

They don't tell you what happens when you're not next of kin. There are so many ways for the authorities and the family to keep you in the dark when you and your partners don't put anything in writing. When you keep your declarations private, that privacy comes with consequences. It takes three days for me to find out that Corrine isn't just missing, she's dead. And then I have to tell Shaw.

I can't get the details my brain needs to paint the full picture and I'm not crazy enough to press her twenty-two-year-old brother for more information when he finally tells me why Corrine hasn't returned from her weekend trip with her girls. There had been no trip. Just another man and a motel off 93 North. Both she and the man she'd been with are gone now, shot to death in the bed they'd shared. The shooter has taken his own life in the very same room. That is all Nathan says when he calls to tell me Corrine isn't coming back to the apartment we share in Boston's Back Bay. That's all the information I have to give Shaw when I tell him we'll never see her again.

Now I'm sitting in the front seat of my Escalade as a few more mourners make their way up the short steps leading to her mother's home in Roxbury. I shouldn't be here. I never meant to come. That's what I tell myself. That's what I told Nathan when he told me to stay away. I just needed the address, because no matter how their mother feels about me or Shaw, Corrine Johnson was the love of our lives. Shaw and I weren't invited to the service, but I can't let this day pass, this moment, without at least trying to express my condolences to Corrine's family. I'd planned to send flowers, but I'd waited until the last minute to order them. Drinking myself stupid as I'd listened to Shaw fighting his tears through my cell's speaker function.

I found a florist nearby, thinking I'd drop them at the gravesite after the interment, but I don't know where they'd laid her to rest. I only have the address to the house. I think of the night, two years ago, the first time I stood at the bottom of those short steps, waiting for Mrs. Johnson to welcome us into her home. The four of us cramming our way into the front room. Taking her gracious offers for drinks, unable to ignore the way she was glancing between Shaw and I.

The sound of Corrine's nervous laugh when her mother finally came out with it and said, "So, which one of you is the boyfriend?"

Corrine had kept her eyes on her mother and her voice

steady. "Both of them, mommy. The three of us are together."

"Mrs. Johnson—" I started. But I didn't get much further. I am still sure her screech of "What?! No. Absolutely not!" could be heard for blocks. Corrine did her best to explain that she knew—we all knew—it was an unusual relationship, but the three of us were in love. Mrs. Johnson wasn't having it though, even when Shaw tried to tell her how much Corrine meant to him and how much I meant to the both of them. That had been her breaking point. Doesn't matter how grown or successful you are, you can only push a Black mother so far before she'll let you know exactly what you're *not* going to do. She didn't raise Corrine this way, she let us know. There were some colorful words I wanted to forget on the spot. Words that hurt Shaw in very specific ways, words that reminded him of the way his own father had rejected him.

She took turns passing the blame between him and me. Me for using the fact that I was a successful attorney as a distraction. And Shaw for, I don't know the fuck what. His obvious good looks that he must use to get whatever he wanted, from whoever he encountered, the Lord Jesus Christ's desires for his Earthly children be damned. Before long though, she concluded that we were both sexual deviants out to manipulate her beautiful, intelligent daughter who had nothing but the brightest future ahead of her. A future with darling children and a husband. One husband. There was no way in hell she'd be spending her time shacking up with two men. Men grown enough to know that what they were doing wasn't right.

She said all this thinking Corrine and I had met at a work event. She had no clue that we met at a rope bondage demonstration thrown by my former dungeon master. She didn't know that *Corrine* was the one who refused to be denied, the one who wanted Shaw and I both. All or nothing. But none of that mattered. We'd told her what was important. We loved each other. We wanted a future together, the three of us. Mrs. Johnson was not having it.

Corrine came to our defense and that's when I'd known it was time for me and Shaw to go. Corrine insisted on staying behind. "I fucked up," she said as she ushered us back down those short steps. "Let me talk to her alone. She'll come around."

Mrs. Johnson didn't come around. Ever. We won over her baby brother, Nathan, and her cousin, Justine. A few of her friends were on board when they saw how well we treated her and how happy she was. But Mrs. Johnson banned us from her home and all family functions. She told Corrine she didn't want to hear about us. She didn't want to see us. She wanted her daughter to want more for herself than fleeting erotic entanglements. Corrine's words. Not Mrs. Johnson's.

My mother overcompensated. Insisted that the three of us come to her when we needed motherly love. Shaw took her up on the offer, but Corrine was hesitant. "Your mom is so... she's a goddess," she told me. "I hope you don't expect me to live up to Lynetta Coleman. My beans and rice will never be that good," she joked. At least I thought she was joking at the time. While Shaw was calling her Lynetta as soon as my mom requested it, Corrine never fully warmed to my mom. She stayed overly polite like an intrusive guest afraid to overstay their welcome.

And now Corrine is gone, her last moments on this Earth spent in the arms of a man who isn't me or Shaw.

I've tried for days not to think of that motherfucker. What his name is, what he looks like, what it is about him that stopped Corrine from telling Shaw and me the truth. What did she need that we weren't giving her?

I let out a deep breath and tell myself to go home. Or better yet, call in for the rest of the week and go to Shaw's. Selfishly, I cut off the ignition and step out of my car, pulling my trench coat tight around my six-foot-six frame as I face the frigid February wind. There's no snow on the ground, but it's still cold as fuck. I grip the bouquet of white lilies and roses in my other hand as I make my way across the street. The front door opens before I step onto the opposite sidewalk and a Black dude around my age steps out on the tiny porch, tugging on his coat over a security guard uniform. Mrs. Johnson is right behind him.

She freezes as I approach the walkway.

"What in the hell are you doing here?"

"Auntie!" The guy calls out as she shoves him out of the way and marches toward me. Mrs. Johnson isn't a small woman, but most people are short beside me. I stand still, bracing myself for the next thing that will tumble out of her mouth. Out of the corner of my eye, I see Nathan coming out of the front door. I keep my focus on his mother as she storms down the walkway.

"Mrs. Johnson, I'm sorry to show up like this—"

"You damn right, you're sorry. With your sorry,

perverted ass. You really think you can show up here today, of all days. Like you're someone anyone in this family wants to see."

Just in time, I see her hand rearing back. Maybe I owe her the release of slapping the shit out of me, but I know the fire in her eyes. I'd only seen it once before when my aunt caught my uncle cheating. That sort of rage doesn't end with a slap. Mrs. Johnson wants to fight me. She's hurting in a way I'll never understand, burying her oldest child way before her time. I don't blame her. She swings at me as I lean back, avoiding the first blow. I step to the curb, knowing all I can do is retreat. She stops in her tracks, but she's still seething.

"You wanna bother someone? Go bother Josh Delinsky's family. He was just like you. All you bum-ass, no-good motherfuckers just wanted to use my baby girl. None of you wanted to make an honest woman out of her. Just take, take, and now my baby girl is gone. I hope you're happy, Vaughn. You selfish—" I miss the last word as she charges toward me again, even though her son and her nephew are now trying to get between us. Still doesn't make her message any less clear. All of this is my fault.

"Mommy," Nathan begs. "Stop."

"Everything okay here, folks?"

I turn to see two obvious cops in their matching black slacks and ill-fitting peacoats. The shorter of the two has a pathetic-looking bouquet of wildflowers in his hand. The taller one has a mustache that makes it clear he's down to violate all kinds of civil rights. He eyes me as his partner steps up on the sidewalk.

"My guy was just leaving," Corrine's cousin says, giving me that look, like 'no matter the situation, brotha to brotha, I don't want to deal with the cops right now.'

"What's your name son?" White-Supremacist Stache says like he's my dad's age and not a hot ten years older than me.

"I was just leaving," I say as I hand the flowers I have with me to Nathan. Before he can take them, Mrs. Johnson slaps them out of my hand.

"Get the fuck out of here and don't you ever come back."

"Why don't you take a quick walk with us?" The shorter one says, stepping between me and Mrs. Johnson. I glance at Nathan as he mouths an "I'm sorry." I glance at his cousin, who flicks his head in the direction of the street. He has no idea what the fuck is going on or who I am, but he's telling me it's time for me to go.

I turn and walk back across the street, the detectives following close behind.

"Nice ride," tall asshole says as I open my driver's side door. I look at them, wondering if they're going to climb in with me. Across the street, I see Nathan get Mrs. Johnson back up those short stairs and into the house. Security-guard cousin is still standing in the yard. He might be late for his shift, but he looks like he's sticking around to make sure I don't start anymore shit. Or to be a witness if I get beat to death by the cops, whichever comes first.

"What's your name?" Mustache asks again.

I bottle up the urge to flick my business card in his face

as a distraction while I choke the other cop out. "Vaughn Coleman."

"Vaughn Coleman! Just the man we were looking for."

"Why?"

"Well, Miss Johnson's little brother there—"

"What about him?" I don't want trouble with the law, but I don't want them bothering Nathan either.

"He was very helpful. And he told us that his sister had two boyfriends. One named Vaughn Coleman."

"That's me. How can I help you?"

"Well, this all felt open and shut, but we were looking into Miss Johnson and Mr. Delinsky a little more and it appears that our shooter, Ryan Morgan, had been sending Miss Johnson emails for some time. Emails about her relationships with various men."

I can feel the confusion hit my face as I scramble my brain trying to search for that name. "I don't know a Ryan Morgan. How did he know Corrine? She never mentioned him or any emails to me."

"Not sure, but it looks like he'd been stalking her for quite some time. Keeping tabs are her movements on and offline. We just thought we'd check with you, see if you knew anything about. What about this other boyfriend?"

"Pretty sure he doesn't know a Ryan Morgan either and he definitely would have mentioned a stalker if Corrine had said something. I didn't know her killer's name until you just told me. I didn't know the name of the guy she was with until today either. I didn't even know she was cheating before this all went down."

"You're saying this is how you found out?"

I nod, swallowing the pain and the anger that's rising in my chest again. "I thought she was with her friends for the weekend. Her friend Autumn's fortieth-birthday getaway."

"Tough pill to swallow."

"Is there anything else? 'Cause I should go."

"That's a good idea. Doesn't look like Mrs. Johnson wants you anywhere near here. Care to tell us why that is?"

I swallow and push my glasses back up my nose. "In a perfect world, every family would get along with every significant other."

"The Johnsons seem like great people. Mrs. Johnson is a saint. Any reason why they wouldn't like you?"

"You'll have to ask her." I know the woman is upset, but I also know she doesn't really think I would want any harm to come to her daughter. And neither would Shaw.

"You live close by?"

"Back Bay."

"Oh, okay. Well, stick around town. We might want to talk to you again. Stalking adds a different element to a murder. So does hiring a hitman. Especially a young one." More confusion clouds my face. How the fuck old was Ryan Morgan?

"How young and what are you talking about a hitman?"

"Eighteen," The short one chimes in.

"Ryan Morgan was eighteen? An eighteen-year-old did this?"

"An eighteen-year-old who's been pretty interested in Corrine Johnson and her love life and you for some time. He was really keeping tabs on her, which seems pretty strange. Would make more sense if a jealous lover put him up to it."

"Why didn't you tell me this sooner?" I ask. I know why. Nathan probably waited until the last minute to tell his mother he knew Corrine was still seeing us. He probably waited 'til the last minute to tell the cops Shaw and I existed.

"We didn't know about you, Mr. Coleman. We just discovered the emails ourselves. Did you get any suspicious emails about you and Miss Johnson?"

I wrack my brain, trying to think of anything, but nothing comes to mind. "No."

"Well, we might have some more questions for you. What's the best way for us to contact you?"

"Just reaching for my business card," I tell them before I even slip my hand into my breast pocket. "Do you mind telling me your names?" I ask. Wouldn't hurt to look into these two jerk-offs myself.

"Where are our manners? I'm Detective Catan and this is Detective Jansen," the short one says, as Jansen studies my business card.

"What kind of mother wouldn't want her daughter to date a... patent attorney? Sounds fancy. Explains the car."

I take my keys out of my pocket, ready to end this fucking conversation already.

"We'll be in touch," Catan says with a nod of his head. I just nod and climb into my car. I slowly pull away from the curb as they step back, watching me like I'm the killer they've been looking for this whole time. I catch Security-guard Cousin watching me in my mirror as I turn down the street. When they are out of sight, I realize how fucking hard my heart is beating.

I pull into the first Dunkins I see and try to calm the hell down. It doesn't work. Who the fuck is Ryan Morgan? Who the fuck is Josh Delinksy? And why...

I stop myself from asking that question. There's nothing I can do about this now. My phone chiming in my pocket snaps me out of it. I check it and see a text from Nathan.

I told you not to come.

I know. I'm sorry.

Let's talk soon.
Just not now.

Okay, man.
Sorry.

I toss my phone on the passenger seat and slam my head against the headrest. This is all too fucking much. My girl is dead. My girl was cheating on me and Shaw. She had a stalker that she never mentioned to me or Shaw. An eighteen year old stalker who was the one to pull the trigger and her mother thinks this is all my fault. I open my eyes, trying to blink back rage-filled tears. I don't blame her. I would have married Corrine. I would have given her children. I would have done anything for her. And I knew down to the bottom of my soul that Shaw would have done the same.

We checked in with her constantly. She was the center of our world.

Clearly Mrs. Johnson was right about something. Clearly I dropped the ball somewhere. I fucked something up, did something to make my Corrine turn to this Josh Delinksy dude. I did something that made her feel like she couldn't tell us she had a damn stalker. Whatever fantasy world Shaw and I were living in, Corrine wasn't there with us. How the hell do I explain any of this to Shaw? How do I tell him that we were somehow the last to know?

I know I need to take a step back and process this new information without the what ifs. I need to grieve. I need to take care of Shaw. I need to let Shaw take care of me in the way only he can. I need to work through more than one level of heartbreak. I need to chill the fuck out before the detectives start to think I really did have something to do with this. Or worse.

But first I need more information. I need to know more about Ryan Morgan and those emails. And I need to know everything about Josh Delinsky.

TWO

Brooklyn

I should have stayed my ass at home.

When they found my fiancé's body—and the body of the woman he was fucking while he was supposed to be on a snowboarding trip to Vermont—I had about twenty minutes to process the news before I had to decide whether or not I was going to nope the fuck out of this whole situation. I saw it, the complete nervous breakdown that's still waiting for me. I saw the moment Josh and I met at a birthday party in Brooklyn. The moment he asked me out. The moment I decided to give this cute white boy who seemed to be the only decent human working on Wall Street a chance.

That moment. That stupid moment, I actually worried what his family would think of me as we drove up to New

Hampshire. Would they want their son with an orphan-turned-special-victims A.D.A. from the Bronx? What would they think of their son wanting to make a life and possibly have children with a Black woman? I had my come-to-Jesus moment. Talked to my sister about her own husband and the trauma of not having a father to walk us down the aisle. Or a mother to become a full pain in the ass while shopping for dresses.

I saw the moment when I realized it was going to be okay because his parents are cool. Total hippie, sci-fi geeks who just want to nerd out and have a good time. One sister, Kelsey, is an Instagram model, who is even more beautiful in person. The other, Meredith, is a tree-hugging, animal rights activist that just wants to know that I care about climate change. I do. I'm more confused about how their financial analyst brother came from such earthy folk. They are proud of Josh. They love him and in nearly no time, they loved me too.

Pattie started to call me her daughter as we were getting closer to the big day. George asked for my opinions for proper Thanksgiving sides. Kelsey and Meredith added me to our own group chat. They are actually pretty good with the memes. None of it is what teen me pictured for in-laws, mostly because I'm not on a yacht being fed grapes by Omar Epps, but I saw that moment. I took a step back, let that deep breath in and accepted the fact that Josh loved me. We were going to get married in the late Spring on my sister's farm and eventually we were going to have kids. And maybe a cute dog.

But none of that is going to happen 'cause as it turns out this motherfucker was cheating on me. Me. Brooklyn Lewis. The baddest bitch from the Boogie Down Bronx and I can't even take this giant diamond ring off my finger and throw it in his face, because he's dead.

"Brooklyn?"

I look up at the sound of Pattie's voice. I force a semblance of a smile as I walk to the other side of the grave site. Mourners are starting to disperse. There will be food at his grandmother's house and more small talk and condolences than I can stand. I should have stayed home. I considered it, but every time I tried to make the call, or worse, send the text, I'd hear Pattie's voice. I'd hear her voice breaking when she finally called me back after I called her twenty times 'cause I couldn't find my fucking fiancé. I'd hear the way she fell apart when she told me he was gone.

She's standing near the edge of the canopy with an older white woman with curly salt-and-pepper hair and tortoise-shell glasses. She's holding the hand of a younger man. Pattie waves me over.

"This is Josh's best friend, John Dipper, and his mom, Lori."

Lori takes my hand. The gesture is overly familiar, even for this moment of communal grieving and it pisses me off even more as I realize who her son is.

"The Dipper?" I ask. He swallows and nods. "He told me he was with you." The second the words are out of my mouth, I want to regret them, for Pattie's sake, but it's been a long couple of weeks. It's been a painful twenty-four hours, pretending I'm not crying for my own awful reason that no one but Josh's sister Kelsey even pretends to understand. I don't want to take it back. Especially with the way John is looking at me. There's something he's not saying.

"I know. I—"

"You know?"

The blood drains from John's face. Phew boy, do I want to know what the hell he's thinking. I dredge up the smile I only use for that asshole Judge Benson and every ounce of home training I have left in my body.

"Lori and John. It was so nice to meet you. If you'll excuse me." I know I shouldn't, but I turn and walk away. I'm not going to stand there next to Josh's fucking mother and let his childhood best friend tell me to my face that he knew Josh was cheating. I make it halfway down the long incline that brings you back to the cemetery drive before I hear John calling my name. Of course he's done the stupid thing and chased after me.

"Brook! Wait up!"

I turn on Dipper and try my best to light him on fire with my eyes. "Please. Go back and tell Pattie how sorry you are."

"I—"

"I mean it. I know Josh was your friend. Pattie needs this right now, your comfort and your condolences. But I don't."

"'Kay. For what it's worth, I told him to stop. Pattie couldn't stop talking about you and my mom couldn't stop talking about the wedding. I never met this Corrine chick." Hearing her name makes my eyelid twitch. "But I told him to stop and I told him to stop using me as a cover. He was blowing me off to hang out with her too."

"For how long?"

John swallows. That tells me what I need to know. "Seven months." I do the mental math. Right after he proposed.

"I appreciate that. Thank you." I have nothing else to say. I need to process this shit and I can't do it around Josh's people. People who love him and knew he was cheating on me and... I let the air between me and John grow extra frosty and when he still doesn't take the hint, I turn and start making my way to a small copse of trees breaking up the expanse of green and headstones. I can't hide, but I can't participate in this at the moment.

I rethink leaning against the trunk of a sturdy pine tree as I take my phone out of my pocket. I pull up my text conversation with my sister, then rethink all of that. Liz is the best, but if I thought she was busy when she had one kid, two have eaten up all her time. Between her husband, the demands of their whole ass farm, Liz's bakery and settling in with a new baby, I'd be lucky to hear back from her within a few hours. I open my group chat, which Liz will get to later, and start to type. Something catches my eye.

A man.

A tall-as-fuck Black man with hair shaved close to his head, the beginnings of a full beard and glasses. There's a hint of authority about him, but he's not a cop. I know cops. He doesn't have that *way* about him. Also, cops don't wear glasses. I saw him earlier, when we first arrived at the cemetery, but I figured he was here to visit a loved one. I'm wrong. He's here for this. Or to check all of this out.

This dude does not blend in. Still, I'm almost positive that's the last thing he's trying to do. I watch him standing in the road next to the row of town cars. Josh's uncle is heading back to his car and I see him stare at the man. We're in the middle of New Hampshire and I'm the only other Black person here. This dude is gonna draw more attention the more people start to leave. I know I should go back over to Pattie, but I don't.

I walk down the small incline and cross the road. He watches me the whole way and for some reason I feel like he's here for me. As I get closer, I see that he's not just tall. He's fine as fuck, not that that matters. He's also dressed way better than a cop. His dark wool coat is tailored to perfection.

"Are you looking for someone?" I ask him. He's looking at me intently. I know what he sees. I'm plus size by definition, but my overall appearance isn't what grabs the attention. My breasts are fighting to get out of my coat. My nickname's been Big Boobie Brook since the sixth grade. Most people notice, not just men.

"I'm sorry to show up like this. Is this the service for Josh Delinsky?" he asks.

"Yup."

His eyebrow arches at my flippant tone. I should have kept my ass home.

"I—uh, I'm looking for Brooklyn Lewis."

"You found her. You have more bad news for me?"

He holds out his hand for me to shake, like we weren't

standing a few feet from a hearse. I know nothing about this man, but I want to know why he seems so hesitant, like he didn't just come looking for me at a funeral. Something like that takes confidence. "I'm Vaughn Coleman. My partner was Corrine Johnson. She was with—"

"I know. I know who she is. Or was. I'm sorry you lost your business partner. This isn't the best time though. Maybe later this week—"

"No. Not my business partner. She was my *partner*. She was... mine."

"Oh. Oh!" I blink, hard, the reality of what he's saying dawning on me. I scoff and stop myself before I smear my eye shadow. The only thing I can do is breathe. I glance over my shoulder and see that Pattie and George seem to be wrapping things up with friends, family and well-wishers. Meredith has found those same pine trees. She's dashing her own tears away as she looks at her phone. There's more. Hours more. I have to keep it together to get through this and then I can fall apart. Then I can deal with Vaughn Coleman. Another deep breath. "Okay."

"I know I shouldn't have come. Her family didn't want me at her funeral. Showing up at her lover's funeral is probably the definition of bad form."

"Well, I just met the guy who was covering for them if you wanna talk about bad form." He looks over my head and I consider pointing John Dipper out to him. Let Vaughn Coleman give him a piece of his mind, maybe a fist to the face, but I don't. "I should get back."

"Right."

"But I do want to talk to you. This is some completely

wild Random Hearts shit and you might be the only one who understands how fucked up it is that I decided to even come to this funeral. We won't talk about the fact that I'm still wearing that asshole's ring. We should definitely talk."

"There's someone else. My other partner, Shaw."

My heart drops. How many people was Josh fucking? "Excuse me?"

He swallows, then straightens his shoulders. "Corrine was in a long term, polyamorous relationship with me and another man, Christopher Shaw. We both loved her very much."

"Wow. Okay. Yeah, I can't do this right now." My vision blurs for a moment, but something in me refuses to pass out. Vaughn reaches out and takes my elbow. His touch brings things back into focus.

"You okay?"

"Yeah. Yeah."

"Here. You can text me at that bottom number." He hands me a business card. I take it.

Vaughn Coleman
Leeds, Parker & Coleman
Patents | Trademarks | Litigation.
Boston, MA.

"You drove up here from Boston?"

"Yeah. I need to talk to you." I hear it then in his voice. He needs exactly what I need. And he's hoping I'm the one who can give it to him.

"Okay, thanks. You should go."

He nods with a tight smile before he turns and walks back to the black Escalade parked near the cemetery gates.

"Who was that, honey?" I turn as Pattie comes up beside me. A wave of exhaustion hits me then. I'm so sick of being polite. I miss my parents. I miss my mom. I miss my sister and my friends. I see that moment again, a moment that almost was, the moment where Josh's people nearly became my people. But they aren't my people, because my people would know how unfair this is for me. My people would have given me options instead of insisting I come to the service to keep up the lie. To tell them that Josh did nothing wrong because, even in death shrouded in infidelity, I forgive him. My people wouldn't look at me with big watery eyes and tell me to keep wearing my ring.

"Oh, it was no one," I say. "He was here to visit someone, but he's going to come back."

"We're gonna head back to Josh's Nana and Pop-pop's house."

"'Kay." I follow her back to the family limo. As we drive back down the pine-covered road toward Josh's grandparents' house, I make up my mind. I never want to see the Delinskys again.

I groan as I hike Iona higher in my arms. It's only been three weeks since I last saw my sister and her family, but this little one is growing faster than a weed. "What are you feeding this kid?"

"Only the finest breast milk, but don't look at me. That

is pure bone density. Blame her big-ass father. Why didn't I marry a short man?" Liz says, letting out a fake cry as she turns off the sink. My sister got all the tall genes our dad's side had to offer. She's five eleven and I feel short beside her at five eight. Her husband is six five and built like a broadside of one of their barns. Small children were not in the cards for them, but damn.

"Some woman asked me if Palila was in the second grade the other day. Puberty is going to be hell for her," Liz sighs.

"No one better to help her through it."

"True. So?"

"So." It's been a month. I'm back at work, in body and mind at least. Being the District Attorney's Special Victims Bureau Chief for the Bronx gives me plenty to keep me busy, but my heart is still broken. I won't say that out loud though. I refuse. Josh doesn't deserve it. Whenever I can, I leave the city. Friends don't know what to do with me and I don't know how to react to them.

I don't want to just sit in my apartment alone, so I go upstate in the car that Josh taught me how to drive after I kept complaining about how annoying it is to close the ninety-minute distance between myself and my sister and her husband's apple farm. I thought my sister was crazy for leaving Manhattan behind, but after her life was almost taken away thanks to an honest-to-god hit attempt in her own apartment, I can see why things were never the same.

It doesn't hurt that she found a hunky farmer to love the hell out of her. I've never seen my sister so happy. She leans against the counter and gives in to her urge to coo at her baby girl for a few moments before her smile fades and she fixes her gaze on me.

"Talk to me. What's going on?"

"Nothing. I'm just pissed."

"And you have every right to be."

"Pattie keeps texting me. She invited me to lunch tomorrow with her and Meredith. I get it, she lost her son but—"

"He was cheating on you."

I rap my knuckles, hard, on the kitchen table. "Am I dumb?"

"What? No!"

I bite my lip and hold Iona a little closer. I'm so tired of crying. "You know how they met?"

"Did you find out?"

"Yeah. I talked to the detectives again. Ugh, I think they know I had nothing to do with this."

"Clearly they don't know you, 'cause if you found out Josh was cheating on you before all of this—"

"I would have killed him myself."

"Look, it's two different things. It's two different, horrible things. You lost someone you love. Okay, three things. You lost someone you love. You found out something horrible about that person in the process and now you don't get a chance to confront him about it. It's painful and it's unfair as hell."

"Four things. His family somehow wants me to be over it so I can emotionally support them through their grief." Almost on cue, my phone chimes in my purse. "Can you grab that for me?"

Liz grabs it, immediately shaking her head. "It's Kelsey."

"See?"

"You want me to text her back?"

"No. I feel like—I feel like they knew."

"That he was cheating?"

"No. I feel like they knew he was kind of shitty and they liked me so much they didn't tell me or tell him to get it together. Like when his buddy John just came out and said he'd told him to do right by me, it's like, you know. You know what someone you've known their whole life is like. You know what they are capable of."

"Maybe they thought he'd changed."

"But that feels so unfair to me."

"It is."

"Right? I should have been given the chance to make the decision. I feel robbed. I said yes to someone I thought was faithful. Actually, let me back it up. Faithfulness never crossed my mind. That's how duped I feel. I never for one second even considered that Josh cheating on me was in the wheel of possibility. I'm sitting here, not processing the fact that he's gone. I'm just not. Can I be honest and say that?"

"Of course you can. Brook, you remember what it was like to lose Mom and Dad."

"Yeah." That cruel, specific pain blooms in my chest again. Almost twenty years and it still hurts like hell. "Am I a bitch if I tell these people to leave me alone?"

Liz shakes her head and gives it to me straight. "No, not if you don't want to continue a relationship with them, but I would maybe be a little nicer about it. His parents are pretty chill people. His dad, at least."

"I don't know," I say as a tear escapes. I dash it away and give Iona some gentle pats down her back. I don't know how I feel about the Delinskys. I can't look at them the same way. I don't know them well enough to fight for something with them and I don't like the way Pattie and the girls are making me feel, like we're all in the same boat. We're not. I'm in a completely different marina. I need time to heal. I need time and space to be angry and I need time and space to beat myself up for missing Josh. For missing him so fucking much.

My chest hurts so bad. I stand and hand over Iona. "Take your adorable-ass baby."

"She is pretty damn cute, isn't she?" Liz says, her eyes filled with love.

"I stopped myself from looking her up again."

Liz's expression sobers. She knows who I'm talking about. The other ghost in the room that Pattie and the rest of Josh's family seemed hell bent on ignoring. That night, after we put Josh in the ground, after Vaughn Coleman appeared out of nowhere, I finally looked her up. Corrine Johnson. I was shocked I hadn't done it already.

I'd already asked the detectives to to fill me in on every detail. Put on my A.D.A. hat and grilled them right back after they'd found Ryan Morgan's emails. Looked into Ryan Morgan's background and learned he'd been in and out of foster care until his aunt took him and his younger brother in. Saw proof that he'd found Corrine's private photos on some 4chan-style message board and decided she was the one for him. I wanted to know what had happened and, in that process, I started to fixate on Corrine Johnson.

What was it about her that my husband-to-be and a stalker found so interesting? It's fucked up. I know. She didn't deserve this. But she didn't deserve my happiness either. She's a lawyer too. Or she was. Family law. I try not to laugh at that idea. I find her Instagram. I fixate on her face. She's pretty. Black as well and thick too, like me. That bothers me. Josh has a type, which he'd never mentioned. Not that it should have mattered, but it did matter, because he lied and cheated and all of that got him killed. I think of Vaughn and then try not to think about Vaughn. I haven't reached out to him. I don't know what to say.

"What are you looking for?" Liz asks. "Why go digging her life up?"

"I don't know. A reason? My brain wants to make sense of it," I say, leaving out the part where I have fake conversations with Corrine where I ask her why. Where I ask her about Vaughn and Christopher. Then I ask her why again. I think about my life, my career. How I'd started researching how to freeze my eggs 'cause I can't leave it to just Liz to carry on the Lewis name and our spectacular racks. And then the moment happened. The moment where I met a cute white boy with this great apartment uptown who apparently didn't think I was enough.

"I think you should talk to someone," Liz says. She's found a great therapist online. I know she'd help me find one too.

"I know, but I'm not ready. I need to be honest with someone and I'm not there yet."

"Just promise me you'll keep talking to me."

"I will. I should get going." The days are getting longer

again, but I don't want to rush back to the city after dark. I still hate driving. I kiss my sister and her baby goodbye. Tell her to send my love to Silas and Palila. I climb up into my big-body Tahoe. I need to see the road, so I refuse to drive anything small. Before I pull out of the farm, I dig Vaughn Coleman's card out of my wallet and I text him.

THREE

Vaughn

I'd offered to drive down to New York and then I'd offered to at least meet Brooklyn Lewis in New Haven or Hartford, but she insisted on coming to me. A little over a month has passed since that day in the cemetery. I knew I'd overstepped. Actually I'd polevaulted over a wall of none-of-my-business, but for some stupid reason I'd thought Brooklyn would reach out to me within a few days. I knew she had questions and I was eager to know what answers she might have for me and Shaw. But nothing. Not a word. Not for a month. Then last Sunday evening, a New York area code lit up my phone. She was forward and direct. She wanted to know if we could talk that following weekend. She preferred to speak in person.

I was just about to leave Shaw's place in Barnstable when her text popped up on my phone. It only took a few minutes for us to figure out the details. And now we are riding up to the tenth floor of the Sheraton Downtown Boston.

I'd extended the offer for us to meet wherever was most convenient for her. She'd suggested her hotel room.

"I think we need to speak in private, but I'd feel more comfortable if you came to me," she'd said. "You seem chill, but not chill enough for me to go to a stranger's apartment." There was no reason to argue.

I look across the glass-and-steel elevator as it stops on the fifth floor. The woman beside me smiles like she notices the tension between Shaw and me when the four of us all climb into the tiny space together. She and the man with her take their rolling bags, heading off to their rooms. The doors slide shut and we're rising again. I glance over at Shaw. He's pissed. He's doing everything to avoid eye contact with me. He's been like this since he arrived at my place a few hours ago and decided blasting the Celtics game was preferable to telling me how the rest of his week had gone. I get that he wants me to leave this alone, but I still want answers. And I know deep down he wants them too.

"Say it before we get up there," I urge.

"Fine." He looks up at me, his tongue rolling over his molars. "This is a bad idea."

"You mentioned that."

"Yeah, but I just wanna go on record, so you know and I know that this is a bad idea. When this blows up in our faces and the detectives show up again and tell us to stop tampering with witnesses or some shit—"

"She's not a witness. And they said the case is closed."

The detectives interviewed me and Shaw, but soon after they dropped it. I honestly had no clue who Ryan Morgan was and no idea why he would stalk Corrine or mention me in his stalking and the detectives couldn't find any clear reason either. It turned out Corrine had never even seen Ryan Morgan's emails. The day he decided to take her from us, the hundreds of messages he'd sent were gathering digital dust in the spam box of an old email Corrine had linked to her barely used Facebook account.

Talking to Brooklyn Lewis about it after the fact wouldn't land any of us in hot water with the police. Unless she'd hired Ryan Morgan, which was extremely unlikely. Talking to her wouldn't impact a case the cops had already moved on from. For them it's over. For us...

We stop at the twelfth floor and the doors open. Shaw doesn't move to exit the elevator. He's still looking at the floor. I put my hand out to stop the doors from closing.

"You wanna leave?" I ask.

Shaw is quiet for a moment, but as his expression softens the slightest bit, I know his answer.

"We're already here," I say. "You can meet her and if I'm not feeling any part of this, we'll leave."

"And if this whole meet and greet starts fucking you up, I'm pulling you out." Shaw and I have been grieving in our own ways. He's shed his tears, but he's said almost nothing. Still, I know he's hurting. He steps past me and I take hold of the back of his neck as we walk down the hall. He's tense as fuck and not from bending over his workbench all after-noon. He stops suddenly, rolling his neck into my grip as he looks up at me.

"I just need a second." He closes his eyes, his long lashes touching his skin. I pull him closer and brush my lips over his brow. His arms wrap around my back and I feel a shuddered breath roll through him.

"We can go. I can tell her I'll meet with her tomorrow. You don't have to do this."

"No." He releases me and lets out a deep breath. He's fighting like hell to hold back some completely appropriate tears and this time he wins. "Come on."

We continue down the hall and turn two corners before we arrive at her suite. I see Brooklyn Lewis just outside her doorway, tipping a young waiter. She's wearing a long-sleeved, black and teal, silk sleep shirt and nothing else. Even her feet are bare.

"Hey," she says, her voice oddly cheerful. "Come on in."

We follow her into the suite. There's a covered platter of food on the table along with a bottle of Chardonnay and three wine glasses. "I didn't eat on the road. Hope you don't mind."

"Not at all," I say.

"And I just got the extra glasses to be polite. I'm gonna fuck up that whole bottle."

I hold back a snort and incline my head toward her. "If there was ever a time to drink, it's now. This is Shaw. Christopher Shaw. Shaw, Brooklyn Lewis."

"Nice to meet you," Brooklyn says as she shakes his hand.

"You too."

"You guys make yourself comfortable," she says as she goes ahead and starts to fill all the wine glasses anyway.

"None for me," I say, but Shaw takes a glass with a quiet thank you.

"How was traffic getting over here?" she asks.

"You want to talk about the traffic?" Shaw says.

"Oh?" I watch her as her neck snaps back in surprise. "Okay." She sets down her glass and slides easily into a seat at the small dining table. I watch as she pulls her leg up so she can perch her foot on the seat as well. Her whole thigh is exposed now as well as the teal silk underwear she has on. She glances over at me before she turns her attention back to Shaw. "We'll skip the small talk then. Let's get right to it. I have my questions, but you're my guests. So please, I'll eat while you grill me."

She pulls the cover off her platter and the monster cheeseburger waiting for her makes her stomach growl. She doesn't seem embarrassed though. She just grabs her knife and cuts the thing in half before digging in. I take a seat in the armchair by the window and take in the way Shaw is watching her.

"We didn't come here to grill you," I finally say. The sound of my voice releases the tension in Shaw's shoulders. He sets down his wine glass and takes a seat on the firm sofa in the middle of the room.

"I'm sorry, Brooklyn," he says, sounding more like himself. Shaw's a prick in his own way. Still, all puffed up with women he's just met isn't really his style.

"It's okay. I've had to stop myself from cussing my boss out like every day. I get the short fuse. This is bullshit and no one understands why. Or even if they do, it's like they are trying to comfort you with a rake."

Shaw chuckles and reaches for his wine again. I watch him take a deep sip before he lets out a breath. His shoulders finally relax.

"I have to say, you two are quite the pair." She nods toward me before nodding in Shaw's direction. "A tall-slim and a swole for no reason. I mean, Josh was cute, but I don't know that I would have given him the time of day with the two of you around. How'd this all come together?"

"How'd we meet?" I ask for clarification.

She nods, her mouth full of burger.

"At a party for a shared client, actually. A scientist from the Cape."

"Kind of an awkward guy. Not a lot of friends," Shaw adds. "He invited his lawyer and his carpenter—"

"You're a carpenter?" Brooklyn asks.

"He's quite the craftsman," I say. Shaw's work speaks for itself. He likes to let it do the talking. In public, I like to brag for him.

"That's cool. What's, like, your speciality? I know shit about woodcrafting or carpentry."

"I mostly make furniture and some custom pieces for wealthy people who like to tell their friends how much they spent on a custom piece of furniture," Shaw says truthfully. He's made a name for himself through high-priced word of mouth. It's given him the financial freedom and independence he wanted his whole life.

Brooklyn laughs into the back of her hand before she washes down her food with another sip of wine. "Rich people do like to brag about their custom shit. That's awesome. You on the Gram? I'd love to see your work."

"Yeah," Shaw nods. "I'll show you."

"But we're not here to talk about furniture are we? Or are we?"

"I mean, I'd rather talk about our recently murdered partners and how they were cheating on us, but furniture is cool too." Shaw takes out his phone, crosses the room and hands it to Brooklyn. She looks at his screen, cocking her head to the side.

"Salted Sea Customs. Oh, this is beautiful." She hands back the phone.

"Thanks," Shaw says before he heads back to the couch.

"Okay, so yeah. Josh Delinksy. Corrine Johnson. The ultimate betrayal, a brutal double-murder and suicide, and absolutely no way to deal with it." Brooklyn sighs and sits back. I ignore the way her legs part, showing off the gentle impression of her labia against her underwear.

"How did you and Josh meet?" I ask.

"Oh, it's pretty boring. We met at a birthday party, found out we had some college friends in common. Dated, got engaged. Then somewhere in there, there was another woman and four shots at close range. And here we are! I'm not surprised he cheated on me, now that I look back on it. Actually..." Her gaze cuts to me, a sudden look of determination touching her features. "That's the pain talking. I'm the shit and I have no idea why he cheated on me."

"I know why Corrine cheated," Shaw says suddenly, almost to himself.

"You do?" I say, trying to keep my voice measured. Why didn't he tell me this sooner?

"The last time I saw her, before she went on her

supposed girls trips, she made a joke. Something about how she needed a break to recharge. A break from us." He considers his wine glass for a moment before he looks over at Brooklyn. "We met her at a rope bondage exhibition. She was..." Shaw doesn't finish, but I know what he wants to say. That she was wild. Insatiable. That she wanted everything she could handle and more. She wanted us and just us. Or so we thought.

"I wanted to ask you guys about her," Brooklyn says. "I thought knowing more about her, it would help, but I'm not sure it will. Knowing anything about her won't turn back time."

"What will help?" I ask her.

"I guess, knowing that you guys are—not hurt, I don't want you to be hurting—but I want to know that you're as pissed as I am."

"I'm pissed," Shaw admits with a shrug.

"There we go. Now we're talking. Let it out!"

Shaw smirks as he goes on. We've been talking, but not as much as we usually do. I hate to think there are things he can't tell me, but sometimes you need a neutral third party to open certain doors.

"When we got together, Vaughn went out of his way to make sure that all three of us were not only comfortable, but happy. Vaughn went out of his way to listen. If she wanted out she could have said so."

"My friend's therapist says cheating isn't about wanting out," Brooklyn says. "It's about wanting it all."

"Huh," I grunt in agreement. "That might be the only thing about this that makes sense."

"Still makes me feel like shit." Brooklyn wipes her hands on her napkin, then reaches for her phone. "You wanna see my wedding dress?" She crosses the room this time and shows Shaw the photo on her screen before she comes over to me. I try not to notice the way she walks or how lush her thighs look barely covered by her silk night-shirt. I can't ignore the way her nipples are brushing through the smooth fabric.

I look toward her phone as she nearly steps between my legs. I take the device and zoom in on the picture of her standing in the bridal shop mirror. I know plenty about custom men's clothing, but I don't know a damn thing about wedding dresses. That doesn't change the fact that Brooklyn Lewis looks stunning in white.

"I paid out the ass to get the alterations just perfect. It's impossible to get any kind of a refund on a custom wedding dress."

"When was the ceremony supposed to be?" I ask.

"In two months. I actually had someone ask me if it was cancelled. Tough to get married when your groom is dead."

"I'm sorry," I say as I hand back her phone.

She gives me a tight smile. "It is what it is." She crosses the room and sits back down in front of her food. The bold confidence she's been showing off since I met her in the cemetery seems to suddenly fade.

"What are you thinking about?" Shaw asks her.

"I don't know. It's not a new revelation or anything, it just shocks me every time I think about it. No one has let me deal with this the way I want to deal with it yet. Well, not no one. My sister and my close friends have been great, but there's still this, this wall. It's like a comfort barricade or something. Of course, no one knows what to say when someone dies and it turns out they were cheating, but everyone seems to expect to only want to hear certain things from me.

"And that doesn't even include Josh's family, who I'm considering completely cutting off because somehow I've been their emotional rock and being the emotional rock for white people in this situation is about as fucked up as it sounds."

"I think we're having the opposite problem. Or an adjacent problem," I say.

"What's that?"

"Corrine's family hates us and they banned us from the funeral," Shaw responds.

"Why do they hate you?"

"Would your mother want you entering a full-time relationship with two men, especially if she thinks it's just about sex?"

"Well, my mom's dead."

"Oh, I'm sorry. I—"

"Thank you, it's okay. And I'm not sure. I think she'd be more concerned about whether or not I was happy and my needs were being met. And if she liked the two guys."

"Yeah, we never got that far." Shaw sighs and leans back across the firm couch cushions.

"I'm sorry to hear that. We've known each other five seconds, but I like to hope that you treated her well. I have not enjoyed dealing with Josh's family, but I think it would hurt way more if they shut me out. What would help you two? What would help you grieve?" She suddenly laughs. "I didn't think this conversation would go this way, but whatever. Tell me what you need."

"I don't know," Shaw says and I know he's telling the truth. He's hurting, but we both know there is no good way to get through this, the grief and the betrayal all wrapped up together. There's no easy answer.

"I just want to see him smile again," I say honestly. I can handle deep pits of my own personal hell, but I can't stand to see Shaw hurting like this. I love him too much. He won't look at me now because he knows that.

"You like titties, Chris?" Brooklyn suddenly says. "I can flash you. I'll show these titties and put a smile right on that face."

"Wow," Shaw said, a laugh rumbling up from his chest. A genuine smile touching his face.

"See Vaughn, you just gotta shock him into it. Next time he's sulking, slap him in the face with your dick. Perk him right up," Brooklyn teased with a wink.

"I can see why his family is leaning on you," I say.

"Oh, I know. I was cursed with a warm, caring personality and an amazing sense of humor. Brings all the boys to the yard. Makes it impossible for them to see you as a person while they are busy basking in your glow. Thought Josh was different, but I was wrong."

The words tumble so easily for her and I can tell she's said them before, but maybe not to the people who need to hear them most. Brooklyn Lewis has a way about her, that's for sure.

"What do you need?" I ask her.

"Not sure if I'm ready to admit that to you yet, Vaughn. This is also why *I* can't go to a therapist and I'm getting secondhand tips from my friends."

"Why?" Shaw asks.

"I'm bottled up too tight. Don't get me wrong, I'm in touch with my feelings. I know everything that's going on inside. The why and the how and how it tastes and how it smells. But I can't articulate it."

"Why?" Shaw asks again, with more tenderness this time. He really wants to know and so do I.

"Uh, let's just say that when the interior is at odds with the exterior, it's hard to get the validation you need. You're a tall, strong man. You work with your hands. Say you're deathly afraid of spiders," she says to Shaw.

"He is," I can't help but mess with him a bit. He smiles a little and my heart inflates a bit more.

"There you go. I'm sure your punk boyfriend—who is just blowing up all your secrets—believes your phobia is real, but if you told most people daddy long legs pushed you to tears and blubbering, it would be hard for them to believe it. They'd have to see you break down and then they'd have to love and respect you enough not to judge you for it. Make that commitment not to make you handle the spiders anymore. Or help you with your fear, if that's what you want."

"Okay, so what's your big scary spider," Shaw asks.

"Well, since we're just spilling secrets to practical strangers, my big scary spider is that fact that even though I am an extremely accomplished woman, I am terrified of ending up alone. When Josh proposed, I was *overwhelmed* by the idea that love had finally found me," she says with a dramatic wave of her hand. "But when I breathe in the general direction of thinking I could end up alone, I have a list of fifty reasons why any guy would be lucky to have me. I agree with everything on that list. That doesn't change the fact that I've only had one serious boyfriend and the fact that that boyfriend, turned fiancé, was murdered while he was busy wanting more. More than me.

"Because like I said, cheating is about wanting more or wanting it all, so clearly I wasn't enough. And I know how that sounds, but it's how I feel and the few times I've even dared breathe a word of something even close to that to my friends and my sister, they rush to assure me that it isn't true. They can't explain how to rebuild trust for myself when I can't even yell at the person who hurt me. So now I feel both undesirable and stupid. That, boys, is my spider."

I look at her as she takes a deep swig right from the wine bottle. And then I look at Shaw as he turns to me. Now is not the time for either of us to mention how good she looks in that night shirt.

FOUR

Brooklyn

I'm doing it again. Being too much, too soon. I know what Chris and Vaughn are thinking and what impression they are going to have of me when they leave. *Oh, Brook's great. She's strong. She's bold. Boy, is she funny. She's going to be fine.* I don't know why I thought meeting them would help. I just added two more to the list of people standing on the other side of the chasm between me and whatever I need to regain my sanity.

I know I won't heal overnight. I know I'll never fully be the same.

I see it with the victims I try to fight for every day in the courtroom. Time doesn't heal shit. Time just allows for more room for pain to twist and fester unless you work really hard at it. It's a constant battle that shapes and reshapes you over and over again. You never get over trauma, you just learn how to deal with it.

And that's what people don't understand. I've been hurting for so long. I'm still hurting from losing my parents and years of thinking I might lose Liz too. To lose Josh like this and to think he never really loved me at all? It's too fucking much.

I ache all the time and I see now, looking at Chris and Vaughn, knowing that when this night is over and they go home to each other, I am truly alone. This is why I can't go to therapy, because I know what a therapist will say. I know what tools they will give me. I'll forgive myself over time. Like how I finally stopped playing the what-if game when it came to my parents. I know, one day I'll look back on this and know it wasn't my fault. I'll be able to say Josh was the asshole in this situation. I'll be able to say it with no hesitation and know that he made a choice, a choice that would have hurt me in different ways if we'd made it down the aisle.

But for now, there's just pain. There's hurting and self-blame and this bone-deep desire for someone to actually love me. To be in love with me. To want me and to mean it. That's the tricky detail I'm not ready to tell a therapist or anyone really, because no one can fix it. No one can make that love appear out of thin air. It's not just that I'm hurt by what Josh did. I'm terrified of the future because of it.

"Brooklyn?" I look up at the sound of Vaughn's dangerously deep voice. For all I know, he's a complete asshole. Maybe he's controlling, inconsiderate. Maybe he never puts the toilet seat down and Corrine was just sick of it, but I highly doubt any of those things. Since the day he first approached me, I knew there was something about Vaughn Coleman. Something warm and kind. Honest. It's what made me think contacting him was a good idea, but now I know I'm just wasting his time.

"Vaughn," I say.

"Do you want us to go?"

"No." I shake my head as the word rushes out of my mouth because I don't. I like Vaughn and Chris, even though he had a bit of an attitude at first. I get it. Strong silent type who's more comfortable with a warehouse full of wood than talking to a stranger about his feelings. There's warmth there too, though. You just have to get close to him to access it. I think he and I have a lot in common. Not that it matters. "I think I just—maybe I came in a little hot."

"Nah, you're good," Chris says.

"You guys hang out. We can order more food if you want. Unless you want to go."

Vaughn looks at Shaw for a fraction of a second before his attention is back on me. "We're in no rush. We can chill for a bit."

"I want to keep talking to you, I—"

"You chill. We can do the talking," Chris offers.

"I can live with that. Or if you want, we can say fuck it and go roll around in that king bed over there." I let out a shaky laugh, feeling like a whole fucking fool for blurting such an inappropriate thing. You can't ask two guys you just met to fuck you. I mean you can, but in this situation you probably shouldn't. It's too late now though.

My words are out and Vaughn is looking at me with

what can only be described as pity in his eyes. Just what you want from an attractive man, even if you're only joking about having sex with him. And I was definitely joking. I lost my libido with Josh. There are still hints of arousal here and there, but I know I can't perform. I'll freeze up and probably start weeping. But Vaughn doesn't know this and he's still looking at me. The pity is still there.

"Have you been with anyone since?" he asks gently. It's a stupid question because of course I haven't, but I can tell he means well.

"No, I have not. How about you?"

His eyebrows come together as he frowns. He's not sure if I'm being serious or not until Chris pauses and looks over at me.

"Right. Duh. You two. Sorry."

"You're good," Chris says.

"I think I can speak for the both of us when I say we would love to spend the night with you, but—" Vaughn says.

"You don't think going from being dumped via homicide to a casual threesome would be the best idea," I reply, ignoring the way my panties have basically flooded at the idea. Is it fucked up in the extreme? Yes. Would I love to get my back knocked out by two men as attractive as Chris and Vaughn? Hell yeah. But he's right. That would just invite more confusion that would leave me more empty inside.

I have needs. Real needs and Vaughn Coleman and Chris Shaw aren't the people to meet those needs. I need to come to terms with this. I need to wrap my head around the fact that I am in this alone. I have to get through this on my own. Hopefully on the other side, there's more joy and a hell of a lot less pain. And sex I might actually enjoy.

"I hope you don't take that as any kind of rejection because believe me," Vaughn says, his eyes wide as he looks me up and down. Chris's gaze is back on the wine glass he's rolling gently between his palms. Still, his lack of eye contact does nothing to dull the heat in his words when he speaks.

"Yeah, finding you attractive isn't the issue."

"I have to say, I am a little jealous. You two have each other."

"You have us now," Vaughn replies. "Not that way, but I think we have a very unique club going on here. Scorned lovers with no closure and whatnot."

"Is it okay if I get your number from Vaughn?" Chris asks.

"Yeah, of course."

It's interesting to see the effortless, silent exchange between them when Vaughn tosses Chris his phone without warning. Chris snatches it out of the air and unlocks it with the passcode. His fingers fly across the screen and then my phone chimes with a text.

"There you go. You have the both of us now."

"Thank you. Well, what am I supposed to do now?" I say as I walk over and flop down beside Chris on the couch. "I was ready for some run-of-the-mill small talk, but now I'm torn between rambling some more and a good old fashioned sob session. But I guess you two don't need to be here for either of those things to happen."

"Nah. No need for that. Here." Chris moves closer and

puts his arm around me. I want to be shocked by it. Especially from the way he came into my hotel room, a little on edge, but I accept the comfort. I lean into him for just a moment before he rethinks his position and takes off his letterman jacket. He's wearing a soft sweater that smells of soap and faintly of wood. It would make a perfect candle. Vaughn stands up and finds the remote next to the TV.

"Let's see what on." He sits on the couch beside me. He doesn't touch me, but I can still feel the warmth coming off him. He rolls through the guide until he finds reruns of *Living Single*, something we can all agree on. Resting against Chris's side, I realize just how fast my heart has been beating this whole time. How hard it's been beating since I hopped on the parkway.

I close my eyes as Regine starts to go in on Max. I try to focus on the rise and fall of Chris's chest. I can't help but wonder how the hell he's so calm. Maybe because he hasn't spent the last twenty minutes rambling and taking half a bottle of wine to the head. I can't help but wonder how Vaughn is so relaxed next to me, with his impossibly long legs stretched out beside the coffee table.

Maybe it's because they have each other. They've had weeks to comfort each other. Weeks to fall apart together and to build each other back up. I know they are not okay. I could hear the pain in Vaughn's voice when he talked about *her*. I could see the hurt in Chris's eyes when he talked about the how and why they were currently in this fucked up position.

My eyes blink open and I close them again. That ache returns to my chest. I want Chris to kiss me. I want Vaughn to put the weight of his whole body over me. I want to feel something other than this. I want reliable human contact that's not asking me to put on a brave face. I fight back the tears and try not to beat myself up too much. I miss my cheating fiancé. I miss Josh.

Chris and Vaughn leave a little before one a.m. We watch TV and talk a little more. I ask Vaughn about his work in patent law. He asks me about the politics of the D.A.'s office. That's all fine and good until we start talking about the upcoming election for mayor. It makes me think of Josh and suddenly I need to change the subject.

Shaw distracts me by showing me his craftsman website where, a few times a year, he posts photos of select projects, step by step. Looking at pieces of wood go from planks or stumps to useful expensive things is somehow soothing. He shares some other craftsmen's Instagrams with me. I watch a guy make a table in his Instastories and feel my heart start to slow a little.

When it's time for them to go, I reluctantly tell them how I don't know how I'm feeling about the next day or if I'll even stay til Sunday morning like I'd initially planned. I apologize. It was my idea for us to meet up, but I didn't manage my own expectations and now I feel like I am just wasting their time. They are both very sweet about it. Too sweet. They go. I tidy up a bit before I remove my lace front so I can wrap my hair, then I fall into bed.

I'm asleep almost immediately, but I sleep like shit.

Hard, deep sleep, but it's full of nightmares. It's full of Josh. It's the same version of the same dream I can't seem to stop. I see him somewhere. At work. On Liz and Silas's farm. Coming out of the men's room in my favorite bar. Standing on the other side of the platform while I wait for the train.

This time he's in my apartment. I am so pissed. So hurt. Everything inside me is boiling. I want to tell him to leave. I want to tell him I deserve a fucking explanation. But I say nothing. I just watch him as he pretends. He sets down his bag. He smiles at me and he lies. He lies about how he missed me. He lies about how much he loves me.

My throat burns with unshed tears. Finally I tell him I know. I tell him I know about Corrine. He just smiles and asks me if I want to walk down to the bodega. More happens. I'm walking with my friend Noa. Some actor I don't even like tells me he wants to take me out, but there are condition. I have to rub his feet. When I jolt awake close to six a.m., my throat still hurts.

I lay awake, scrolling endlessly through the explore tab on Instagram. Watching video after video of cake decorating, crafts for kids, stuff the algorithm feeds me for my baby Palila. I go and look at pictures of the kids and that makes me feel better for a moment. I fall back asleep. When I wake up, I regret not drinking a little water with my burger and wine.

I suck it up and drink the two bottled waters in the mini bar that are going to cost me fifty dollars a pop before I use the restroom. I go back out into the sitting room of the suite, thinking about how Chris and Vaughn looked filling the space. I go to the window and look out over the river. I have no fucking clue what river I'm looking at, but people are walking along it, enjoying this cloudy Saturday morning.

I'm going to stay, I decide. Give myself at least another twenty-four hours to be alone with my thoughts, away from work and away from the city. This is how my weekends are now. I have to be away. Usually at Liz's, but I remember that since they have Silas's cousin Mason and his wife Xeni visiting from L.A. for the weekend, that's why I'd made other plans. Last place I thought I'd end up is Boston.

I don't watch baseball, but a century's long feud with racial overtones is to be respected. As soon as Liz told me her plans, I knew I needed to escape. I could have dragged my friends away, but I don't know. I just don't. Rayna is busy with her boyfriend, who she keeps breaking up with. It's smack in the middle of Claudia's two weeks to be in NorCal with her husband and Noa... Noa is too healthy for me right now.

I see Noa and I envy her. She's trying so hard. Her last breakup was horrible. But she grieved and then she bounced back in this way that's just—I mean what the fuck. She's a picture of mental health. Putting herself first. Actually seeing the therapist Claudia recommended. Eating well. Going to workout classes. Crafting! I know her life isn't perfect. I know she's human. She has her bad days too, but sometimes I look at her and I can't.

It would kill me to put in that kind of effort. Mostly because no one actually wants to see me better and happy right now. It's still too soon. I mean it is, but I wonder what the time frame is. How long must the general public see me as the grieving widow-to-be? Six months? A year? Two?

Forever? I carry Josh's ghost and the ghost of our relation-ship with me everywhere, through my waking hours and when I'm asleep. Fucker won't leave me alone long enough for me to join Noa for cardio hip hop.

That's why I text her. 'Cause she is who she is and I know she won't judge me. Noa is made of good friend material.

> *When can I start dating again?*
> *Not like LOVE*
> *But when I can look at a man as a distraction?*

I hit send and flop back on the fluffy white bedding.

My phone chimes a moment later. I stare at the ceiling, thinking about Vaughn Coleman's glasses. Then I think about Josh. I breathe through that ache in my throat again, then reach for my phone. The reply isn't from Noa.

Hey Brooklyn.
It's Shaw. Chris.
Are you still around?

A sudden warmth settles in my stomach, an odd sense of relief mixed with something else I can't really name at the moment. I was putting off texting him and Vaughn. I'm glad he's reached out first.

> *Hey. Yeah.*
> *I'm going to lay in this bed*
> *all day probably.*

What's going on?

If you're cool with it, I'd like to see you.
Just me and you.

A different kind of lump lodges itself in my throat. It could be nothing, but it feels like something. I say yes.

I'll be there in an hour.

K. I'll put on pants.

You don't have to.

I know then that I absolutely have to. He might be flirting, but I don't trust my judgement, so I save the jokes and don't respond. I shower and get dressed and do my five-minute face. I glue my wig back down and adjust my baby hairs just so. Then I search for a breakfast spot within walking distance. An hour later, down to the minute, there's a knock on my door. I open it and there is Christopher Shaw, somehow better looking than the night before. Same letterman jacket, different sweater. This one is a black and grey argyle and he's wearing dark-wash jeans that fit him perfectly over a pair of fresh sneakers. I have no plan to let him inside. I'm rushing him out of this hotel and we're going to talk over some French toast and burnt coffee.

"Hey, Chris," I say as I step toward him. I expect him to back up as I go on. "I found this place called Breakers—"

Chris doesn't move. Instead he becomes this wall of

man and muscle. I barely avoid walking right into him, but I don't back away as he looks down at me. His gaze roams over my face as his tongue slips out and wets his lower lip. I don't even think about stopping him as his strong, rough hand slides gently under my hair and up the side of my neck. I just focus on not passing out or blurting some stupid shit because I know that will stop him from doing what I want him to do next. My eyes drop to his perfect, full lips framed by his perfectly manicured beard and mustache. I think about tugging on his beard and pulling him closer. Before I can lift a finger, he's kissing me.

His lips move against mine and I completely give in, kissing him back. He teases my tongue with his and I let him. I perch up on my toes and try to reach the altitude where he resides. I press my tits against his chest and do my best not to moan as my nipples ache for direct contact. His other hand slides around my back, under my coat. He grips my ass and pulls me closer. The position is wrong, but if it weren't for the height difference and the way he's bending down to meet me halfway, I know I'd be able to feel his cock hardening against my stomach. When he pulls away, we both have a hard time breathing. I look up at him, my lungs craving more of his woodsy soap smell. He moves his thumb to my lower lip and my pussy clenches hard on itself as my tongue darts out and licks the pad of his skin. His nostrils flare when I do it again. He swallows and then he speaks.

"Call me Shaw."

FIVE

Shaw

"What are we doing here, Shaw?" Brooklyn says. She looks up at me, her gaze still hazy as her focus drifts back down to my lips. I want to kiss her again, but I've already fucked things up. When I told Vaughn I just wanted to come talk to Brooklyn Lewis, we both knew I was lying. I did want to apologize to her for the way I came at her the night before. We smoothed things out, but I'd stepped into her hotel room sideways and it took way too long for me to get my shit together. I'm still trying to cope with my own grief and not to lash out at Vaughn when things get to be too much.

But the apology was only part of it. I wanted to see her again. Losing Corrine destroyed me. I didn't realize until last night that my grief was turning me into a special kind of an asshole.

"I came here to apologize." I say as I drop my hand from

her neck. I don't step back. I'm not ready to leave her space. Brooklyn frowns, dropping her gaze as she starts to smooth my sweater over my chest. My muscles jump under her touch.

"Apology accepted, but what are you apologizing for?"

"For last night. I thought Vaughn was kidding himself about a whole bunch of shit. I didn't understand why he wanted to see you. And I didn't understand what I was feeling about it. I shouldn't have bugged out on you."

"I appreciate you saying that, but I still don't know what you mean. Can we go get breakfast and you can explain it to me?"

"Yeah. Let's go."

I follow her down the hall to the elevator, fighting the urge to slip my hand along the small of her back, to take her hand in my grip. It's the thing Vaughn and I have been dancing around. We've been dealing with the fact that Corrine was fucking murdered. Trying to wrap our minds around that. That she had a stalker we knew nothing about. Of course we miss her and there are layers of emotions. All the stages of grief and trauma, but I still can't get over the weight of her physical absence. I can't deal with how addicted I was to Corrine and what she and I had with Vaughn. What Vaughn and I had with her.

When Vaughn told me about Brooklyn Lewis, I thought he was grasping at straws. I thought he was out of his fucking mind even wanting to be around her. What the fuck purpose would it serve? If we need outside support, there are groups for that. Counselors and shit. Bonding in our trauma won't do any of us any good.

"Why did you kiss me?" she asks as the elevator doors close.

"Is it okay if I don't have a good answer other than I wanted to?"

"I guess I'll have to take that. Let me kiss you next time, okay?"

"Do you want there to be a next time?"

"I'm not sure yet. But let me make the move. Okay?"

"Of course."

"And don't apologize for kissing me. I *did* want you to kiss me, in the fantasy files of my brain. I just wasn't expecting it."

"So, it was a good surprise?"

"Yeah. At least I know my pussy's not broken," she says with a little smirk as the elevator chimes at the lobby floor. I follow her out of the glass door back to Dalton Street. We walk down to Newbury Street. I glance in the comic store window as we pass. It's still closed.

"You into comics?" she asks as we continue up the block.

"More into the movies, but Vaughn buys them when he can."

"What's his drug of choice?"

"Batman."

"I can see that," she says as we arrive at Breakers. "He has a way with that tailored trench coat."

I smile to myself as we join the short line at the door. He was wearing a similar coat the first time I saw him. "Fighting intellectual crime suits him," I say.

"I'm sure it does."

There's a wait for larger parties, but the hostess can seat parties of two immediately. We sit by the window. I watch Brooklyn as she peels off her jacket and starts to look over the menu.

"Hmm. I love eating my feelings," she says. I should be looking at the menu too. I've had coffee, but nothing to eat and it's past time to fill the tank. I can't take my eyes off her though, even to see how much two sides of eggs is going to cost me. I know it's a little on the foul side, but I can't help but look. I couldn't help but look last night either. Brooklyn Lewis has some of the biggest natural tits I've seen in real life.

I pride myself as a lover of the human body. I'm also a genuine tits and ass man. Vaughn told me she was beautiful with a figure to match, but damn. I'd love to get under that pink sweater. I know that won't happen. Still, my mind deserves a break. Even just for a few hours.

"Okay. I know what I'm getting." She sets down her menu and crosses her arms on the table, resting her tits on top of them. She's not doing it to show them off. She just seems comfortable that way.

"So tell me, Shaw. What's your deal?"

"Where do you want me to start?" I say.

"Wherever you like? I think I see how you and Vaughn fit together. I thought you were fire and he was ice, but it's the other way around. He's sweet and warm, and you're—"

"A confusing asshole?"

"A little, but I think I can let first impressions go for now. You're a pretty good cuddler too, so that doesn't hurt your case. But no, tell me about you and tell me why Vaughn isn't with you."

"Vaughn isn't here because I wanted to talk to you alone."

"Was there something you couldn't tell me in front of him?"

"No, it's not like that. Vaughn knows everything. I don't have an issue sharing things with him, but you're a D.A. You know phrasing matters."

Her eyes narrow and she leans forward a little more. "An A.D.A. You want to talk to me without hurting his feelings."

"I don't think what I would say to you would hurt his feelings. I just—"

"No, I get it. One-on-one conversations are important."

"Vaughn and I have different versions of closure. I think yours and his align more than mine."

"How so?" she asks.

"Vaughn wants answers he won't get. I think you do too. I want to move on. I feel a lot of things and none of them will bring her back or change where we are now."

"And what does moving on look like for you?"

"Figuring out where Vaughn and I go from here."

"Well, I think if you want Vaughn to be in your future, you need to let him search fruitlessly for those answers he's not gonna get and when he and I are ready," she says with a little shrug, "you two can rethink that future and reshape your happiness."

"That's the smart thing to do."

"I know it is. I'm a genius. So tell me literally everything else about you."

"I'll skip a few things. Grew up here in Boston. Came close to joining the Navy. Dad caught me with my neighbor's dick down my throat and kicked me out before I could make it to boot camp. My mom didn't try to stop him. Spent the summer on the Vineyard with my grandpa, who's a carpenter. He taught me a few things. Introduced me to a few people. Including my agent."

"Your agent?"

"I used to model."

"Oh. That I believe. You're, like, stupid hot. So, no more modeling, then."

I shake my head. "The scene wasn't for me. But I saved up enough money and met enough people to buy my own place out in Barnstable. Close enough to my brother and sisters, far enough away that I can justify never running into my parents." I pause as the waitress comes over to the table. Brooklyn orders some special and asks if they have a brand of hot sauce in the back. They don't. She does her best to take that news well, but she doesn't stop herself from scrunching up her nose in disappointment.

I confirm the size of the pancakes, then order six blueberry with a half dozen scrambled eggs, some salsa on the side and the biggest glass of orange juice they offer. Once we're alone again I finish what I was saying.

"Anyway, I met Vaughn at a party. He was cool with me being sexually fluid and I was cool with him not being sure what he was yet. We started hanging out. Some time later, we met Corrine. Vaughn expressed his interest in her. I expressed an interest in her. She expressed her interest in us. Fast forward and I'm having breakfast with you."

"Hmm." She doesn't say anything else. She's thinking.

"Not what you wanted to know?"

"Just trying to decide how invasive I want to be."

"My tongue was just in your mouth. Ask me anything."

She chuckles, casting her gaze to the floor before she lets out a deep breath. She looks back at me, considering me for a few long moments. "I mean, I have questions, but they are invasive and pretty juvenile. And I think I probably know the answers."

"Who knows? I might surprise you."

"Okay fine. It's kinky right? You guys aren't just poly? You weren't. It was more than that."

"Correct. Brooklyn—"

"You can call me Brook. Everyone at work calls me Brooklyn. We don't need to be that formal."

"Brook. It is kinky. Do you want details?"

"Sure," she replies, her tone light.

"Vaughn is a switch and so was Corrine. I'm a Dominant. So, we do play with Dominance and submission."

She cocks her head to the side, gazes to the ceiling like she's trying to do the math on that, and nods. "Yeah, I can see how that works."

"We also participate in rope bondage. I can take it or leave it, but Vaughn and Corrine really enjoyed it and Vaughn's pretty good with knots. I'm even better."

"Of course you are. You almost joined the Navy. I'm pretty vanilla, I guess?"

"There's nothing wrong with that."

"I'm trying to picture... Corrine," Brook says, like it's a struggle to mention her name. "It's hard to imagine participating in all of those fun activities with the two of you and then having the energy to take on a whole other relationship on the side."

"To her credit, Corrine was one of the more insatiable people I've ever been with. She wore Vaughn and I both out routinely. I shouldn't have been shocked that she had energy for more partners."

"I like to get down, don't get me wrong, but I don't know that my sex drive is that high."

"It wasn't a judgement."

"I didn't think it was. I was just thinking out loud. Maybe—" She cuts herself off as our food arrives. The pancakes are bigger than I expected, but I'll make short work of them. I get the butter situated just the way I like it, then drown my plate in syrup.

"Maybe what?" I ask before I take a big bite. Breakers may have a weak hot sauce selection, but their pancakes are pretty good.

"Nothing." She sighs, sitting back from the table like she's just lost her appetite. "I keep thinking the same shit over and over, and at some point I have to understand that it's getting me nowhere. Josh cheated and Josh is gone. Both of those things are true and I have to accept them and let the feelings that come with these true facts roll over me like a dump truck. Truck. Truck." I almost choke on my food and that wins me a slight smile from her. I swallow and successfully clear my throat with a sip of juice.

"You mentioned last night. About not feeling like enough," I say.

"Yeah?"

"I'm still turning that around in my mind. Me and Vaughn not being enough. *And* the two of us being too much for her."

"I mean, it's like I said last night. It's the wanting it all. Josh and I were happy. Or I thought we were, so the idea of wanting it *all*, or even a little more than what we had, seems excessive. It's crazy to me that I was so happy and thought I was so lucky to have finally found someone I actually wanted to marry and the whole time Josh was just doing all this other shit. We were never on the same page. Did you have even the slightest hint that she was unhappy?"

"Real talk? I don't know. I try not to look back, but I think that's why I wanted to say this to you."

"Say what?"

"I'm being hypocritical as fuck, but whatever. Josh was an idiot. He should have been straight up with you or cut you loose. I try to put myself in Corrine's shoes and she probably didn't want to break two hearts, but no combination of our situation was about to walk down the aisle. Josh asked you to marry him. He made the decision to honor you and only you. In a very specific way."

"I mean, the three of you were monogamous right?"

"We were. We all took our agreement very seriously, but we hadn't had a commitment ceremony or even a talk about locking it down on a permanent basis. Cor and Vaughn lived together, and sometimes I think that was just so they could keep each other company. We were rolling with a good thing. Being honest and open. That's why what Corrine did was fucked up. She didn't have to lie."

We both clam up then and focus on our food. The waitress comes back and I order another juice and more water for the table. Brook orders some coffee. She finishes her special, leaving a piece of overly fatty bacon to fend for itself.

"I think about him all the time," she says suddenly, like she's confessing to an awful crime. "I have these weird dreams about him where I'm trying to yell at him."

"Is he smiling at you in them?"

"Yes! How did you know?"

"I have the same kind of dreams about Corrine. I'm watching Vaughn, he's trying to talk to her and she just blows him off and smiles. I ask her over and over why she's lying. She just keeps on smiling." I haven't told Vaughn about these dreams because I know they would just make him feel guilty. "I feel like I saw something. I know I saw something. She wasn't unhappy, but she was—there was something. I can't put my finger on it. I saw it, but I trusted her to tell us. And then I convinced myself it was something else."

"Do you think she was going to leave you two?"

"Eventually, yeah. I think she wanted another life. Her mom definitely wanted her to have another life. I'm not sure what other life Corrine wanted, but it was something that ain't have shit to do with us."

"You know what's sad? I know I would have left Josh if I found out he was cheating, but this part of me that thinks about him all the time? I look at her and wonder if I would have let that shit slide just so I could keep him."

"The what-ifs are going to really fuck us up, huh?"

"Yup." She takes a sip of her water and sits back. "So, is that why you kissed me? To show me my worth?" she jokes, sort of.

"Nah. I kissed you because I wanted to do more, but I know that's not going to happen. Not right now."

"How can you be so sure that you want more? You barely know me."

I shrug. "A gift, I guess. I just know."

"And what about Vaughn?"

"He trusts me. And he's attracted to you, too."

"Well, I have to say, I've never had anyone tell me that two fine-ass men want me. And so casually over breakfast. But since it can't be more, why tell me?"

"I'm gonna say something and I don't want you to think I'm being condescending."

"Okay," she laughs. "Go for it."

"When it comes to men, you have options."

"Oh, I know. That was never the problem. I need viable options, Shaw. I wanted to be loved. And I mean loved. Like, loved the fuck up on. Just loved, loved, loved. Then I need, like, a few hours to get my hair done, visit with my sister and my nieces, but the moment I come back, it's time to love up on this bitch again. It took me thirty-five years to find someone who I thought really loved me and then to have him taken away and to find out it was a lie? Let's just say, you can kiss me, but it's going to take a while before I can field even the most serious requests for my love and affection."

I smirk and shake my head, digging back into my pancakes before they get too cold.

"What?"

"Nothing."

"You know you never told me what you needed last night. Neither did Vaughn. Other than answers and a fast-forward button. What do you need emotionally?" She draws out the word like she needs to add levity.

Corrine liked to add innuendo to every situation. Everything out of her mouth was about keeping me and Vaughn hard. Every waking moment was making sure we knew she was wet for us. I miss it. Well, some of it. The parts that weren't a lie. I don't hate the silly way Brook carries herself, though. It's refreshing. She tries, in her way, to clear the heavy air out of every room. I take another bite as I consider her question. She waits patiently, watching me before she picks up her fork and toys with that last piece of bacon.

"Vaughn is a walking heart. I've never met anyone who loves the way he does."

"Hmm." I can tell she's trying to picture what that looks like coming from him.

"If you knew his mom it would all make sense. She's— that woman is so full of love and she really passed that on to Vaughn. The man is a lover. I can see Corrine getting sick of my shit, but not Vaughn's. He's the real thing."

"Don't tell me that. I already feel terrible for you guys."

"Look. When he told me he was going to find you, I told

him he should fuck you for good measure. Don't feel bad for me."

"Shaw!" she laughs.

"I was upset, aight. At the time, I figured if Josh could fuck our girlfriend, we should be able to fuck his fiancée. Street justice and what not," I say, throwing her a humorless wink.

"You're kind of a pig, aren't you?"

"Not where it counts."

"So, I don't have to worry about your voting record?"

"Hey, I'm not the one who is two steps away from being a Fed."

"Damn, dude! You know how to cut deep," she laughs. "Also, I work in special victims. I'm one of the good guys who actually wants to stop real bad guys. Not send young people away on minor drug charges."

"I know. I've seen all twenty seasons."

"Anyway." She rolls her eyes. "What did Vaughn not-the-total-pig say when you told him to hit me with that payback dick?"

"He told me he had questions for you, but he really wanted to make sure you were okay. I mean, of course you weren't, but he saw how fucked up we were. He wanted to make sure you had someone who understood what you were dealing with."

She's been jokes all morning, handling this tough conversation like a damn G. But I know that look, that feeling. When reality swoops back in and punches you in the fucking chest. Tears start to fill her eyes.

"I don't. And I'm not," she says. "Everyone wants me to

be back to normal, but not too normal. No one cares that I might never be the same or how long I need to get there." I grab a napkin and hand it to her. She carefully dabs her eyes, but she still fucks up her eye makeup a little. I tell her, so she's not embarrassed later. She excuses herself to the bathroom. When she comes back, her makeup is fixed, but her eyes are more red and puffier than before, like she fought a hell of a fight not to have a full breakdown.

"Sorry about that," she says.

"Don't apologize. Let's talk about something else."

"You want to see some cute-ass pictures of my nieces?"

"Yeah. Let me see."

She spends the next ten minutes talking about little Palila and baby Iona. They are some cute fucking kids. She tells me about her older sister, who Brook clearly loves, and her husband Silas who owns some apple farm. She sounds happy for them, but there's a sadness that's settled on her shoulders and she can't seem to shake it. I'm the dick who put it back there with our heavy breakfast conversation.

I pay for our meal and we head back to her hotel. She's tired again, she tells me. I think it's best if I leave her in the lobby.

"I'm gonna maybe take a nap and then head back to the city later this afternoon."

"Okay. Let us know when you get back so we know you made it alright."

"I will. Thank you for breakfast and thank Vaughn. You've both been great."

"I'll tell him."

She sighs before she looks up at me. "I can't see you guys again."

"I know."

"The three of us all want something that we can't have. Commiserating won't bring closure. Nothing will. And that's if we don't try to make it something else to take the edge off."

"I know."

"And I did try to think of reasons why it would work. Like, just the sex or just the hanging out, but that's not enough. It'll never be enough."

"Brook, I know."

"I'm just thinking out loud."

"Text us when you get home and if you do want to talk to us again, you know you can."

"I know. And I appreciate it. I should go."

She doesn't say goodbye. Just turns and walks to the elevator. I don't watch her go. I love the idea of Brooklyn Lewis. But at the end of the day, I just want my girl back.

SIX

SIXTEEN MONTHS LATER

Brooklyn

I manage to hold a polite smile on my face until Deek is finally out the door. I ran into him two weeks ago near our old building and he stopped me and talked to me about my parents' apartment. The one we hold on to. I promised Liz I wouldn't give it up, just like she's holding on to her place in Harlem. Gentrification will probably come for both places some day, but for now we're both subletting. Living space in any borough is precious and costly.

Deek heard about my tenant, Missy, moving to L.A. and wanted to know if I'd be willing to rent the place to his two little sisters. He promised he'd make sure they pay on time. I remember his little sisters, sweet-faced little dickheads who were always ready to throw hands over the dumbest shit. I will not be renting to Deek's little sisters. Even though I passed, he asked if I wanted to catch up. We haven't seen each other in a while.

I thought about the crush I had on him in high school and how I'd wished he'd paid any attention to me. I knew he just wanted to hit and I was okay with that. I haven't had sex in over a year. I invited him to my new place. I made it very clear that I was using him. He flashed that smile that really would have worked on me fifteen years ago. It's the smile that let me know he was using me too. We took it to the bedroom and I immediately regretted this decision. Deacon Wright has the stroke game of a clumsy teenager. I let him finish. I thanked him for a great time and then I sent him on his way.

I sit on the edge of my couch, looking around my apartment, numb. It's done. Josh is no longer the last man to touch me, the last man I've let inside me. As soon as the thought passes through my mind, I think of Shaw and how it had felt when he kissed me. How for weeks I fell asleep with my hand or my vibrator between my legs, picturing what it would have been like if we had skipped breakfast and if I'd invited him in. If we'd called Vaughn over. What would have happened and how I would have regretted it.

I look at my phone. It's barely ten o'clock. So much for the all-night fuck-a-thon I was hoping for. I think about texting the girls in our group chat. They'll take my mind off the continued tragedy that is my love life. Maybe I can meet Noa and Rayna for a midnight snack. For some stupid, stupid reason, I text Shaw.

I just had the worst sex of my life.

A weird sense of shame settles over me as soon as I hit send. Talk about a bad move. I'd made it clear that I didn't want him in my life. That trying to even be friends with Shaw and Vaughn was something that, not only was I not ready for, but would actively hurt more. Texting him like this? About another dude? It's just tacky.

I'm sorry, I start to type. *I shouldn't haven't reached out like—* but before I finish, he replies.

He still there?

I stare at the response. Look at the words I still have typed on the screen. I can still send them. I can still apologize and then delete his number. And Vaughn's number too. I've made a lot of progress in the last year, but that doesn't change the reality of what we are to each other and how we met. I need to leave Shaw alone. I need to turn to my friends and my sister in this time of comically bad sexual disappointment. But I don't. I delete the apology I started and open myself up to a conversation with Shaw.

No. He just left.

I jump as my phone starts ringing in my hand. I answer with my heart still beating in my throat.

"Jesus, Shaw," I laugh.

"I just wanted to hear your voice when you explained why you had the worst sex of your life when you could have called me or Vaughn."

"Well, I think we both know why I didn't call either of you."

"But I think I can guess why you're texting me after. What happened?" His voice is so soft and deep. I close my eyes against the sound of his simple question.

"Just an old friend from the neighborhood. The forever-single, always-in-trouble-with-three-or-four-women type. I'm sure you know a few guys like that."

"More than a few. Was this the first time since Josh?" he asks like he knows that if it weren't the first time, if I wasn't warring with weird emotions I couldn't explain, I never would have texted him.

"Yeah," I admit. "I guess it's good that it was bad. The bar is nice and low. It can only go up from here."

"Yeah, don't put that shit out into the universe," he says.

"Good call." I laugh because he's right. It's the same conversation I've been having with Noa and Claudia for months. I can want good things for myself. I can want real happiness. I can want whatever the fuck I want. If I want sex to be a part of my life again, why wouldn't I want it to be good? No use in wishing for mediocre.

"Come out to the Cape and come see me," he says, his tone easy and calm, like it's something we do all the time.

"Just like that?"

"Just like that. Vaughn will be here Friday night. You should come."

"And do what?"

"Whatever you want. My place is on the beach."

"Public or private?" I ask for some weird reason.

"My neighbors have access to the same stretch, but they aren't that close and the shore bends. It's pretty private."

"So, I come to your place and we go to the beach?"

"Brook," is all he says. He's telling me to cut the shit. I know what he's not saying and if I thought it wasn't true, I would never have texted him. I want to see him and Vaughn again. When I said I needed to walk, I'd needed time and space. I'm ready now. The specifics are just a little hazy. But Shaw's trying to make it clear. If I drive up to his place there will be sex. Sex between the three of us.

"You have to promise me something," I say.

"What do you need?"

"I need you to be honest with me and I'll be honest with you. If we're not feeling this, that's fine, but I don't want to have a false sense of anything."

"I can do that. And I know Vaughn can too, but you should talk to him yourself."

"I will."

We're both quiet for a few long moments. I have a lot I want to say, but I want to say those things in person.

"Are you okay with dogs?" Shaw asks.

"Yeah, I kinda have to be. My sister and her husband have six."

"That's a lot of fucking dogs."

"They live on a farm so it makes sense, but still. You have a dog?"

"Yeah. Adopted him about six months ago. His name is Roger."

"That's a cute name. I'd love to meet Roger."

"Bring yourself and your swim trunks. We'll take care of the rest."

"Sounds like quite the weekend."

"I promise no part of it will be the worst anything of your life."

"What did you just say about putting bad shit out into the universe?" I laugh.

"Brook, bring those big titties up and let us make it worth your while."

"Okay, okay."

We say our goodbyes and later, Shaw texts me his address and gives me some pointers on the best routes to take. I promise to check in with him along the way. I go back to my room, change my sheets and crack a window as I put on the fan. Deek wears the same cologne he wore in high school and it's all over my bed.

***

"Thank you for keeping me company," I say as I pull up to Shaw's driveway. It looks exactly the same as the Google Earth pictures I'd pulled up the day before.

"No problem. I'm almost done with my puzzle, so we did each other a favor," Noa says through the speakers.

"Promise me you'll go out with Rayna tonight," I laugh.

"I will!" Noa's been on a real puzzle kick lately. It's the most wholesome hobby ever, but she's gotten real competitive about it with some random dude she was playfully shit talking online. Now every Saturday, she won't leave her apartment until she finishes a new massive puzzle. This week's is Pugs In Space. She sent me a picture of the box before I got on the road.

I pull up the hedge-lined driveway, right to the massive colonial. It's a gorgeous house from the outside. Two stories, with what looks like a one-story addition. The grey wood shingles are weathered in this perfect way and the white trim looks brand new. I see Vaughn's SUV parked in the driveway and try not to laugh at the fact that we practically have the same car. I stop my Tahoe right beside his Escalade in front of the garage. Off to the right in the middle of the yard is a big red barn, half covered with ivy. I'm guessing that's Shaw's wood shop. Movement to my left catches my eye and I see Shaw step out of the side door. A sleek chocolate lab pokes his head out to see who's arrived.

"I'm here," I tell Noa.

"Okay cool. Have fun with your nerdy lawyer friends. I need nerdy lawyer friends with beach houses on the Cape."

"Add it to your vision board, boo."

"Not a bad idea. Okay, check in with me or the girls. We love you!"

"Love you, too." I end the call and let out a deep breath. Okay, so I may have asked for honesty this weekend and then immediately lied to my sister and my friends. I told them where I'm going. I gave Noa and Liz's Vaughn's information and explained that we are meeting up at his boyfriend Shaw's place, but I didn't tell them all the dirty details. I didn't tell them who they really are. Who they are in relation to Josh. Sixteen months. It's taken sixteen months to get to this point where I don't feel bad about wanting my own life anymore.

I cut off the engine and open the door. "Hey," I say as I climb down from the high cab.

Shaw comes down the wide brick path leading up to the driveway. Roger follows at his side, wagging his tail. "How was the drive?" Shaw asks as he takes my weekend bag from my hand and kisses my cheek, all in one smooth motion.

"It was good. Your directions were perfect."

"Good. This is Roger. Roger, sit." The chocolate lab immediately drops his butt to the gravel and looks between the two of us, hoping he did good.

"Okay, that's fucking cute. Can I pet him?"

"He'd be offended if you didn't."

"Hi Roger," I say, scratching his head. "Aren't you a good boy."

"He's trying to make up for this morning," Shaw says as he rolls his eyes.

"What happened?"

"He ate half of Vaughn's breakfast and knocked his coffee over his laptop in the process."

"No!" Roger barks as if to confirm my horror.

"Yes. His laptop is okay, but it was a tense couple of hours."

"I bet."

"Come on in. Vaughn's making lunch. You hungry?"

"I could eat."

"Good. You're gonna need your energy."

"Oh, it's like that."

"It's like that. I hope you stretched too." I think he's joking. He might not be.

We walk into a mudroom with a slate floor where we

leave our shoes. I follow him into what might have been a sitting room at one point, but now it's an office. I look around at the mix of old and new. Shaw pauses, letting me take it all in. A large but shallow stone fireplace with a useless mantle takes up one whole wall. There's a big window with a nice view of the yard. Against the opposite wall is a desk with Shaw's computer and another drafting table, where plans for something or other are spread out. He has a really intense looking printer and shelves stuffed with books and files and little wood carvings.

On the wall are framed blueprints of the original structure of the house and the blueprints of the addition, added in 1977. I stop and look at the little metal plaque embossed at the bottom of the frame. The Thomas Haskins House 1705. I don't know what I expected from Shaw's home, but this old colonial farm home wasn't it.

We continue on and I watch as Shaw has to duck as we walk into the newly remodeled kitchen and dining area. I didn't realize how low the ceilings are. There's another original fireplace, but it looks like it's just for show. Roger's dog bed is in the hearth. He happily takes a seat and busies himself with the giant rubber bone waiting for him.

The kitchen's slightly higher ceilings provide Vaughn with an adequate amount of headroom. He looks good, but different. Like this year since I last saw him kicked his ass a little. Still, he looks good. A few greys have populated his beard and he looks sharp in his tailored Bermuda shorts and polo shirt. I feel a certain way about Shaw. A way I'm not willing to put words to yet. I don't know how I feel about Vaughn. We haven't spoken since that night in my hotel room. In my mind, I know I can push Shaw. I can test him. Things are different with Vaughn. I don't want to hurt either of them, but I feel like I need to protect Vaughn.

When he turns from whatever he's making and smiles at me, my whole body warms. *He's full of love*, my memory tells me and I know it's true.

"You made it," he says, before he pushes his glasses up his nose. I don't know how Batman is his hero of choice when all I see is a perfect Black Clark Kent. I cross the kitchen and walk into his arms, wrapping myself around his slender, muscular frame.

"Thank you guys for having me. What's for lunch?"

"Crab cakes and a summer salad. There's also strawberry shortcake."

"That sounds amazing. You a good cook, Vaughn?" I tease.

"I think I'm okay."

"Man," Shaw sucks his teeth. "He's a great cook."

"What can I say? My mama raised me right."

"I'm not mad at that," I laugh.

"Why doesn't Shaw show you to your room? I'm almost done here."

"This way," Shaw says, nodding to the doorway at the other end of the dining space.

We walk into a formal sitting room with nice blue and white furniture, then head up this narrow-as-fuck staircase.

"Tight fit, huh?" I laugh as Shaw ducks his head all the way up.

"It's a heritage home. I can't make any changes to the original structure."

"I love it, but I'm worried about your poor necks."

"I spend most of my time out in the barn. It's fine. Here you are." He shows me to a large bedroom that gets plenty of natural light. I wonder if Shaw designed and furnished this whole place himself or if he had help. It's a lovely, beachy farmhouse, but none of it seems like him or Vaughn.

"Vaughn has his room right across the hall and my room is down on the other side of the house.

"You guys don't sleep in the same room?"

"We do, but if he's pissed at me or if I'm being a moody dick about a piece, he'll tell me to fuck off and sleep up here."

"It's good to have options, I guess."

He shows me the bathroom that's been remodeled. Before he leaves, he steps in close to me, invading my personal space like he did that morning in the hotel. He cups the side of my neck as he looks down at me, his brown eyes calm and searching intently all at the same time. He licks his lips and I think of the way he kisses. After sixteen months, I can still feel the way his lips moved against mine. It's the best kiss I've experienced in my whole life. My whole life. I've known this for sixteen months, known that Josh's lips never felt that good, never tasted that good. Josh made me happy for a while, but Josh never made me feel like I was on the edge of something that could drag me down or liberate me in equal measure. And from the way Shaw is looking at me, it's like *he* knows.

Sure, he knows I'm still hurting. He knows I'm still lonely. But now it's clear he knows the hope I've brought with me to the Cape. The hope that he's exactly what I need.

"Come down when you're ready. We'll talk over lunch and then after, we'll get started."

"Okay," I say, but it comes out more like a breath. He doesn't kiss me this time and as I watch him duck his head to go back down the narrow stairway, I remember why. *Let me be the one to kiss you next time.* He didn't forget.

I sit on the bed and take a deep breath and stock of my current situation. I'm going to spend the weekend with Vaughn and Shaw. I'm going to do things I've never done with one man, let alone two. I'm going to do my best not to think about Josh. I'm going to set aside the complex feelings I have about how I lost him. I'm not even going to think about the fact that I'd already lost him before a single shot was fired. This weekend is mine. I'm past due some real selfish pleasure and I think Shaw and Vaughn are more than capable of giving it to me.

SEVEN

Vaughn

"Everything okay?" I ask as Shaw comes back into the kitchen.

"Yeah. She's good. She just needs a minute."

"I sent the list to the printer," I tell him.

"Thanks. I'll grab it." Shaw walks into his office and is back a moment later with the revised checklist we went over the night before. It's been a long time for the both of us, working with someone new, but we agreed. We need Brooklyn to be fully informed so she can feel free to explore what she wants this weekend with us to look like.

I've been thinking about her for months. Resisting the urge to reach out to her, just to say hello, to see if she's alright. When Shaw told me they'd spoken and that she'd agreed to come up and see us, I wasn't sure how to feel. The last six months have been rough. Shaw and I took a break.

After meeting Brooklyn and seeing how right she was, that there was no quick fix to our grief, along with the ongoing silence from Mrs. Johnson, we thought it would be better to give each other some room before we said or did something we'd regret. It only lasted three weeks, but it was long enough for us to both come to the same conclusion. We were both still feeling pretty fucked up, but we weren't ready to walk away from what we had together, not yet. Almost a year later and we're still playing it by ear.

There are more conversations we should have, but we don't. Shaw got a dog. Things are okay now. Not back to normal, since that'll never happen. I'm lonely out in my Back Bay apartment, but Shaw is staying put and I don't know how to solve my loneliness in a way that isn't inherently selfish. Shaw sees how I'm struggling. He's kinder now and puts me first in ways I didn't know I needed. It's not enough, I start to see after a while. Still I appreciate it. And I appreciate that he knows I'm excited to see Brooklyn.

Time changes things. The way you look at someone. Your intentions. My attraction to Brooklyn Lewis was instant, but I knew what she clearly laid out for Shaw the last time they saw each other. At that moment, the three of us crashing together would have made things worse. I'm glad Brooklyn took the time she needed. I'm also glad she reached out.

Two works. Two works great, but there's something about three. I still have fucked-up feelings around Corrine. But I can freely admit that I miss aspects of the dynamic we had. Even though this weekend isn't headed in that direction, I'm glad we get to play with a beautiful woman again and I hope Brooklyn leaves feeling well fucked and well rested. That's my main goal.

Shaw and I wait. And wait. Ten minutes goes by and still no Brooklyn. Maybe she's not ready.

"Should I go—" the sound of the stairs creaking stops me.

Brook comes into the kitchen and scratches Roger's head as he trots over to meet her. "Sorry," she says with a little smile. "Just needed a moment to freak out and then I had to text my sister."

"You're good," Shaw says.

"Let's eat." I walk them through my overly elaborate menu for a "quick" Saturday lunch and then we take our seats at the dining room table. I threaten Roger with a stern look and he goes back to his bed before I get him in a head-lock. Still haven't forgotten about breakfast.

"Should we skip the small talk?" Brooklyn says with a nervous laugh once we're settled. "I mean, I love small talk. Don't get me wrong. I just—yeah."

"If that's what you want." Shaw goes over to the counter and grabs the three-page checklist. He hands it to her along with a pen. "This list encompasses most of the possible elements of Dominance, submission, bondage, discipline, sadism and masochism. Are you familiar with all of those terms?"

"Yes," Brooklyn nods. "But before we go there, there are just a couple things I need this weekend."

"Of course. Go ahead. "

"Well first, thank you so much for inviting me. Seriously, I love your house. I hope I get to see your workshop and I secretly hope you'll teach me how to whittle."

I almost choke on my iced tea as Shaw cracks a slight smile. "I can show you some basic carving tricks."

"Yassss," she whispers. "Second thing. I don't know where you guys are emotionally, but I don't want to talk about Josh. I've done a lot of work there and I just can't with ghosts-Josh's-past working their way into every moment. I get to feel my feelings, but bringing him into my present and my future does absolutely nothing for me."

"We don't have to talk about what happened, unless you need to," Shaw says.

"Intense sexual activity sometimes brings up intense emotions. We don't want you to force yourself not to talk about Josh if you need to," I add. "We've been intimate with each other, but haven't been with a third person since—before. I don't know how that is going to make me feel and I want to be able to talk about it if I need to. That's part of aftercare."

"Right. I read a little about aftercare. You think I'll need it?"

"It's required," Shaw says. "Even if we just slow dance and watch a movie. You're gonna feel some type of way about it afterward. It would be very bad for me—for us to tell you to fuck off to bed without seeing how you're doing emotionally or physically."

"You could strain your neck just looking up at me. What kind of friends would we be if we didn't make sure you were okay?" I say, messing with her a little. She smiles.

"That's true. Okay, if I need to talk about him, I will.

But, like, let's not jump in with a 'remember that time we were all cheated on and they both got murdered.'"

"Deal. What else?" Shaw asks.

Brooklyn looks at me then. "I told Shaw on the phone and I'm sure he told you that I need honesty. If you guys aren't feeling me or if I'm not feeling you as we move along and get to know each other more, tell me. I can handle rejection. I don't want to be lied to, even if you're trying to protect my feelings."

"I can agree to that and I hope you'll do the same for us. Even if you're the slightest bit uncomfortable, please tell us," I say.

"I will. Okay. Let's talk about this list."

"So we modified this list to exclude our hard limit items," Shaw says. "Things that Vaughn and I are absolutely not into and won't experiment with."

"Like what? If you don't mind me asking."

"Knife play. Blood play. Certain kinds of breath play. Certain bodily fluids."

"Ah, yes. Okay."

"Also, we like to push each other's limits, but safety is very important. Even if you're interested in certain things, that doesn't mean you'll feel safe doing them. Keep that in mind," I say. "We always want you to feel safe. I like a good choking, but I don't feel comfortable experimenting with electric shock."

"Yeah, nope. Okay, let me see." She takes a bite of her crab cakes then picks up the pen. I modified the list so she can select what kind of experience she has with different things.

"Just circle what you'd like to try. Or try again. What-ever the case is."

"Jesus. I never really thought about how many ways there are to gag someone." Her gaze slashes to Shaw. "Do you own a pair of manacles?"

"No, just leather cuffs, but we can order some."

"Nah, I think that's a little bit above my pay grade." She flips to the last page and then back again. "Yeah, this is a lot."

"You don't have to rush through it," Shaw says. "We're just trying to get the ball rolling."

"Sorry. My lawyer brain is taking over. I need to take this back to my team for a consult," Brooklyn says.

"You can't rush a lawyer when it comes to contracts," I say with a chuckle.

"What's a typical Saturday of bondage and sadism like for you guys?" she asks.

"It depends on what Vaughn needs," Shaw says.

"Last weekend I was worn out, but also restless, so Shaw gave me a task. Friday night, he tied me up using nylon rope and then I had to make him come without my hands or my mouth. In the morning, I was still on edge so he strapped me to our fucking machine until I couldn't take it anymore."

"Knocked him right the fuck out for the rest of the day," Shaw said. It was true. I slept all day Sunday and was ready to go back to work and deal with a pain-in-the-ass client first thing Monday morning.

Brooklyn sits back and picks up the list again. She flips to page two and lets out a very formal hum of approval. "I'm trying to open my mind to what I want. Not just what I need. Be a little wild here, Brookie," she says to herself. Then she picks up her pen. I watch her and Shaw as we finish our lunch in silence. Brooklyn takes her time going through the list, slowly eating her food. I clear the table, then continue to wait as Brooklyn checks and rechecks the list.

"Okay." She sets down her pen and lightly slaps the table. "We can amend this in the future. Or, like, in an hour when I realize the fucking machine is not for me?"

Shaw and I both laugh. "Yes. We can amend it anytime. And we don't have to start with the fucking machine," Shaw says.

"Okay, cool. Real talk, I do like the idea of ropes and being tied up, but I'm not there yet. I'd like to watch, though."

Shaw and I both share a nod. "We can work with that," I say. "I like to watch too."

"Cool. I can do outdoor stuff, but not public stuff. I'd like to keep my job."

"So would I," I say, thinking of the one time I asked to jerk Shaw off in public and how quickly we almost got caught. The thrill wasn't actually worth the risk.

Shaw takes the list back from Brooklyn and gives it a thorough once-over, making a few notes before he hands it to me. I'm happy to see that her interests overlap nicely with ours. She's interested in submission, but doesn't have any experience with it. I smile at the little stars Brooklyn has drawn next to her big yes items. She's hesitant about impact play with certain implements, but is open to hand spanking and flogging. She's interested in playing with various toys that can be inserted. She's made a note that she face slapping is a hard no for her. I had added a part that covered physical affection. She's selected everything, but put a circle around hand-holding, hugging and kissing.

"Let's head down to the beach," Shaw suddenly announces.

"Right, the beach," Brooklyn says, her smile still a little unsure.

Brooklyn

I try to just breathe as we make our way down the shrub-lined path, through the trees behind Shaw's house. Roger leads the way and I follow him, trying to ignore the way it feels to have Shaw and Vaughn at my back. I don't know what I expected. Maybe to show up and find them both in all leather, dicks hanging out, ready to slap me across the cheeks as I beg for permission to do, well, anything. But nope. We have lunch. We talk. There's paperwork. I change into my red bikini that shows off every inch of my fat body and just barely supports my tits, but makes them look sexy as hell at the same time.

They both told me I look nice in their own way when I came back downstairs. Vaughn actually took off his glasses and did a double take. Shaw seemed less interested in my body, but I think that's okay. He'd promised to tell me if we have a problem and that includes if he's not ready to handle my truly plus-size figure. We're just going to the beach to relax. I have my towel and a worn copy of JAWS I grabbed off the shelf in the sitting room. I listen to them talk about baseball and I keep my opinion of the Red Sox to myself, since it's supposed to be a nice weekend.

Shaw tells me the beach isn't far and, before long, the dirt path we're walking on gives way to fine, white sand. Up ahead, the beach stretches out all the way down to the deep blue ocean. I feel like maybe I need more time to think. This quick walk didn't give me enough time to really consider everything I'd checked off on that list. Maybe I should have said something before we left the house. Do I want to submit to Shaw? I think so. I just have no clue what that's going to feel like or if I even want to *like* it. Neither he nor Vaughn are pressuring me, though. We're just walking to the beach. No big deal.

The trees turn to tall grass and, sure enough, we're standing on a nice stretch of private shoreline, a whole two-minute walk from Shaw's back door. I have to know how much he charges for his custom pieces. Beach-backed property ain't cheap.

"Hold up one sec," he says as he peels off to the left. Pressed into the edge of the grass is a hand-made wooden cabinet.

"Isn't this a bit magical," I say, expecting a witch or a centaur to step out of the thing.

Shaw pulls out his keys and opens the big padlock that secures the doors. "Beats having to lug shit back and forth from the house." Inside are four tall beach umbrellas, some beach chairs and a half-empty bag of charcoal. I sling my towel over my shoulder, ready to grab a chair, but Shaw grabs all three and then Vaughn politely moves by me and grabs two of the umbrellas. I follow them to a nice spot and get out of the way as Vaughn sets up the umbrellas to shield us from the bright sun. There's a nice breeze, but not a cloud in the sky.

"So you weren't kidding about this beach being private," I say to Shaw as I look around. Way, way, way down the beach, I see the specks of two white people with a child. In the other direction, there's nothing. The shoreline curves a bit, but I can't see beyond it. Just tall grass and trees. I close my eyes and breathe in the sea air. It's been a long time since I've been on a beach. It's been a long time since I've taken a real deep breath.

"Here ya go." I open my eyes again at the sound of Shaw's voice. Our little sitting area is all set up.

"Thanks." I spread my towel on the chair on the left, drop my book onto the seat, then walk down to the water to dip my toes in. "Oh my god!" I scream as I run back up the hot sand.

"You gotta let yourself work up a bit of a sweat," Vaughn says with a sweet smile. "Then you run in and cool off. Repeat the cycle again."

"Oh, you have a system."

"Of course." He takes the frisbee he's been carrying and finally throws it for Roger, who says fuck it and runs right into the waves after the bright orange disc.

"Wow, he really doesn't mind the cold water," I say as I

bend to call him to me. I stop as soon as I see Shaw shaking his head.

"Nah-uh."

"What?"

"Sit here with me. You can play fetch with the dog later."

"Is that an order?" I tease as I walk about over to him. I try to ignore the fact that he's taken off his shirt and he's more jacked than I remember. He's also covered in tattoos, from forearms to collarbones, down his chest and stomach. I keep my drool in my mouth, but my pussy has been on hold all damn morning and she's sick of my shit. She instantly starts to ache as my fingertips start to twitch. I need to touch this man.

He looks over the frames of his sunglasses at me. "Yes. It is."

"And what will you do if I disobey you?" I plop down in my beach chair with a groan. It's hot as fuck out. I'll be sweating in no time if I don't get some shade. And yeah, fine, okay. I didn't come all this way not to be close to Shaw.

"There are plenty of ways to punish you, Brook. Trust me."

"Oh, I believe you, but I've been following the Man's rules for a long time now. Maybe I want to run free."

"Try me. See how it works out for you."

"Yeah, yeah. I'll sit by you, I guess." I shrug out of my cover-up and pick up the worn paperback I've borrowed.

"They filmed that close to my grandparents' place."

"Oh yeah?"

"Yeah. They raised my dad in Oak Bluffs. We lived there for a bit before we moved back to Boston."

"I've never been to Martha's Vineyard."

"We should go."

I glance over and think for a moment that Shaw's eyes are closed, but he's watching Vaughn as he tosses the frisbee back into the water. It's hilarious to watch Roger belly flop after it. I try to stop myself before I think there's no need for me to be here. There's no way I can improve upon this picture of two beautiful men and their loyal pup. Then the part of me that's been working like hell to remember that I didn't do anything wrong chimes in. *They want you here. You want to be here. Just enjoy this.*

"How long's the ferry ride?"

"Not long. You'd enjoy it. You stand on the upper deck on a misty day and just breathe that salty air in."

I try to picture it, but all I can think about is acting the fool with my friends on the Staten Island Ferry. "I think I have some generational trauma with boats and open water."

He sits up, but still doesn't look at me. "That's why all of the men in my family went back to the sea. My five-times great-grandfather was a whaler and every Shaw man after him has worked on the sea in some capacity."

"And you?"

"He's an old salt at heart," Vaughn calls out.

"I'm trying to picture you dressed up like a sea captain."

"Well, you did mark down roleplay," Shaw says. "We can make it happen."

My pussy seems to like that idea. "Don't men think women on ships are bad luck?"

"And that's why I'd have to take you to the Captain's quarters and show you what happens to stowaways." My mind flashes to the image of Captain Shaw and his crew running a punishment train on me. I hope this trip to the beach doesn't last too long. I'd like to get to the naked portion of the day. I scrunch my nose up at him instead of opening my mouth, 'cause I'm not sure what thirsty ho shit might come out of it. I let out a sigh, trying to exhale my sexual frustration.

Settling back in my seat, I think it's time to read the classic novel. Really, I'm just skimming the first paragraph over and over as I try to ignore the energy coming off the man sitting next to me. Shaw's head lolls back, probably settling in for a nap. A moment later, he holds out his hand.

"Move your chair closer to mine," he says quietly, but firmly. He's still watching Vaughn and the dog. I swallow, setting down my book, grabbing the base of the chair and shifting it a few inches across the sand. Shaw's forearm comes over my leg and he gently uses his elbow to push my thighs apart. His long fingers waste no time moving my bikini bottoms to the side.

EIGHT

Brooklyn

I know he can feel how wet I am as soon as he spreads my lips apart. His strong fingers are surprisingly gentle as he explores my whole pussy. The whole thing. He eases down to my aching entrance, spreading my juices around before he moves back up to my clit. Shaw has that magic touch. That soft caressing touch that my clit craves when it comes to direct contact. I can come like this. I know I can, in a heartbeat, but I don't want to come yet, not so soon. It's been so long, though, I may not have a choice. It's different when it's someone else's skilled hand. It's different when it's someone you've wanted to touch you for months.

I press my head back into my beach chair, dig my heels into the sand to stop myself from squirming too much. If I don't control myself, I know I'll be humping Shaw's hand, begging him to let me come. I'm not there yet.

A gasp slips out of me and my eyes fly open as I feel his lips against my neck. "How does that feel, Brook?"

"Am I required to tell you?" I whimper as he pushes one finger inside of me. He works it in and out.

"Yes, you're required to tell me."

I tilt my head back so I can look him in the eye, but my gaze drops to his full lips instead. "It feels good, I guess," I manage to say.

"You guess?" He slides his finger out, then uses his whole hand to cover my slit and give it a firm squeeze. My eyes roll back in my head at the feeling. I'm so slick and wet, and I can feel how wet his fingers have become thanks to his exploring. My clit presses up against its hood. I'm starting to understand how this game works. "I thought we were being honest with each other, Brook." I jump as he gives my pussy a harsh slap. It catches me off guard, but I definitely don't hate it, especially when he does it again. I moan, my pussy soaking with a fresh wave of arousal.

He does it again and two more times before I grab his forearm, whimpering his name.

"Tell me again," he says, his voice shockingly calm.

"It feels good." I blink a few times, trying to breathe, when I realize Vaughn has suspended his game of fetch with Roger. The dog is still frolicking in the waves, but Vaughn seems frozen at the edge of the water. Shaw picks that exact moment to reach with his other hand to move my bikini top off my breast. He leans over me, drawing his tongue over my puckered nipple. I reach up and run my fingers over his fresh fade, holding him closer as he continues to suck on my breast.

Vaughn is watching us, the front of his shorts tenting out. His erection looks impressive from nearly twenty feet away. I almost laugh as he takes off his glasses and rubs his eyes, like he's not sure if he's hallucinating or if Shaw really is pushing two of his skilled fingers deep into my pussy while he switches to my other breast with his equally skilled tongue.

"Should we—" I try to speak, but he just fucks me harder with his fingers, adding a third. "Should we include Vaughn in the fun?"

Shaw looks up and I shiver as my wet nipple is exposed to the warm air. Then he looks back at me before sucking my nipple back into his mouth. His tongue swirls over the tip and a tiny orgasm rolls through me. This is already better than the pitful sex I had with Deek. I know Shaw feels the tremor because his fingers ease up on my clenching cunt and his mouth moves to my neck.

"Who says he isn't having fun?"

"It just doesn't seem fair." Vaughn is still standing there, looking like a sexy math teacher, pushing his glasses up his nose again. He goes to adjust his erection, but stops himself at the last second and puts his hands on his hips. "Is he not allowed to touch himself without your permission?"

"He can do whatever he wants, but there are certain consequences if he touches himself without permission, yeah."

"That's cruel," I moan as he lightly squeezes my clit.

"It's what he asked for. Vaughn, come here."

Vaughn walks over, coming up the beach with long,

sexy strides. God, his legs drive me crazy. He should have been a model, not a patent lawyer.

"You rang?" he says, his voice thick. Poor guy is hard as a rock and I'm starting to see a little dark spot on the front of his fucking shorts.

"Brook thinks you feel left out."

"I'm right here. Why would I feel left out?"

Shaw leans up and uses the hand that was knuckle-deep inside me to reach into Vaughn's shorts. He doesn't pull his dick out, but I watch Vaughn's eyes fight to stay open as Shaw jerks him off beneath the fabric for a moment. He releases him and turns his fingers' attention back to me.

"She's worried about that, I think," Shaw says.

"I like to wait," Vaughn replies.

"As long as you're happy," I say.

"The view is better up close, though. You have a beautiful body, Brooklyn," he says. His sincere compliment is nice to hear. It still trips me up a bit and I wonder if he speaks to everyone this way. "May I?" he asks Shaw.

"No, you may not. But you know what you can do." Shaw breaks away from me again and I try not to complain. I'm glad I didn't when he hooks his thumbs into his swim trunks and pulls them down to his thighs, releasing his monstrously large cock. Out of the corner of my eye, I see Vaughn licking his lips. I don't blame him. Sucking dick isn't even my favorite thing to do and I feel my mouth watering at the mere thought of wrapping my lips around that thing.

"Come here."

Without hesitation, Vaughn drops to his knees and takes Shaw's dick in his mouth. He doesn't hesitate, swallowing the thing down. I watch as Shaw watches him, lightly scratching the back of Vaughn's head as it bobs up and down. Vaughan's glasses slide down his nose again, but there's something so sexy about the way he keeps them on as he goes to work. I slide my fingers between my legs to ease the ache that Shaw has built up. I barely brush my clit before Shaw knocks my hand out of the way. He seemed so focused on Vaughn, I have no idea how he even saw my hand move.

"Move your fucking hand," he says. I don't know why, but his words sting a little. That emotion catches me off guard and I find myself frozen. I don't mind rough, dirty talk at all and it's sexy as hell coming from Shaw, but maybe in the moment, I'm not ready for that just yet. I drop my hands to my lap and feel myself retreat.

Shaw senses it immediately. He looks over at me and does a double take when he catches whatever my face is currently doing. He leans over and cups my neck, pulling me closer as he kisses my cheek and then my ear. "I'm sorry," he whispers. He pulls back and looks me in the eye. "I want you to wait for me."

"Okay," I say thickly, fighting back tears. I don't know what the fuck is wrong with me.

"Here. Vaughny." He taps Vaughn's shoulder and Vaughn immediately lets Shaw's dick fall out of his mouth. "You're gonna make me come and then you're going to make Brook come."

"I can do that," Vaughn nods at me, seeking my approval. I don't hate that idea.

"Okay," I reply, feeling that odd tingle of relief settle over me. Vaughn goes back to work, stroking and sucking Shaw's perfect erection. Shaw drapes his arm over my leg again and starts to massage my upper thigh. It's not the brutal pounding or gentle stroking I was hoping for, but it helps erase that tight feeling. Helps take my mind off those shitty feelings that threatened to ruin the moment.

I try to keep still and be patient, but it's hard. Being fingered on the beach is good. Watching Vaughn suck dick is the sexiest thing I've ever seen. I feel myself squirming, my hips and my clit impatient as hell, even with a reward coming my way. Shaw spreads my thighs again and gives my pussy several light taps as Vaughn sets a steady pace.

Shaw turns to me. "I'm still waiting for you to kiss me," he says.

I look at his lips, desperate to suck the bottom one between my teeth. "I haven't kissed Vaughn yet. That doesn't seem fair."

"You're gonna be a problem, aren't you?" he says, unleashing this megawatt smile that threatens to melt my ass right to the sand. I just give him a little smile back and nod. He keeps on patting my pussy, driving me closer and closer to the edge as Vaughn draws him closer to his own orgasm.

Suddenly Shaw leans back, almost tipping his beach chair over as he grips the back of Vaughn's head with one hand and my thigh with the other. "Oh fuck!" he cries, coming into Vaughn's mouth. I watch as Vaughn swallows the first load then goes back for more, sucking every drop from the tip of Shaw's still hard erection.

"Brook wants to kiss you, you know?" Shaw says, still breathing hard with his eyes still closed. Vaughn doesn't wait for further instruction. He makes his way over to me and I know what's coming next. I'm ready. I want it. Vaughn gently cups my neck, tilting my chin up with his thumbs and presses his wet lips to mine. I open, letting his tongue and Shaw's salty cum slide into my mouth. It's filthy as fuck, but I love it, which is clear by the way I'm moaning into our kiss. And damn, can Vaughn kiss. I don't want it to end, but I break away, looking down as I feel Shaw's hands moving between our bodies.

Vaughn's shorts are down around his thighs now, he's holding up his shirt with his other hand and Shaw is sliding a condom onto his long, thick, erection.

"I want you to fuck Brook," he says, all cool and calm.

"I also want you to fuck Brook," I add.

"It's crazy, 'cause I definitely want to fuck Brook," Vaughn says before he's kissing me again. He's just as good a kisser as Shaw, but it's different. More tender, more careful like he wants me to fall in love with this kiss. He wants me to remember the way he took his time with it.

Vaughn pulls back and smooths his large palms over my exposed breasts. "Lay back for me." I sit back in my chair and let him grab my legs behind my knees until he's gotten me into the right position, my ass half on the chair. With Shaw's help, they push my knees up until my thighs are pressed against my chest and my pussy is nice and exposed. I watch the concentration in Vaughn's eyes as he fists his dick and gentle rubs my clit with its engorged head.

I fight to keep my eyes on him, fight to roll my hips against the sensation, but both are impossible. I whimper, making the most pathetic noise, and almost beg Vaughn to get on with it. I remember what Shaw said, remember that they have this under control. There's no need to rush this, even though the only thing I want in this world is Vaughn's cock inside of me. He doesn't make me wait much longer. I open my eyes again as he prods at my entrance, which is now dripping with arousal. I watch, biting the tip of my tongue as he pushes his way into me, inch by gloriously thick inch. Everything on Vaughn is in proportion to his impressive height. I don't think I'll be able to take it all. Doesn't mean I don't want him to try.

Shaw settles back into his chair and watches as Vaughn pumps in and out of my desperate pussy. It's hard for me to breathe in this position, with my legs trapping my breasts practically against my chin, but I can't remember a time I've been so turned on. I can't remember a time I've wanted to come so badly and wanted a man to keep fucking me all afternoon long. And I don't want him to look away. I want him to enjoy this as much as I am, as much as I think Vaughn is too.

"How does that pussy feel? She's nice and warm, isn't she?" Shaw says.

"Yeah," Vaughn groans as his head falls back.

"You should give it a taste," Shaw says. "See how it feels on your tongue."

Vaughn doesn't skip a beat. Just slides out of me and in

the next second, he's bent over with his tongue inside me. He's pushed my knees up even more, using his grip on my thighs for balance. It's too much sensation. His mouth moving over my gaping slit, my breasts squeezing against my legs. I'm gasping for air before the orgasm hits. And during? I black out. When I can hear and see again, Vaughn's pushing his cock back inside me. Shaw is saying something about how they should add my pussy to the menu. How there should always be a mouth on me at all times.

It's too much. Too fucking much. I come again at Vaughn's rhythmic stroking. His thick head pounding against all the perfect places inside my aching cunt. Through my blurred vision, I see Shaw sit up and kiss Vaughn deep. I watch, my eyes focusing in on the way their tongues move together and I can't handle it anymore. I slam my hips down, rocking myself hard as hell against Vaughn's strokes. He breaks their kiss, sensing what I really want. His fingers go to my clit as he starts fucking me hard and faster than before.

I grab his wrist, digging into his skin with my manicured nails, as I squirt all over his lap, all over the beach towel. I'm not sure how close the neighbors are, but I hope they can't hear me coming. Vaughn lets out a deep grunt of his own and I feel his erection jerk as he fills the condom. A sick part of me wishes he wasn't wearing one. I'm that keyed up. That high on the orgasms that are still rippling through me. I want to know what it's like for him and Shaw to fill me up. I want to stick my fingers in my cum-filled cunt and just live in that moment. I keep that to myself, though, as Vaughn slowly pulls out and gently eases my legs back down.

Shaw comes closer and helps me sit all the way up in my beach chair. I catch a glimpse of Vaughn as he takes off the condom and drops it in a recycled CVS bag he has in his backpack. I like that they don't litter.

"How you feeling, little thing?" Shaw asks me as he rubs my legs all the way to my toes.

I just smile and give him a thumbs up.

"Come with me."

I let Shaw help me up to my wobbly feet and stand there, my eyes only half open as he fixes my bathing suit, adjusting the ties behind my neck and covering my sloppy, wet pussy again with my bikini bottoms. My ribs are a little sore and my thighs are letting me know that I need to spend way more time stretching. I can't bring myself to care, though. I feel amazing.

"Can your hair get wet?" He asks.

I shake my head. "Not with salt water." My braids are actually a lace front that cost me half a kidney. I'd rather not have to do a full wig wash routine. I'm still riding a sex high, but I'm not that out of it.

"Cool. Come on." He walks me down to the water and I realize how hot I am before the cool waves even hit our toes. We've been in the shade, but it's beyond warm out and we've worked up quite a sweat. June weather on the Cape is no joke. "Water's cold, but you'll get used to it. Just stick with me."

I let out a little yelp as he tows me into the light waves. It's cold as fuck, but Vaughn was right. It only takes my body a second to adjust and then all I can focus on is how refreshing it is. We wade out until the water is almost chest high and then Shaw pulls me to him, grips my ass and hoists me up. I wrap my legs around his waist, my still-humming pussy pressing up against his rock-hard abs. I look into his dark brown eyes as he scans my face. I see a now shirtless Vaughn out of the corner of my eye, making his way for us. I turn and look at him as he rubs his fingers gently down my back.

"Tell me something I'll hate about you both," I say.

Vaughn lets out a sputtering laugh. "Why?"

"Because I need a reason not to come back. If this is what it's like with you two, quality beach dick and amazing food, I may quit my job and see if Shaw needs a full-time wood apprentice."

"Wood apprentice, huh? Is that a real position?" Shaw asks.

"Something I made up. You show me how to whittle and then I spend all night riding that wood."

"Well, now we know something bad about you," Shaw replies. "You're corny as hell."

"Oh, it gets way worse. Trust me. Where's the dog?" I ask.

"He's down there," Vaughn nods. I look down the beach and, sure enough, Roger is having a grand old time running in out of the waves with a piece of driftwood hanging out of his mouth.

"We'll stay down here a while then head back and chill until dinner," Shaw says as he gives my ass a little squeeze under the water.

"And tonight?" I ask, thinking about what it would be like to take them both at the same time.

"Tonight we'll see how much more you can handle," he says.

The sun beats down on the three of us as the waves ripple around us. The smell of the salt, the sand and Vaughn's sunscreen. I can't imagine a more perfect day.

NINE

Vaughn

"Here's what the fuck I don't get," Shaw says as we walk back up the path. He's walking in front of Brooklyn and I, with Roger leading us all like he's our guide. "How is Captain American's shield made of vibranium and he's got all this super strength? If he throws that thing, it's cutting motherfuckas in half. They always play it like you'd just get the wind knocked out of you. You'd be dead and in separate pieces."

"Something tells me you can't get away with PG ratings by chopping people in half," Brooklyn laughs. "Not really Disney's style."

"Why not!" he shouts sarcastically.

"He's technically not Captain American anymore. Maybe Sam will do the right thing and use the shield to really murder some people," I say.

"We don't need another Black man getting arrested, even if he's doing the right thing. I just want one henchman to walk over and say 'oh shit, he's dead and his legs are over there.'"

"What I don't like is how these movies do Thor," Brooklyn says. "Forget the fact that fandom acts like Hemsworth isn't fine as fuck, but Thor is a literal god and I have to spend, like, ten movies watching him play third fiddle to Tony Stark's bro quips. Pass!"

I hear a chirp then and immediately know the sound. "Shaw. Your phone."

"Ah shit." He stops on the path and pulls his cell out of his backpack. "Fuck, I missed a call. There was a problem with Wilson's delivery." He starts to turn, but hesitates, his fingers flying across his screen.

"Go," I tell him. He kisses me on the lips and then Brooklyn on the cheek before he turns and runs back to the house. Roger runs after him. He doesn't want us to leave Brooklyn alone while we're sorting this all out, but I got it from here.

"He sent this table that seats twenty-eight people to Vermont and he knew they were going to have a hard time reassembling it, but his contact was confident they had it."

"Clearly they don't," she replies.

"Wanna join me in the outdoor shower?" I ask when we reach the rinse shower installed in the backyard.

"Ooh, an outdoor shower sounds amazing. Let's do it." We'd spent most of the afternoon on the beach. In and out of the water, tossing random shit for Roger to play with and watching Brooklyn closely for any signs of a come down. She was handling things well, but that didn't mean she wouldn't have an unexpected reaction or be overwhelmed later on. Of course, we would give her her privacy if she asked, but it was never a good idea to just dump someone alone with their feelings after their first threesome with a new Dom and their submissive.

I also know this wouldn't be the best time for me to be alone. I'm trying not to dull my response to Brooklyn, but it's difficult. When the time is right, I'll explain it to her in a way that won't scare the shit out of her. My initial instincts are usually spot on when it comes to my own feelings. It takes me between five and ten minutes to decide how I feel about someone and that rarely changes.

I explained this to Shaw years ago. He was skeptical at first, but after a while he started to trust my instincts and to pay closer attention to the little things people did and said to reveal parts of their personality. Negative self-talk, unchecked confidence or humble selflessness. People usually give that shit up right away, but you have to pay attention and you have to remove your own feelings.

I had tried for a long time not to think about how my instincts had failed me with Corrine. Finally, I was able to forgive myself and let the past be the past. Brooklyn had been right all those months ago. I wanted to talk to Corrine. I wanted an explanation. An apology and a chance to apologize, but that wasn't going to happen.

All I could do was move forward, keep Shaw close and not murder Roger for his many attempts to ruin my breakfast. I'm still moving forward, that's the plan. Somehow being with Shaw lately though has felt like standing still. Like he's afraid to make any sudden moves, like we both are. But now Brooklyn is here and I can tell we both like her. I'm not sure what that means for us, for me.

We walk to the back of the house and set our things down on the benches Shaw built a few years ago.

"This is so fancy. Like an old-timey spa. How did Shaw find this house?"

"Just popped up on the market at the right time. The previous owner liked the idea of him making furniture out in the barn, so he sold it to Shaw without fielding any other offers."

"Wow. That's amazing. And you just come out on the weekends?" She asks as she turns on the water. She jerks her hand back and I'm sure it's freezing cold.

"Yeah. Unless work gets in the way, I head out here most Friday nights and stay through the weekend. When Shaw isn't busy with a piece, he'll come into Boston and stay with me or visit with my mom."

"That sounds nice." She freezes, her mouth hanging open a little, as I take off my swim trunks. I hold them under the slowly warming spray and ring them out before I lay them on the metal railing. "Everything okay?"

"Yeah, sorry. You were literally inside me two hours ago and I'm still shocked by your nudity."

"You want me to put my suit back on?"

"No, no. you're fine. I'm just—I'm a little off kilter," she says with a nervous laugh. She reaches behind her neck and unties her bikini top before stepping out of her bottoms. I watch her, trying not to drool over her luscious curves, as she moves by me to rinse her bathing suit and hang it beside mine on the railing. She steps under the spray, careful not to get her braids wet.

"What's throwing you off?" I ask gently.

"I almost said that I shouldn't say it, but I guess I'd be violating that whole honesty rule I threw down."

Brooklyn came her face off down at the beach and didn't hesitate letting me and Shaw hold her for nearly half an hour after it was done. I didn't think for a moment that maybe she hadn't enjoyed herself or maybe we'd thrown too much at her too soon. Maybe she wasn't feeling any of this.

"What's on your mind?" I ask, keeping my tone casual. She grabs my hand and pulls me under the water with her. Her hand goes to my chest and she lightly traces the fraternity brand on my pec.

"I'm having the best time I've had in awhile." She's looking down at her feet when she utters the words.

"Is that a bad thing?" I lightly tuck my finger under her chin and encourage her to look up at me. She does without hesitation, but I see something in her big brown eyes. She's sad again and that shit doesn't sit right with me.

"Damn, you're tall," she says as she rests her chin against my chest.

"It comes in handy when you need me to reach for things. Trust me."

"I bet. Anyway, I was just thinking about how I'm going to feel when I go home. Like, the return to reality will be the biggest letdown."

"I don't like leaving here either," I say.

"Right, but it's different for you."

I take her gently by her shoulders, turning her around before I pull her back against my chest. I wrap my arms around her and she reaches up and wraps her fingers around my forearms. A moment later, I feel her lips brush against my skin. I can't resist the temptation to lean down and press a kiss to her temple. Her chest rises and falls as she lets out a deep sigh. I'll stand like this for the rest of the afternoon if she needs me to.

"How is it different?" I ask.

"Because you know you'll be back in five days. You know Shaw will be here waiting for you."

"No, I don't," I say bluntly.

Brooklyn spins around and takes a step back. "Vaughn. I'm sorry. I didn't—"

"No, you're good. I'm just saying. We aren't promised tomorrow. Not saying there's another stalker with an itchy trigger finger out there. But what if I get in a car accident? What if Shaw is in his workshop alone and hurts himself? What if he decides he just doesn't want to fuck with me anymore? What if I decided this situation isn't for *me* anymore?" I don't like to think about any of these things too much, but it's the truth.

"You're right."

"I take what time I can with him and that's all I can do. You should do the same thing. Do you like being here with us?"

"I do. A lot. I'm having the time of my fucking life. And please don't tell my sister that, 'cause going upstate to her house is fun and all, but it's not quite like this."

"I promise not to contact your sister. I like having you here and I know Shaw does too. If you want to come hang out with us some weekends, then let's keep doing that."

"Yeah," she says.

"There's more."

"Of course there's more. Do you see me? Do you see this face? Do you see all these emotions?"

I laugh as I smooth my hands over her shoulders again. She relaxes into my touch as I massage her skin. "Tell me, tell us, when you're ready."

"I will. And what about you? You seem to be handling all this perfectly well. Please tell me you're struggling with all kinds of difficult emotions your therapist will love to hear about later."

"You know I am, but I'm trying to take things slow. In the name of honesty, I don't want to scare you. I can come on a little strong sometimes. It's why I feel more comfortable letting Shaw lead."

"What do you mean?"

"I'm very... decisive."

"In what way?"

"I know what I want and what I don't. Once my mind is made up, it's made up. Obviously, if I'm given new information, I can adjust accordingly."

"So, why do you have to give the reins over to Shaw? There's nothing wrong with being decisive."

"Because sometimes it turns people off. Shaw is more patient with that kind of thing. He's got his own intense way about him, but he seems to have control acting on how he feels."

"Is that why you came to the funeral alone?" she asks.

"Yeah. It's why I went to Corrine's service alone, too. He knew we shouldn't, but I'd made up my mind that I was going to try and pay my respects to her mother. Didn't work out that way, though."

"Okay. So what decisive thing are you holding back from me?" she asks.

"That I could see myself loving you very easily."

"Shaw said you were quite the lover. He said your heart can seat twenty-eight, easily."

"He's not wrong."

"And how do you feel about that?" she asks. She steps out of the spray and I notice she's shivering even though I'm pretty warm. I cut off the water and wrap her in one of our beach towels.

"Thank you."

"Let's go inside." I grab the rest of her things and let her lead the way. She encourages me to keep going once we're back in the kitchen.

"Finish what you were saying. About your max capacity for love."

"It's like this. Some people—actually most people—are looking for one person to love. I'm sure plenty of people would like a wide variety of people to fuck, but most of us are looking for that special someone to love."

"Right."

"I don't know if it's my mental wiring or if I have some sort of weird reverse grinch heart." She smiles at that. "But I met Shaw and I loved him as much as he could stand it."

"And then what?"

"I felt like I genuinely had the output to cover four more people. At first I thought it was actually a phase , but now I see that being polyamorous is really important to me."

"Have you guys ever thought about having kids? Legit question. Wouldn't solve the poly problem at all, but you seem like one hell of a nurturer."

"We have and we might one day. For now, things are the way they are."

"Okay. Go on."

"I feel like I have so much in me, like it's a physical thing in my chest and I have no idea where to put it. That's why submission is so important to me and why it works so well with Shaw. He helps me burn off that excess energy."

She stares at me, her eyes narrowing. I've seen this look once before, that night in the hotel. She's trying to do the mental math on me. "But you can't just give this love out to anyone."

"I mean, I guess I could, but who likes having their heart stepped on?"

"Wow. That's—I'm trying to picture what that feels like. I want—I think I want one person, like just one person to be strong enough to hold me together when I can't do it myself. It seems impossible to find that. I can't imagine having the energy to spread what I feel inside around to more than one person. But I think that's because I've never really been loved."

I want to say to her, *Let me love you Brooklyn. I have this here for you. Let me give it until you can't stand it anymore,* but as the thought passes through my mind, so does Corrine's face and the same thought I've had since

Shaw's confession in the hotel room. That Corrine may have been overwhelmed by us. That she may have been overwhelmed by me. She'd needed a break, time to be involved with just one man and not two containing the power of ten. And she'd found that relief, that lack of pressure in another woman's fiancé. I won't do that to Brooklyn now. I won't put my needs in her lap and chase her away.

"We don't have to talk about this. I know you said no ex talk," I say.

"No, that's not it. Let me just put on some clothes and check in with my sister. I'll be back in a few minutes."

"I'm right behind you." I follow Brooklyn upstairs and head into my spare bedroom. I wash my face and lotion up before I head out to the workshop to check on Shaw. I turn right the fuck back around when I hear him shouting from the driveway. Someone's fucked up real bad. I busy myself in the kitchen and wait for Brooklyn to finish getting dressed. She comes back in a pair of leggings and an oversized t-shirt. She looks fresh, but tired.

"You want to watch a movie? Shaw's still on the phone."

"Yeah, sure."

We set up in the den and she takes her time going through the available movies on our streaming service. "Who was watching *Phantom of the Opera*?"

"Shaw. He's big into musicals."

"Oh really?" she says with a smile. "Let's watch that." She hits play, then settles back against me. I pull her close and toss a blanket over her legs. When Shaw comes back into the house twenty minutes later, she's dead asleep.

Shaw

I still want to punch someone, but the music of the night soothes me as I walk into the house. I come into the den, ready to belt out the final chords, but catch myself before I wake Brooklyn.

"Shit, sorry," I whisper, easing into the room. I take a seat beside Vaughn and look over at her. She's still knocked out.

I won't lie and say shit hasn't been a little tense between Vaughn and I the last few months. He knows I love him and I'm trying not to fuck things up between us even more. But I didn't know not having Corrine around would be this tough, in this way. I'm glad Brook's here and it's selfish. For a lot of reasons, but mostly because of the way she is with Vaughn. Shit's new and temporary as fuck, but I can tell she likes him and she makes him smile. I think we need some of that if only for a weekend.

"How's it going?" I ask him as I look at Brook's beautiful face.

"Okay."

"Just okay? What's wrong?"

"I'll tell you later. What happened with the table?"

"Nothing. Fucking nothing. They left the leaf on the truck and the client was pissed 'cause they put it together and it was, like, four feet too small. I had to talk them down and then it took forty minutes for them to get their video chat together so they could show me the fucking thing and then it took them another fifteen minutes to find the leaf.

Everything is good now. I'd be real pissed if it was my guys, but the client hired them so it's their choice if they want to use them again."

"Glad it's sorted out. What time do you want dinner?"

"We can just order pizza. Tell me what happened."

I watch as Vaughn's long fingers ease over Brooklyn's shoulders. Something in her face twitches and I realize she's not really in a deep sleep.

"Hold that thought." I stand up, go to the other end of the couch and lift Brook's feet. Setting them in my lap, I lightly take hold of her big toe.

"This little piggy—" I jump back as she slaps my hand away.

"Don't even think about it, Shaw." She laughs as she stretches and sits up. "Crap, I missed like half the movie."

"Sorry to wake you up. We have some important shit to discuss."

"I'd love pizza for dinner."

"I knew you weren't sleeping."

"I was, but then something about a leaf woke me up."

"That was my bad." I grab the remote and pause the movie just as Raoul tells Christine there is no damn Phantom and take a seat on the coffee table in front of Brook.

"Listen, we have to have a serious talk," she says.

"Yeah and then I'll let you kids watch one more hour of TV before dinner. I'm just playin', but I do want to talk. Down at the beach, I almost made you cry. Can you tell me what that was about?"

"Oh that," Brook says, her eyes wide. I glance over at

Vaughn and he's doing his best to hide his own shock. He was busy sucking my dick when it happened. He didn't see the fear or the tears that had sprung up in her eyes. I know he's dead, but I'll dig up Josh Delinksy and whoop his ass if he did anything to make her fear men, especially in a sexual context. Brook sits forward and makes a dramatic show of putting both her hands on my knees.

"Shaw, I think you've uncovered my dirty little secret."

"And what's that?"

"I am very sensitive. A lot of people don't believe that, for a lot of reasons, most of them being extremely racist. I know you didn't yell at me, but you caught me off guard. I don't like it when people raise their voice at me, especially in a personal context."

"Would it bother you if I raised my voice at Vaughn?" I ask her.

She cringes. She's holding back. "I don't know. Maybe. My parents didn't yell. I mean, they would beat that ass, don't get me wrong, but neither of them were yellers, so I just—"

"You don't have to like being yelled at," Vaughn says.

"Do you not like it?" I ask him. We've never talked about this. I do get loud with him when scenes get intense, but he's never said anything about it.

"I can take or leave it. You seem to get excited, so I figured it was something you needed as a part of your outlet."

"Huh, interesting. I won't raise my voice, then."

"Listen, I didn't come here to shake things up. If you're a yeller, you're a yeller," Brook replies.

"No," I laugh. "I thought Vaughn was into it. I don't have to yell and I definitely won't get loud with you. That's no problem."

"Okay," she says sheepishly. I can tell there's more, but I'm not sure I want to push her just this second. She's given a lot of herself in the past few hours, been very open. She doesn't need to bleed her herself down all in one day. "There's one more thing. I realized it later, when I was getting dressed."

"Okay."

"And you get to cash in an 'I told you so', but there was one thing that used to happen with Josh and you made me think of it today on the beach.

I don't like the sound of that shit. "What was it?"

"Josh used to rush me."

"Rush you how?"

"He had this thing about making me come first, but he always wanted me to do it so quickly. I didn't feel like you guys were rushing me at all, but when you kinda snapped at me, it put me back in this place where it was like 'stop go, stop go' and it didn't matter how I actually felt. I didn't like it."

"Thank you for sharing that. How about this? We keep talking and we keep figuring out what does work for you."

"I like that. And, I mean, if you're into something I might not be at first, let's talk about that too. Intent matters. I don't like to be yelled *at*, but I don't think I would mind if you were loud, if that makes sense. Like, you don't need to whisper," she says with a little smile.

"Fair enough. Vaughn, anything to report?"

He looks at me, his jaw working. "Not at this time, sir."

I know he's fucking lying, but I don't push him. Not now, 'cause I know what he's going to say. I can see it all over his face. I could see it in the way he was holding her. He wants the go-ahead to fall in love with Brook.

TEN

Brooklyn

I've made my way to the other end of the house, to the addition with its new floors and higher ceilings. There's a bedroom here and Shaw's playroom. Shaw and Vaughn have been amazing so far. I don't know what to do with these open, positive conversations we keep having. I decide to file away this open communication as something I want with a future partner. It's something I didn't have with Josh.

I also file Vaughn's love of full nudity away as well. I'll keep it right in the front of my brain for the next time I'm alone and think about calling someone like Deek.

I join them in the playroom. It's a large, modern space with high, vaulted ceilings and one of those rubber, gym-type floors, I assume for easier clean up and traction. Shaw's in a cabinet in a far corner looking for something, still wearing jeans and the henley he put on before dinner when the temperature started to drop. Vaughn is butt-ass naked, coiling a length of rope around his elbow and thumb. They've given me a choice. I can watch or I can participate. Truthfully, a bitch is scared. I want to say I feel free to dive right into whatever freaky shit Shaw has in his mind to do to Vaughn, but from the moment I stepped into the room, I've been speechless.

I'm not naive. I have a sense of what sex dungeons look like. I've crafted the finer points of one in my imagination. Still, standing on the threshold, trying to take in every piece of furniture and contraption and the miles and miles of rope hanging on the walls, has me overwhelmed.

"Did you make all this stuff?" I asked Shaw. The room has stocks, some massive wooden X thing, three chairs with different holes and headrests, and two different benches with metal rings that I'm guessing are for rope and chains. There's a sex rocker too, one of those seats that lets you strap a dildo to it so you can fuck yourself with a swing of your hips.

Shaw closes the cabinet doors and comes back across the room. "No, we bought most of it. I like to keep my work and play separate. Also, it's much quicker to order something than to make it."

"Fair enough."

"I did make that bench, he says, nodding toward the wooden seat near Vaughn. "I couldn't find what I wanted to work with Vaughn's long legs."

"Ah."

"So. How are you feeling?"

I feel my brows draw together as I frown. "I'm still not sure."

Shaw takes my hand and walks me over to the bench in question. There's plenty of room for us to sit beside each other. "Talk to me."

I glance over as Vaughn hangs the rope back on the wall, then comes over to join us. It's hard to take my eyes off his rising erection. He stops in front of us. Something about his cock being at eye-level and just fucking out there while I'm trying bare my soul to Shaw should feel inappropriate, but it doesn't. Vaughn seems happy. He seems comfortable. I want him to be naked and happy. And I don't mind that his half-filled cock is inches away from my face. I don't mind it at all.

"I think I'm limiting myself because I'm scared."

"What are you scared of?" Vaughn asks.

"In a larger sense, the lasting, global impact of white supremacy. But, right now?"

"Yeah, right now," Shaw laughs.

"I want to trust you both enough to let myself do whatever, but I'm just not there yet." I stop myself before I apologize. I don't need to be sorry for that. Vaughn and Shaw are great, but I'm taking a risk being here alone with them in this way. I don't think they are gonna kill me or anything, but...

"What's one thing you want to do tonight, but you're afraid to ask for it?"

"Well, I still feel like I'm getting in your way. You're both just so ready. I feel like I'm slowing down your night."

"Vaughn, does your night feel interrupted?" Shaw says.

"No. Yours?"

"Fuck no. Try again."

"Okay, fine. I want you to tie me up, but not in a way that's gonna make it difficult for me to walk tomorrow and I want you both to fuck me at the same time. I also want to watch you two fuck each other. I think I would feel weird literally standing there watching, though."

"Okay. Vaughny, what do you need tonight?"

Vaughn glances at me and I see that he's holding back because of me. I reach up and take his hand. "I'm a big girl. If it's too much for me, I'll say so. We'll still be friends."

He squeezes my fingers before he looks over at Shaw. "I need impact. Lots of it, but I don't want Brooklyn to think she needs to get involved if it makes her uncomfortable."

"What's your flavor?" Shaw asks.

"Dealer's choice."

I look at Shaw as his gaze falls to the floor. His throat bobs as he rocks his head a little. He's thinking.

"What do you want?" I ask him.

He rocks some more, a scowl drawing his features together. "I'd need a clone of myself to do it all, but considering the circumstances, I think we need to warm you up. I think you need to watch. I heard everything you said and I have your whole checklist locked up in the brain vault. I won't push your hard limits, but I think we need to at least get you into the shallow end. Can you trust me with that? Can you trust me to course correct if you're not feeling it? I do want to tie you up, just your arms and tits. I'd also love to gag you, but we'll work up to that."

I think about it for a moment. If anything goes wrong, I

can still run away and activate my phone with my face. Not that I think we'll get there, but a girl can never be too safe.

"Yeah, we can do that."

"Good. Vaughn, tell Brook your safe word," Shaw says as he stands. He heads back to the large cabinet.

Vaughn gives my hand a little tug and helps me to my feet. "I use yellow when I need to slow down and red when I need to stop. Shaw will check in with you periodically. It's good practice to use green when you're good to continue. It forces your brain to slow down."

"Okay. Green, yellow, red. I got it."

Shaw comes back with two bundles of black-and-yellow rope hanging over his shoulder and a large dildo in his hand. He holds it out for me. "Good size?"

The thing is solid black and maybe ten inches long. It's thicker than a Coke can around. It's bigger than any toy I own. I know I can walk this back and ask for something smaller. Plus, I've already had Vaughn's long dick inside me earlier that day. I shrug. "Let's do it."

Shaw lightly takes my chin and tilts my head up so I'm looking him right in his dark-brown eyes. "We're about to start. And there's one thing you need to know. We have rules in this room, if you're going to play with me."

I don't know what it is about his sudden change of voice, but the gentle thunder in it, which I know he's adapted just for me, goes straight to my clit.

"You need to show me a little more respect, when you're here with me. It's yes, Shaw or yes, sir. Okay?"

I think about telling him to stick his sir up his ass, but my whole pussy is blooming at his words. My imagination can see the full potential of tonight. The intense authority in Shaw's voice is getting me exactly where I need to be. I swallow again, looking up into his eyes, before I nod. "Yes, Shaw." I manage to squeak out.

"Good girl." He leans down and kisses me before he pulls back, drawing his thumb along my lower lip. I actually moan at the small action. Shaw smiles.

"Vaughn," He hands over the rope. "Make her look nice and pretty for me."

"Yes, sir. Come here." Vaughn takes my hand and walks me over to another bench against the wall right below some small coat hooks.

"I'm going to take off your clothes. Are you wet?"

"Yes. Do I have to call you sir?" I ask as he pulls my t-shirt over my head. He hangs it on one of the hooks, then turns back for my bra.

"No, Vaughn works just fine. Unless you want to come up with a nickname for me." He pulls down my pants and my underwear together, offering his shoulder for balance as I step out of them.

"I like Vaughny," I say quietly.

"I do too." My heart flutters a bit when he winks at me. "I'm going to bind your arms behind your back and lift your breasts. It's for restraint, not pain. If you want it tighter, we can do that."

I let out a deep breath. We are really doing this. "Okay." Vaughn is quiet as he goes to work. I stand still as he very gently puts my arms into place, giving me a sense of what their final position will be. It's odd, but not uncomfortable. I focus on breathing as he makes his way around me in small, intentional circles, looping the rope over my shoulders, between my breasts and around my wrists. He takes his time and, once he's done, I'm starting to get it. He's run the rope on either side of my breasts, then loops it around so a strip of the woven nylon is running on either side of my now-hard nipples. The rope is softer than I expected. Its silky fibers feel great against my skin.

He steps back and looks over his handy work.

"How are we doing?" Shaw says as he steps behind me. "Is she suitable for the bow of my ship?" For some reason, I don't turn my head. Feeling the fabric of his jeans brush against my ass is enough.

"Ready for your inspection, sir," Vaughn says.

"Bring her here."

"Come on." Vaughn hooks his fingers into a loop in the rope behind my back, then turns me around. He walks me over to this massive mirror that's on a tripod of wheels. I gasp a little at the sight of my reflection. Gravity wins every battle versus my huge tits, but Vaughn managed to create a nice shelf of rope for my breasts to sit on. My nipples are perfectly on display, but my favorite part is the way he's looped the ropes in the shape of a heart just below my collarbone. He only used the black rope, but I can just imagine how nice other colors would look against my skin.

I look up at Shaw, just as he bends down and shoves his fingers between my legs.

"Shit," I hiss between my teeth before I catch myself. He glares up at me and I remember the rules. "Sir."

I try to hold still as his middle finger slowly rubs back and forth over my slit. Whatever wetness my labia was hiding from the open air is now on his hands and he's spreading it over my skin, around my clit. I know what I said earlier about wanting to slow down, about needing time. Still, I wouldn't be upset if he shoved his dick inside me and put me out of my misery.

"Come over here with me," he says.

He takes hold of the twisted rope behind my back and walks me over to the sex rocker where he's secured that large dildo to the base mount. "I'm gonna take care of Vaughn and you're going to watch and take care of yourself."

I nod, biting the inside of my lip. That seems to be a sufficient response for his house rules. I follow his lead as he maneuvers me over the padded seat of the rocker, then helps me squat until the dildo is pressing against my entrance. My thighs are strong, but not strong enough to hold this awkward squat for more than a minute. Maybe two, if I'm really determined. Shaw knows it, too. I look up at him as his eyebrow arches, questioning what plan I seem to have in mind. I let out a deep breath and sink down on the silicone cock.

"Fuck!" I cry out as it presses against my cervix. It hurts, I won't lie.

"Sit back and adjust your feet," Shaw says. I let my ass settle fully back on the red cushion supporting my thighs, then scoot my feet forward a couple inches. That does the trick. The dildo presses perfectly against my g-spot. The pain is replaced by a perfectly sweet ache. Shaw takes my chin again, his go-to move that I don't hate all. I watch him as he scans my face.

"You set the pace. Go as fast or as slow as you like. Come your fucking face off or don't come at all, but keep this in mind. When I'm done with Vaughn, I'm gonna dick you down until *I'm* ready to stop." I remind myself that I still have my safe word. I still have red on my side if I literally can't stand it. For now though, I accept the challenge. That's the point of all this. I want to be pushed to my limit. I can have boring sex and three minutes of quality time with my hand at home. I nod again and a small voice in my mind tells me to beg. Yes, beg Shaw to kiss me again. I don't know what is wrong with me, but it's what I want the most right now. One of his rough, commanding kisses.

I miss my moment, though. He turns and walks over to the cabinet and busies himself, most likely looking for what he needs to take care of Vaughn, who is now pacing through the middle of the room. I can't help but notice that he won't look at me. It's okay. I have no idea what Shaw has in store for him. I'm sure Vaughn needs more than a few minutes to get his mind right.

I sit on the rocker and focus on my breathing and every tiny motion of my hips. My pussy is so full and I know all I need to do is rock forward and rock back. I know I can make myself come, but I don't want to move. Not yet. Maybe this is part of Shaw's lesson. I can sit on the sidelines. I can watch and give myself a certain kind of pleasure. Or I can dive fully in and play with these boys.

I look over at Shaw again as he leans back and calls out to Vaughn. "Do I need to tie you up?"

Vaughn stops pacing, considering the floor before he looks up and shakes his head. "No, sir. I need to move."

"Fine by me." Shaw closes the cabinet and crosses the room, heading in my direction. He squats in front of the rocker, holding a handcrafted wooden paddle across his palms.

"I did make this," he said, clearly proud of his work with the dark-stained wood. It is very beautiful. "I'm going to use this paddle on Vaughn."

I swallow and nod, encouraging him to go on.

"Vaughn is very good at communicating his needs to me. When he has a lot of emotions built up, he likes pain. He enjoys rough strikes. I want you to remember that before we get started. What I'm about to do is what he asked for."

"Yes—yes, sir," I squeak out.

"We are in a scene together, though, all three of us. If this becomes too much for you, use your safe words. Okay? Voyeurism also needs consent. I'm not going to force you to watch something you don't want to watch."

"Okay, sir."

"Good." He winks at me before he stands to his full height and turns back to Vaughn. He pushes up the sleeves of his henley and stretches his neck. My eyes are drawn to his inked forearms. In the back of my mind, I realize I want more of Shaw. All of him. My eyes move to Vaughn as his shoulders and chest rise and fall. I can see his whole body. Taut, even muscle, his toes moving against the floor. I know this stance is a type of mental preparation. I almost laugh when I realize where and how I've experienced it before when I'm anticipating a horrible day in court. Vaughn is gathering his strength and his focus. I realize that I'm afraid for him, even though I shouldn't be.

Shaw huffs out a breath through his nose, then fixes his gaze on Vaughn's pacing. "I'm ready to begin," he says.

Vaughn lets out his own deep breath, walks over and grabs the edge of the stocks with his hands as he bends over. Shaw carefully walks up behind him. I brace myself for the first strike, ignoring the thrill that shoots through my pussy as my whole body clenches down. Shaw doesn't swing, though. He waits. I look at Vaughn and his mouth is moving, but no sound is coming out. Suddenly he moves his head to the side and I hear a small pop as he cracks his neck.

"Begin, sir," he says, nice and clearly.

I blink, my neck snapping back in surprise as Shaw lands the first blow.

ELEVEN

Vaughn

I have a high tolerance for pain. Higher than most people. When I received my fraternity brand, my line brothers were disturbed for months by how calmly I'd handled the whole process. Shaw's first strike is nothing, but it helps reset my brain. We're trying our best to loop Brooklyn in. To be honest with each other and honest with her, but he knows that I'm already struggling. He knows that she's pressing all of my buttons. He knows I'm on the verge of fucking this all the way up.

I'm a fucking pig, thinking I can claim her this soon. As if that's something she wants. Thinking that I, *we*, are all that she needs. That she just needs to give us a chance to show her. Shaw knows I'm close to breaking. He knows I'm already beating myself up. I wasn't put on this Earth to save anyone, save any woman. But I can't go back in time and change anything that's happened, including the conversations we've had today. Brooklyn is one of the most—no, she is *the* most open woman I've ever met. I can see now why she demanded honesty, because she gives it so freely. How can I not love that? How can I not want to protect that amazing part of her?

She's not yours to protect, I think to myself again before Shaw's paddle connects with the right side of my ass even harder. I jolt forward a bit, but I don't let go of my grip on the edge of the stocks. My cock is already swollen. It's been full and hard since I had to stop myself from licking Brooklyn's luscious breasts as she graciously let me bind her. I think of the innocent look in her eyes as she let me work. She has no idea what she's getting herself into with us. I want her to red out of this situation so we can stop. I trust she will if she's not into it, but as Shaw lands his third, fourth and fifth strikes, all I hear from the direction of that rocker is her heavy breathing.

I see now how much she's been hurting. Not just from losing Josh and being betrayed by him, but from feeling alone and misunderstood her whole life. I go to trial maybe twice a year. I can't imagine showing up day after day on behalf of abused children and assault victims. Part of her is made of pure steel. But what happens when that's all anyone ever sees? She laid it out, plain and simple. She wants to be fucked senseless. She also wants to be kissed and caressed. She wants to be held. She wants to be loved. But she hasn't chosen us yet. We're just not there. And outside of this room, I still don't know if Shaw and I, together, are strong enough for her. So I'll let Shaw beat the sense back into me, give me the release I need so I keep my mouth shut until she decides.

My body settles into the pain around the tenth lick. Eleven is different, though. So fucking hard, I shoot up as I curse out loud. Shaw knows to give me space. I slowly walk over to the door, breathing harshly, scrubbing my hands over my face. My ass is on fire, my whole body is sweating, and my cock... I look down as a string of precum stretches to the floor.

"Are we done?" Shaw says, his voice rough as I walk back in his direction. I look at Brooklyn and she's practically panting. Her chest is rising and falling in harsh, heavy waves and her eyes are fixated on me. I don't miss the fact that her hips are swinging back and forth. She's fucking herself nice and slow.

"Green," she says quietly, before she says it again a little louder. Reminding me that Shaw is waiting for my answer. "Green."

"No, sir. I'm not done."

"Then get your ass over here and let me finish."

I join him back at the stocks and assume the position again. The paddle blasts against the left side of my ass, the pain vibrating through my body straight to my cock.

"How does that dick feel?" he asks before he strikes me again.

"Full, sir," I groan out. "Heavy."

"I think you should empty in Brook's mouth. What do you think about that? You want to fuck Brook's pretty mouth til you fill it with your come?"

"I—I'd like that," she huffs out. "I'd like that, sir."

Shaw doesn't respond. He just paddles my ass until I'm cursing at the top of my lungs. My cock is dripping, creating a small puddle on the floor between my feet. If I didn't think my patience would be rewarded with Brook's full lips and perfect tongue, I'd nut right then and there, without touching my dick. All Shaw needs to do is say the words and I'd spill it all. But that's not what I want. Not right now.

Shaw delivers another, harder blow and a shiver runs over me. The endorphins rush through me, my head's light and all I can think about is coming. It's on Shaw now because I've hit that euphoric point. I won't tap out. He knows he has to pull me back. One more blow and I hear the paddle clank down on the nearby counter. A second later, his rough palms are smoothing over my ass. I can feel the tension in his body. He never answered Brooklyn's question, I realize. He never said what he wanted. Typically, I'd drop to my knees or ask permission to drop his pants so I could fuck his tight asshole until his gives us both permission to come, but things are different now.

Brooklyn is here.

Shaw's hands smooth down my back before he swats my ass with his bare palm. He wants to take the edge off, but neither of us want me to come down yet. I brave a look at Brooklyn at the light sound of her desperate moan. She's not looking at me. She's looking at Shaw as she rocks back and forth on that padded seat. I can see the look on her face. She's so close to begging. I'm just not sure for what.

"You want to come in her mouth or you want to come in her pussy?" Shaw says. Brooklyn moans even louder before I can respond. The answer is a no brainer. I've already sampled that sweet cunt earlier in the day. I'd give anything to be back inside her again, in any way she'll have me. I stand and do my best to breathe. I look at Brooklyn and she looks back at me, her hips stilling. I think she's trusting me to make the right call.

"In her pussy," I say so she can hear me.

"Grab the condoms and some lube," Shaw replies. When I come back from the supply cabinet with a handful of protection, Shaw is squatting beside Brooklyn again, running his hand over her shoulder before he reaches down and starts to toy with her breasts. Her eyes slam shut for a moment before she recovers, her gaze flitting between us.

"How are we doing, kitten?" he asks her.

"Good, sir." My cock twitches at the sound of her breathy voice. She's going to cry. I can hear it. She's too pent up. Her mind is processing too much. She needs a full release and I know that will bring cathartic tears. The tears she fought to hold back at the beach.

Shaw tilts his head to the side and looks between her legs. "Made a little mess there. Did you enjoy watching me paddle Vaughn?"

She nods again. "Yes, sir."

"It was nice having an audience," he says as he reaches up and roughly grabs my cock. My breath hisses between my teeth as Brooklyn gasps. I can't come. I can't come. He swirls his thumb over the tip of my erection, gathering my precum before he takes the shiny drops and spreads them out over Brooklyn's bottom lip. On reflex, her tongue sweeps out and laps it up.

"Ooh. You like that, huh?" Shaw says, pushing his

thumb deeper into her mouth. When he pulls it out, Brooklyn doesn't respond, but he does it again, gathering more clear precum from my dick and wiping it on her lip. Her tongue darts out again and I know it's not enough for her. She wants more. Shaw glances up at me before he turns back to Brooklyn. "Next time, I think we need to call in some more dudes. I don't think a dick in her pussy and a dick in her ass is enough for her. We gotta fill her all the way up."

Brooklyn moans again, her eyes slowly closing as she rocks forward and back. Shaw will let her come, rocking herself on that thing. He doesn't care. He's still gonna fuck her once her pulls her off of it. He leans forward and whispers something in her ear and she practically melts against his shoulder, nodding. I know that feeling. That desperation. The sight of it has more precum leaking from the tip of my dick.

"Vaughn. Take that shit and go lay down on the bench."

I go over to the custom mahogany bench Shaw made for me when we first met and set the condoms and lube on the floor. I have a sense where this is going, so I lay down on my back just as I hear another of Brooklyn's soft cries. A moment later, Shaw has her standing beside me. I look over at her and catch the glistening wet spot on her thighs. Shaw makes quick work of getting a condom on me before he pulls his jeans halfway down his thighs, exposing his own erection. He puts a condom on himself, then guides Brooklyn over my lap, but he doesn't make her sit. I don't mind the view. Her soft stomach and her large breasts hover right in my line of sight. I look at Shaw behind her, towering over her shoulder as he coats his fingers with lube.

"You took that fake dick just fine," he says as I see his hands move down to her ass. He's spreading the lube around. "I know you can handle me."

"I can, Shaw," she breathes out as she forces her shoulders to drop. She's trying to relax. I wait, watching them both. Damn near dying because her warm pussy is just an inch above my cock and I know I can't move, can't sink into her until Shaw gives me the okay. I watch her face, her lips dropping open as he slowly pushes his way into her ass.

"Shaw," she moans before she lets out a little high-pitched noise. I watch the focus on his face. The way his fingers dig into her round hips. He doesn't stop until he's all the way inside of her and then he lets out a quick breath like he knows. He knows he's in trouble 'cause she feels so good. I swallow as he starts to pump in and out of her, my dick still straining and eager. I know he won't make me wait forever, but he has no problem making me wait for a while.

"Okay, Vaughn," Shaw groans. "You can fuck her."

Slowly, with his hand on her lower back and a hand on her stomach, Shaw bends Brook over. I reach up and gently take her upper arms in my hands, giving her the support she needs. All on her own, she wiggles her way onto my cock, rubbing herself along the head until I find her entrance and push my way in.

"God damn," I say through gritted teeth. Her pussy is so tight and I can feel Shaw. I can feel his large erection filling her up from behind. He starts moving again. Setting a steady pace that's easy for me to catch on to. No alternating in and out. We move in and out together. We both rock back and forth in tandem, Shaw cupping her bound breast and me supporting her arms as she cries out between us. I feel her pussy quiver as an orgasm runs through her. Her forehead drops and presses against my chin.

She seems too overwhelmed to speak, but that doesn't stop moans and sighs from coming from her mouth. She cries out, clenching down hard around my dick, right before I feel a fresh rush of wetness on my lap. Shaw takes that as his cue to go harder and faster. I follow his lead, waiting for my turn to let go. Waiting for the moment where he can't hold himself back.

We fuck Brook until she can't stand. I see it in Shaw's face and feel her weight starting to go limp in my arms. She's still coming, her pussy leaking all over my thighs, but we want her to be able to walk the next day. We want her to want this again. I hear the way Shaw's breath leaves his mouth. He's about to come. Sure enough, he goes still for just a fraction of a second before he pumps into her, harder and faster. I can't keep up with his rhythm anymore. I jerk up, trying to meet the pumping of Brooklyn's hips. She arches her back, whimpering his name and then mine before coming again. I close my eyes and think about everything but how badly I want to nut inside this woman. How badly I need to come. Lights flash behind my closed lids as I remember the most important thing. It's Shaw's call. Shaw says when.

I hear a rough "fuck" come from his mouth and, when I open my eyes, he's pulled out of Brooklyn. I take her full weight and hold her against me as she tries to breathe, her arms still bound. I lose sight of Shaw as he crosses the room. When I hear the sink running, I know he's taking a minute to clean up.

I smooth my hands down the sides of Brooklyn's neck. "You okay?" I ask her.

"Yeah. Yeah, I'm good," she breathes before she swallows hard.

Shaw is back with us a few moments later, pulling Brooklyn off my lap. "Stand up," he tells me. I get up slowly and stand beside him as he sits Brooklyn down on the bench. There's a small puddle on the floor now, bigger than the spots of precum I've left around the place. This is all from Brooklyn. What's not on the floor is on my lap and my thighs, soaking my skin.

Shaw lightly takes her chin and turns her head toward my crotch. With his other hand, he pulls the condom off my still hard, still aching dick. "Look what you did to poor Vaughn. Dick's all hard. Crotch all wet. Do you think we should leave him this way?"

"No, sir," Brooklyn whimpers. If I had no clue where this was headed, I'd give up my red just so we could give her break. But Shaw is almost done with his first lesson of the weekend. He strokes me some more, trusting me to hold back as long as he needs me to. My nuts are fucking killing me. I might red for myself and go beat off in the corner while I have my own cathartic cry.

"She can't really move, Vaughn. Why don't you help this sweet kitten suck your dick. Make sure you nut in her mouth. Brook, I don't want you to swallow."

"Yes, sir."

I step forward, taking the base of my cock as I slide into Brooklyn's waiting mouth. She bobs her head a time and a half before my balls seize up my still burning ass tightens. I come all over her tongue. She seems to find her last energy reserve. I would have tapped out, but she's not done. She bobs forward as she sucks out every last drop. I step back because I feel like my soul is considering leaving my body too. My vision is hazy when I open my eyes and watch the way Shaw sticks two fingers in her mouth and lightly pulls her bottom lip down. The sight of my come drooling out of her mouth, my nut dribbling between her tits is almost enough to make me black out for real. Her big round eyes peering up at Shaw. She's so close to begging.

"Untie her," Shaw says before he heads for our fridge filled with water. I make quick but gentle work of the rope. I ease her arms back down to her sides and start to rub her down. Her back, her shoulders, her finger tips. I make note of how beautiful the impressions of the rope look on her skin. Shaw waits until I give my okay before he holds the water up to Brooklyn's mouth for her to drink. Then he pulls her to her feet and takes a seat on the bench, pulling her into his lap. He holds her close, bracing a hand on her thigh. I crouch on the floor in front of them, my fingers lightly stroking her calf, watching her as she looks between Shaw and me. There's still a trail of drool and jizz down the middle of her chest. We're all gonna sleep well tonight.

She takes another sip of water.

"We're done, little bird. How are you feeling?"

"I need one—I need one more thing."

"What's that?"

"I want you to kiss me."

Shaw doesn't hesitate. He leans down and claims her mouth, kissing her roughly in a way that seems to awaken her all over again. It's not long before she's writhing on Shaw's lap. My dick is somehow twitching at the sight of it. She may have needed a little break, but I have a feeling Brooklyn Lewis will be up for round two in no time.

TWELVE

Brooklyn

My bladder wakes me up around two a.m.. My arms and shoulders are a little bit sore, but the rest of my body is still liquid when I open my eyes. Shaw and Vaughn had walked me through their post-game routine, cleaning me up and talking sweetly to me. Rubbing my whole body, making sure I had plenty of water to drink. When Shaw asked me if I wanted to sleep up in my room alone or down in the massive custom bed he and Vaughn often share in the addition, the answer seemed like a no brainer. He grabbed my things for me and after I put on my night shirt and wrapped my hair, I climbed into the giant bed between them. I wanted to stay awake and keep chatting with them, but I passed out sometime after Shaw brought up how he hoped Kayne was done releasing his ugly-ass clothing lines.

Now, there's no Shaw. Only Vaughn, sound asleep beside me with his boxers riding low on his hips. He's snoring. Loud, but it's so cute and I can't really blame him. We had a night. A long, intense night where he took the brunt of whatever Shaw had in mind to dish out and then helped Shaw take care of me. If anyone deserves some loud, restful sleep, it's Vaughn. I use the bathroom by the kitchen and on the way out I see light spilling across the kitchen floor. I investigate and find Shaw sitting in his office, the faithful Roger passed out by the fireplace.

Shaw looks up from his tablet and sets down his stylus pencil.

"Trouble sleeping?" he asks me.

"Something like that. What are you working on?"

"Nothing exciting. Just a desk for a new client."

I step closer and look at the beginnings of a digital sketch. It does, in fact, look like a desk. "That's cool."

"Thanks."

Shaw leans back, one eyebrow reaching for the edge of his fade. I stare at him, trying to hide the smile that wants to take over my lips. He leans back even further, inclining his head toward me. I get it. I'm not fooling anyone. I didn't wander into his office to ask him how the drafting program on his iPad works. I want to be near him again. I'm wondering what's keeping him up and why he's not busy making a Brookie sandwich with Vaughn. Mostly I'm wondering if I should ask him to finger me while I sit on his desk. I decide to keep that all to myself though. We've done enough for one evening.

"Well. Nice chatting with you." I turn to leave. I'm sure Vaughn will welcome me back to bed, even though he's busy snoring his tender, bruised ass off.

"Brook."

"Yep," I say before I turn back. When I do, I realize my mistake. I should have kept my damn mouth shut. I should have crept back to bed and left Shaw to his work. I should have counted sheep until I dozed off again. There's still time for that. I can still escape with my dignity intact.

Shaw swivels the base of his chair and my eyes go right to his lap as his thighs fall open. He's wearing a pair of plaid pajama pants and a different henley than he was when he put Vaughn and I to bed. It's just sleep wear, but it looks so good on him and that thirsty thought is the least of my problems. I take in the way he's eyeing me, opening another door with just a look. Waiting for me to do something, to say something, and I know all of it is bad news. I can't do this with Shaw. Shaw is trouble.

I don't flee like I know I should.

"How do you do this all the time?" I ask him.

"Do what?"

"This."

"What? Working in my office in the middle of the night?"

"No, you ass."

"Listen, you wanted honesty. So, use your words and stop playing games, you *ass*."

My eyes roll all on their own. "Fine. How do you exist at this heightened level of horniness all the time? How do you walk down the street without people of all genders throwing themselves at you? Is that why you live so far out here alone?"

"Well, for starters, there's a woman wearing no pants in my office right now, so that might have something to do with my level of horniness. And for the second part, I don't think people come on to me anymore than they come on to anyone they find attractive. That doesn't make me special."

"Uh huh. Sure," I laugh, but it dies on my lips almost immediately. Shaw isn't laughing. He's frowning at me. "What?"

"What part of this is the part you think you don't deserve?"

"What are you talking about? I didn't say that." I know I sound defensive, but that stung. An uncomfortable heat spreads over the back of my neck.

"No, but you're suggesting that I have something you can't have or can't imagine having, even though my dick was literally in your ass a few hours ago." I stare at him in shock, my brain trying to sort through what he's saying. My silence isn't enough to stop him because he just keeps right on going. "If it's me you think you can't have, you're wrong 'cause you've already had me. If it's a relationship like Vaughn and I have, well..."

"Well what?" I don't mean to snap, but I snap. I'm fucking annoyed.

"Josh is gone, Brook. Corrine is gone. He hurt you. She hurt me, but the brutal truth is they can't hurt us again."

That heat on my neck flashes up my face and down my

throat. I was wrong about Shaw and it's better for me to walk away right now. "Copy that. I'm gonna go back to bed. Goodnight." I make for the door, but he's still got more shit to say.

"Brook."

I spin around, my hands going to my hips. "What?" I say with a mirthless scoff. What the fuck could he possibly want from me?

"Come here."

"No."

"Fine. I'll say this while you stand over there. You wanted honesty. I want to stop punishing myself, I want you to do the same and I definitely don't want you to punish Vaughn."

"I didn't—"

"He's falling for you. Already. You were a fucking dream in there. I don't want you to tell him this feels too good to be true or ask for more proof of how good this can be, 'cause he'll show you. And he won't stop trying to show you until I stop him."

"You think you need to protect Vaughn from me and my insecurities?"

"No, I think you're going through a lot and it's bringing up a lot of emotions. I'm just telling you where I'm coming from. Josh did you dirty. But Corrine did us dirty too and I know Vaughn blames himself. He'd do anything to make it up to a ghost. How far do you think he'd push himself to make it up to a woman standing right in front of him?"

"Fine. That's fair. I'm saying I hear you and now I'm going back to bed."

I don't give Shaw a chance to stop me again. I find my way through the mostly dark house back to the narrow staircase and spend the rest of the night tossing and turning in my assigned guest room. I know I'm being dramatic, taking my beef with Shaw out on Vaughn by leaving him all alone. It's better to rip the band-aid off now, though. I'll be gone in the morning and I won't be coming back.

Shaw

"You got everything?" Vaughn asks. We're standing in the driveway, saying goodbye. After my fucked-up conversation with Brook, I couldn't focus on work anymore. I couldn't say I was surprised to find Vaughn alone in bed when I finally came to join them. I'd considered going up to her room to apologize, but I knew I'd pissed her smooth the fuck off. She didn't want to speak to me and pushing the issue would just make her more upset.

So I gave her space and first thing in the morning, while Vaughn was busy making a ten-course breakfast, Brook arrived in the kitchen, fully dressed, fully packed and ready to get the fuck out of town. She begged off, claiming she wanted to beat traffic and get some rest so she was fresh to handle her week's caseload, but I knew she just wanted to get the hell away from me.

Vaughn was hurt and confused for about three seconds before he realized the way she wasn't looking at me. He knew I did something, said something shitty. He knew I'm the reason she wasn't in bed with us when he woke up. I'll admit it. I fucked up. Maybe she wasn't the only one in the business of self sabotage.

Vaughn puts her weekend bag in the back seat while she sets her purse and phone on the center console. I file the adorable image of her short, full body trying to climb into this massive SUV away for another time when my foot isn't halfway down my throat.

Brook smiles up at him and slips her fingers into his. " I got everything. Thanks."

"Are we going to see you again?" I hear the desperation in his voice. He's kept his word and not blurted out how badly he wants her to stay, but this is Vaughn. He can't hide the way he feels. It's not a part of his programming and she had asked for honesty. He can keep things to himself, but Vaughn's truth is that he's falling for Brooklyn Lewis. She's gorgeous, funny, bright, with a body I don't want to keep my hands off of. It's hard for both of us to see her walk away. Still, I hang back and keep my mouth shut. I've done enough.

"I had an amazing time, but I need to think about it, okay?"

"Okay."

"I just want to be all good. In every way, you know? Leave as much baggage as I can at the door and I think I still have a few trolleys full."

"You can still call us. You know that, right?"

"I know." She stands on her tiptoes. I watch as Vaughn bends over and accepts a soft kiss on the lips. I shouldn't be jealous, but I am. Last night, she was begging me to kiss her and now I know she's never going to let me kiss her again.

"I will call you when I get home, okay?" she says, keeping her voice light, doing her level best to look every-where but at me.

"Okay. Drive safe."

"I will." She leans over, fixing me with a deranged smile. "Bye, Shaw! Thanks for having me. This place is great." *Thanks for ruining a perfectly good weekend.*

"Of course. You're welcome anytime."

Her response is another tight grin before her expression softens and her gaze goes back to Vaughn. "Bye."

She climbs up into her car and we wait as she slowly backs down the driveway. We both wave as she pulls out on the street and we wait a few breaths before she turns on the road and drives away. I brace myself and wait for Vaughn to cuss me the fuck out, but he doesn't. He just turns and walks toward the house.

"Hey, wait."

"For what?" He spins around and I swallow at the blank expression on his face. Vaughn doesn't do loud and angry. Vaughn ices you out and I'm getting frostbite standing in my own damn driveway.

"I know you're pissed at me. I know. Let's just talk about it."

"Oh, like you talked to Brooklyn last night? What the fuck did you say to her?"

"She wanted me to tell her this was all some fantasy that was too good to be true and I wouldn't do it. She got mad."

"Is that all you said?"

There's no point in giving him half truths. If he talks to Brooklyn later all he has to do is drop the magic word, honesty, and she'll tell him everything I said. And I know how he'll take it, even though I was just looking out for him.

"I told her the truth. That you would give her your all and it wasn't fair for her to make you prove it."

"Can I ask you something?" Vaughn says.

"Sure."

"Negro. Are you high?"

"Okay, man. What—" I try to walk by him 'cause I already had one fight with a lover in the last twelve hours. I'm not in the mood for a repeat performance.

"No." Vaughn grabs my arm, hard, reminding me that he's taller and stronger and his submission is willfully given. It's not my right or something I can intimidate out of him. It shouldn't be a turn on, but it is and it gets my attention. I stop and turn to face him, settling in for the chewing out I deserve.

"For real, what the fuck is wrong with you? Of course I need to prove that I'm worthy of her. On what planet do you think it's cool for us to ask any woman, any person, to take the two of us on and for us *not* to show them that they can trust us? Yeah, Corrine cheated, but you have to see how much Josh hurt her. She was days away from walking down the aisle. He embarrassed her in ways neither of us can understand because we're men."

I sigh, keeping my mouth shut. He's right. I know he's right.

"What you and Corrine and I had wasn't a secret, but

we weren't out there, Shaw. She was ready to become a part of his family. Everyone in her life knew about it. On top of that, she's a plus-size Black woman. How many times a day do you think she's getting some messaging that she's undesirable? Fifty? A hundred? She can be confident, but she's a fucking human. So, I think it makes sense that if we want her to be with us in any long term way we prove to her that we aren't using her and that her needs and her very real fears are being met."

"Okay, okay, you're right."

"I know I am. I'm going to take Roger to the beach and enjoy this weather before I have to go back to work. Maybe when I'm gone, you can think of a good way to apologize to her. Whatever she decides, you owe her that much."

"I will. I promise." I grab his hand as he turns to walk inside. "Are we good?"

"I guess. You still fucked up, though. You're not off the hook."

"I know. I love you and I am sorry for fucking up your morning with her. She likes you a lot and I know you both wanted more time together." I laugh and Vaughn turns at the sound, catching Roger's face pressed up against the screen door. "He doesn't want us to fight."

"No. He doesn't want you to be a dick."

"Fair. I deserved that."

Vaughn pulls me close with an arm around my waist and kisses me soft, but deep. He's still angry, but he loves me. We'll have an argument again, probably soon and it'll be my fault. I've been on a roll lately. One day he's going to be sick of my shit and he's going to leave me too. I need to be better for him, if I can just get the fuck out of my own way.

That night, when Vaughn is long back in the city and Roger is dead asleep under my desk, I grab my phone and find Brooklyn's Instagram. I've been there already. Thoroughly checked out all of her social media in the months since she followed my business account back.

She's added a new picture. One she's snapped from the side of the road on her way through Buzzards Bay.

Beautiful weekend on the Cape. Great food. Great company. One cute doggy.

She doesn't tag Vaughn or me, which is clearly the smart move. No shame here, but no one wants to explain how we know each other and why we're hanging out. I keep scrolling, looking at pictures she's posted while out for drinks with her coworkers. Pictures of her watching *The Bachelor* with a small group of women. Pictures of flowers her friend Noa sent her for Valentine's Day.

I think about that night, how I'd sent Roger to the dog sitter, then drove into the city and took Vaughn out to the dinner. We'd spent the night at his place trying to reconnect. Well, fucking and affirming how badly we want each other in our lives. We were honest about Corrine. Honest about how much we missed her even though it still hurt to think about her and what had happened. Vaughn opened up about how weird his apartment felt since shipping her things back to her family. I know he feels her ghost in every room of the place.

I think about what that night must have been like for Brook. How she was supposed to have been celebrating her first Valentine's Day with her new husband. I keep scrolling and see the months and months of posts after Josh's death where she's just trying to prove that she's still alive, still trying to see the good things in life. Pictures of her nieces playing with a fuck ton of dogs. Almost two months of posts of just cakes and pastries, promoting her sister's farm bakery. I scroll back until I find pictures of her and Josh, pictures I'm sure she's conflicted about deleting. I find a picture of the ring.

Feeling some type of way about Mom and Dad missing this amazing moment, but I know they are smiling down on me and my amazing husband-to-be. I love you, @Josh-Del603_2NYC. Can't wait to share forever with you.

I keep scrolling. There are more pictures of them together. At Yankees' games. At her sister's farm. Shopping for books. Sharing ice cream. Waiting in the line for the latest Stars Wars movie. Josh looks like such a basic white boy, I can't imagine what someone as amazing as Brook saw in him, but I know what Vaughn would have to say about it. They were in love and it's not for me to judge how that came to be.

For the first time, I realize I'm pissed at Corrine, not for cheating on us, but for stepping out with someone else's man. For hurting Brook. She knew better. She knew how that kind of betrayal stung. She'd been cheated on before she met us and we had spent years making up for it. Maybe that's why I'm so protective of Vaughn. Maybe it's me with the trust issues. Me with a skeptical eye on this new woman in our lives. It's not fair. It's not Brook's fault and I need to make it up to her.

I switch over to my never-ending conversation with Vaughn and shoot him a text.

Hey babe.
You hear from Brook?

Yeah. She's back in her apartment.
Got home a couple hours ago.

K cool
Luv u.

<3

I switch over to my conversation with Brook and try to choose my words wisely.

Hey. I'm sorry about last night.
Let me know when you're cool to
talk. I'd like to apologize.
I wasn't being fair to you.

I let out a deep breath as those three little bubbles suddenly pop up on my screen. I realize how badly I want to talk to her and how badly I want her to forgive me. I don't want this thing between the three of us to be over. I blink when I see it, then reread the text that pops up on my screen.

Fuck you, Shaw.

THIRTEEN

Brooklyn

"Biiiiiitch," Rayna says, laughing at me.

"What?" I grumble.

"What is with your face right now?"

"Nothing is wrong with my face," I say, deepening the scowl clouding my expression even more.

"You should see it." She chuckles again and takes the bowl of chips I hand to her. We were all busy Monday night and missed our regular group viewing of *The Bachelorette*. We have some catching up to do.

"Sorry. I've been cranky as fuck all week."

"Work stuff?" Rayna asks. She takes care of her grandmother full time and hasn't worked in an office in years, but she knows being a special victims A.D.A. is literally never sunshine and roses.

"No. It's—it's nothing. I'm just pissy, I guess."

"I thought you'd come back from the Cape so relaxed," Noa adds. "I've only been up there twice for weddings, but it's so beautiful."

"No, I had fun. I just—" I shake off the dark cloud that's been hanging over my head since I told Shaw to blow it out of his ass. "I'm fine. Let's watch someone else make bad choices." I pull up the most recent episode in my streaming app and settle in for the worst reality dating shows have to offer. I'm glad I have this. I'm glad I have the girls. It's not the same without my sister and Claudia, but this bit of normalcy has kept me grounded since everything went to hell. It'll bring me right back down to Earth as soon as I get over the mistake that was Me, Vaughn Coleman and Volderdick.

I've spoken with Vaughn every day since I left the Cape. He checks in on me and I ask him how he's doing. I sent him some cool Batman art I saw on Twitter and he sent me a hilarious drawing of Thor fucking Thanos. I let him apologize for Shaw's behavior twice before I told him I don't really want to talk about it. The day we spent together was amazing. Let's just leave it at that.

I'm back home, back to work and I think sometime soon I'll tell my friends and my sisters that I'm ready to start dating again, because I am.

I focus my attention on this chick Stacene who is about to make out with this awful pilot who recited the Pledge of Allegiance as soon as he climbed out of the limo. I'm terrified he's going to make it to hometowns. Right after the first commercial break, a text vibrates my phone. I pull it out

from under my thigh and smile as Vaughn's name lights up
my screen.

Hey sweetheart.
I'm sorry to bother you.

Hey babe.
You're not bothering me at all
What's up?

You don't need to forgive him,
but Shaw wants to apologize to you.
And I think he should too.

I stare at my phone, considering whether or not I'm
ready to hear from Shaw again. He does owe me an apology,
but if he thinks he can be all condescending and shit, he's
got another thing coming.

I'll send you nudes if that helps
butter you up to the idea of a conversation.

I cover my mouth as I snort out loud.

Your nudes or his nudes?

Both?

I'll call him.
Give me a few to consider the nudes.

He sends back a heart and a thumbs up emoji.

"Okay, who are you texting? 'Cause girl, you are blushing." Rayna asks.

"Phssst. Please. I don't blush."

"Fine. Your cheeks just doubled in size. Are you talking to a maaaaaan?"

"I'm just talking to my friend... Coleman. Corny lawyer jokes. It's all very boring. I'll be right back."

"You want us to pause it?" Noa asks.

"Nah. Just tell me what happens."

I walk into my bedroom and close the door. I take a seat on the far side of my bed, then pull up Shaw's contact. I'll hear him out and then I think it's time for me to end this situation once and for all. We had our fun, but this isn't sustainable. Between the reality of how we came into each other's lives, the distance and Shaw's clear attitude problem, I just can't. In a perfect world, I'd ride into the sunset strapped to two amazing men. But this is the real world and Shaw is a jerk.

"Brook. Hey." The sound of his voice makes my stomach clench. The sexy dickhead.

"Vaughn said you wanted to apologize. So apologize," I say, trying to sound bored. Christopher Shaw isn't getting under my skin again. No fucking way.

"I'm sorry for what I said. I didn't—I don't think you are any danger to Vaughn and I shouldn't expect you to be a hundred percent confident in a situation that's new to you with two men you barely know. We've trauma bonded and I think that blurred some lines. It did for me and I'm sorry."

Okay, well, that was a good apology, but I'm still upset.

"You really hurt my feelings, Shaw," I say plainly.

"I know. I get very protective of Vaughn sometimes. I was pissed when he reached out to you in the first place. I love him and I guess, in my pig-headed brain, I think it's my job to protect him."

"Well, Vaughn's a big boy and I think you need to stop speaking for him."

"Okay."

"He's been very open with me. I know he's vulnerable to heartbreak, but we all are and it was unfair for you to say that shit to me."

"You're right. It was." God damnit. Why is his voice so sexy?

"And I think you need to admit that you're afraid of getting hurt too. Using the way Vaughn puts himself out there as a shield for your own emotions is not okay. Yes, I want to protect Vaughn's heart, but it's strange for you to act like you don't have one when Corrine clearly broke it." Okay, maybe that was too far. I bite my lips and listen to beat after beat of silence on the other end of the line. It stretches on so long I double check the display just to make sure he hasn't ended the call. "Are you still there?"

"Yeah. I'm just swallowing my pride or some shit."

"Or some shit. I refuse to believe that Vaughn doesn't call you out when you're acting like this, 'cause I know he does."

"He does. Look, you're right. I am protective of Vaughn, but I was guarding my heart too. It's why—" he cuts himself off. There's something he's afraid to admit.

"Shaw tell me," I say gently.

"It's why I wasn't in bed when you got up." He's quiet, but this time I don't push. His tone is different when he speaks again. Sadder. "Things with Vaughn and I have been kinda fucked up lately and I thought—not that you would fix things, but he wants our shit to be poly. He needs more partners and I didn't realize I wasn't ready to spend the night with someone new between us."

"Oh. Well, why didn't you just say so? Shaw, I can leave you two alone and we can just be friends. Or I can be friends with Vaughn and continue ignoring you or whatever."

That makes him laugh. His laugh makes me smile, but only a little. I'm still kinda pissed.

"I'm not trying to be in the way of you or Vaughn figure things out." I go on. "We tried a thing, just to try it. It clearly didn't work for you. You try to turn it around on me and now I'm upset and Vaughn's upset. I'm sure Roger wasn't too happy about it either."

"He gave me a lot of shit after you left."

"I bet he did," I laugh a little, trying to cover up the way my voice is starting to quiver. I know we can't keep this going, but Shaw's reaction to and rejection of me still hurts. "I won't say no hard feelings, but I get it. We can just, ya know, not all sleep together again."

"That's not what I want."

"Oh?"

"I want to see you again. I want to be with you again," he says.

I wasn't expecting him to say that at all, but it does change things, 'cause I would absolutely be lying if I said I wanted to quit Vaughn or Shaw cold turkey. I know we can't skip off into the sunset together and I'll walk away from them if it's what they want, but it's not what I want. I don't want it to be done even though I know this can't last forever. Still, Shaw threw down a lot of rules when we were in his sex room of pain and pleasure, and if this is gonna happen, we're gonna do things on my terms.

"I want to see you without Vaughn," I reply.

"Okay."

I know how it sounds, but I've made up my mind about Vaughn. If it were just the two of us, I'd be having serious conversations to see how he feels about finding a firm in Manhattan. He's sweet and thoughtful and goofy. He's kind to animals, even when they eat his breakfast, and I know Liz would love him. Hell, so would Silas. I can just picture Vaughn asking him all kinds of questions about the farm and giving Silas the space he needs when he's had enough people time. Vaughn fits my life perfectly. Who I'm not too sure about is his asshole boyfriend.

"The three of us hanging together is a possibility, but you need to give me room to walk away from this, 'cause I don't know yet. You're not giving me time to figure it out."

"That's fair."

"I know it is. Jesus, you drive me nuts."

"Come up this weekend."

"Um no. I'm going to see my sister tomorrow. Why don't you come down here the following Friday and we can talk. If we make up, you can sleep on my couch."

"That's ten days from now."

"So? I want to see my sister and her kids. Is that okay with you, sir?"

"Yeah, fine."

"Good boy."

"You're gonna pay for that," he growls, his voice straining.

"If I let you. Now, I have people over, so I have to go. Go jerk off to the fact that you could be fucking me this weekend if you'd just been nicer and we'd made plans sooner."

"Bye Brook."

"Byeee."

I know I'm being petty and immature, but I don't care. Shaw hurt me and I plan on being a pain in his ass until I feel better about it.

I know it sounds silly, but the massive wraparound porch of my sister's farmhouse is my new happy place. As kids, we rarely left the Bronx. Just to visit family in New Jersey and the one summer we went to our cousins in Texas. Liz and I are the Bronx through and through and while I can't see myself living anywhere but New York, this small town upstate where my sister has settled down with her farmer man is so peaceful.

I look out over their yard where Silas is pushing Princess P on her tire swing, little Iona perched on his hip. Their dogs are skipping through the grass having a grand old time.

It's a warm summer evening and the sun is still in the sky. I'm already covered in bug spray. Liz is beside me and we're shucking corn for dinner, including a few dozen more ears to hold Silas over for seven minutes or so. I'm still tense over my conversation with Shaw. I do want to talk to him, but I'm disturbed by how badly I want to fuck him. He upset me and giving him a bit of that back gave me an unexpected rage boner that I still don't really understand. I want to cuss him out to his face and then sit on that face just to shut him up. It's a fun fantasy, but it's not healthy. I don't want a relationship like that.

"Ah Jesus," Liz suddenly says. I follow her line of sight to her Silas.

"What?"

"No, I just realized something."

"What?"

"I'm gonna let this man put another baby in me."

"You are?!" I laugh.

"Yup. I just—TMI or whatever the hell. But he comes home every day after working his ass off and I just can't keep my hands off him. Even right now. You go to sleep, kids go to sleep and it's on."

"One, gross. I don't need to know you're fucking while I'm here. Two, that doesn't mean you need to get pregnant again."

"Oh, but it does," my sister says deadpan.

I chuckle and turn back to the corn in my hand.

"I can't explain it. I mean, it is no walk in the park, but I like being pregnant and just look at him."

I look over at Silas again. He's huge, a Brawny paper

towel ad come to life, with this chubby cheeked toddler on his hip. He pushes the tire swing again, then strokes Iona's head before he kisses it. "Okay, fine. He's a great father."

"He's a great father. We have this big house. All this freaking land. It's not like how we grew up. There's room for kids to move around here. He told me he was open to as many kids as I want."

"Well, look at you."

My sister glances over at me and whatever she sees on my face brings her gently back to Earth. "I know. If the boys at the firm could see me now." Corporate litigation used to be her bread and butter. Now she's a full-on farmer's wife, raising two beautiful girls and six dogs, running her own bakery.

"I've never seen you this happy."

"Shit's good, isn't it?"

"It is."

"I don't know. I figured I'd marry some business jerk, Mr. Big, kinda guy, but like Black and not afraid of commitment. I never pictured this. It suits me, though. It feels right."

I just smile and keep my eyes on my corn.

"It'll happen for you, Brook," she says softly as she nudges my shoulder. "Soon. I know it."

"Ehh, I don't know about all that, but I appreciate the positivity."

"Things will get better."

"Will they?" I say, my tone dripping with sarcasm.

"Yeah, they will. You're amazing."

"Well, he better hurry up. I slept with Deek a couple weeks ago."

"Nooo!" Liz yells so loud, Silas, the girls, the dogs and a few random birds all turn and look at her.

"I'm sorry. It's fine! Everything's fine!"

Silas gives a thumbs up and goes back to pushing the swing.

"Okay. I'm gonna put my head together with Claudia and Noa, and we're gonna find you someone. Hell, I'll even ask Scott. He knows all the big city lawyer types."

Liz and Silas's twin brother have a complicated history. Mostly because he'd been in love with her at one point, but hadn't confessed his feelings until after she and Silas had slept together. Things had been tough, but now Scott was doing his best to be a good uncle. Truth be told, I'd fuck him if he wasn't a messy douche. He was just as hot as Silas, but the corporate, cleaned-up version, minus the beard and the long hair, with a few Tom Ford suits added. Corporate law fit him a little too well for my liking.

I considered Silas's cousin for a hot second. A cute, burly Scotsman who used to run the farm's diner, but he was married to the place and then literally married someone else and moved to Los Angeles. I hear they are very happy. Must be nice.

"I'll pass. No lawyers for me," I say, lying my ass off. I'd been sexting with Vaughn just the night before. He'd texted me to say goodnight and somehow got on the subject of what he'd do if he was in my bedroom waiting to tuck me in. I fell asleep with my fingers still between my legs, thinking of Vaughn. And Shaw.

"I met one guy, but it's messy and he can be a jerk. I still really want to let him hit it."

"Listen. You've had a really shitty year and half. If you wanna let a meh dude hit, let him hit. But not Deek. And be sure you hit then quit. Sound legit?"

"Ahh, you really are a mom. All unfunny and shit."

"You know what I mean. You just know not to catch feelings for lousy dick."

I almost tell her that my confidence in that department is still a little shaken considering I almost married a pretty lousy guy.

Yeah, but at the time you didn't know, a little voice in my head reminds me. *Don't beat yourself up.* Little voice is right.

"In the meantime, I'm glad I have you and Silas and the girls."

"And we love having you, my Brookie Babe." I look over at her and she looks just like our mom. The thought reminds me that I'm not alone with these kinda crappy feelings. My sister has my back. It's not necessary, but I know she'd fist fight Shaw for me too.

FOURTEEN

Brooklyn

Okay fine. So, Shaw was right. Ten days is a long time, made even longer by the fact that I was basically sexting Vaughn the whole time and playing this other sick mind game with Shaw. He knew Vaughn and I were talking and made an effort to also connect with me. My initial rejection of that idea turned into a perverse back and forth where he'd try to ask me intimate questions and I'd respond with short, clipped remarks. It quickly became clear that Shaw was getting off on my sly responses and my dumb ass really leaned into it. By the time I left the office that Friday, I was practically crawling out of my skin.

I shower and spend way too much time thinking about what I want to wear to have a civil conversation with Shaw. I have my AC unit on, but it's been eighty degrees all week. My favorite yellow sundress that shows off my ass and barely contains my tits is good enough. I put my fresh set of box braids up in a ponytail and check my barely there makeup no less than seven times in my bathroom mirror. At 8:15, he calls to let me know he's downstairs. I buzz him in and then wait the few minutes it takes for him to come up to my floor. I check the peephole right after he knocks and try not to faint at the distorted image of Christopher Shaw standing in my hallway.

I open the door and the real thing is much more devastating. He's wearing a pair of dark wash jeans and a light green t-shirt that's tight on his biceps and shows off the perfect round slopes of his pecs. His hair is freshly lined up and his beard is nicely trimmed. His brand new white sneakers shouldn't be a turn on, but I do love a man who knows how to dress fresh for the summer.

"Hey."

I glare up at him. "Hello, Shaw. Did you find some place to park?"

"Yeah, down the block."

"Good. Come on in."

I move so he can walk past me and then watch as he drops his keys next to mine in the little bowl I have on the edge of the counter. It's strange having him in my apartment. Mostly since I haven't had a whole bunch of men, or any single man really, hang out in my place in such a long time. Deek doesn't count. I don't want to acknowledge the other part. The time we spent together at Shaw's house still feels like a fantasy. Having him drive down here and step into my place makes things feel more real.

"Just you here?" he asks.

"Yep. Just me."

"It's nice. You grew up here?"

"Yeah. Well, no. Not in this building. We were a few blocks over. My sister and I sublet the place. Figured we'd hold onto it after I moved out just in case."

"Smart. Real estate is no joke."

"So."

He turns and looks at me. "So."

I motion for him to proceed. "Do you have anything you want to say?"

"I am still sorry for the way I acted, but I think there's something more pressing we need to discuss."

"What's that?"

"Why I'm here in the first place. You said you wanted to see me alone."

"I don't know. I just did. I know where I stand with Vaughn."

"And where's that?"

"At the moment, it's none of your business."

"Is that right?"

"Yep."

"So, you wanna keep sending my man saucy texts—"

"Saucy?"

"You heard what I said. You want to keep hitting my man up but you want me to stay out of it?"

I bite the inside of my lip and try to decide how long I want to let his foolishness go on. Of course, I'm not trying to carry on with Vaughn without Shaw. I know they are a package deal. Still, that notion goes both ways. Just because Vaughn and I get along doesn't mean Shaw gets to just skate on bad behavior. I walk by him and take a seat on my couch. He follows, but stands in the doorway, watching me.

"Do you like me or not?" I say, knowing full well I sound like a teenager.

"Yes, Brook. I like you."

"So then, what the fuck, Shaw? Why are you making this so hard?"

"Let the record show I was trying to make this less hard on you last week. You were the one dragging this battle of the wills out."

"Yeah, sure. Fine. Whatever. Come over here and let me touch you."

He laughs quietly, shaking his head, but that doesn't stop him from crossing the room. He doesn't join me on the couch, though. He reaches for my hand and pulls me to my feet.

"Where are we going?"

"To your bedroom. Unless you want me to fuck you on this couch."

"Who said I wanted to have sex with you?"

He quirks his head back, staring at me, his eyes comically wide. "Maybe I read this wrong. But I thought I was coming down here for a kiss and makeup type situation?"

"Yeah, okay, fine. Let's go."

I head for the bedroom, but Shaw catches me and pulls me close into his arms. I look up at him, the intense look on his face shocking the breath right out of my chest. "I get it. You're still mad at me, but stop acting like you don't want this as badly as I do. I'm sorry, Brook. Do you forgive me?"

I don't tell him. I show him, perching up on my tiptoes

so I can press my lips to his. He leans down to meet me halfway, gently pushing his tongue into my mouth while both of his hands grip my ass and hold me closer. I feel his erection growing between us and all I want to do is rip his pants off. It's been a long ten days and all the texts with Vaughn did not help. My pussy is aching and I can't wait anymore. I find my footing and start nudging him backwards. He takes my hint, breaking the kiss so he can steer me around in front of him, giving me room to lead the way.

It's warm in my bedroom, the summer heat from the day still lingering. I do not fucking care. We can get nice and sweaty while we do this. I collapse on the sheets and shimmy up my bed, keeping my eyes on Shaw's hungry gaze. I reach under my skirt and pull off my underwear.

"Is Vaughn home? Is he at his place?" I ask him as I toss my draws on the floor.

"Yeah. Why?"

"Call him on Facetime."

"'Kay. Hold on." Shaw pulls his phone out of his back pocket. He toes out of his sneakers as the sounds of the Facetime alert echoes through my room. My eyes stay on him as he kneels on the edge of the mattress just as Vaughn answers. At the sound of Vaughn's voice, my hand slides between my legs. I didn't realize how much I missed him.

"Hey. Whoa. Hey. Are you at Brooklyn's?" he asks, confused.

"Yeah. I think someone misses you. Say hi, baby."

"Hi Vaughny," I wave to the camera on Shaw's phone and spread my legs a little wider.

"Can't say I hate that view. What are you two doing?

Did you kiss and make up? From the look of things, Brooklyn's forgiven you."

"We're getting there. We're skipping right to the good part and I think Brook wants you to watch."

"I do." I say.

"Here." Shaw hands me his phone. I can't help but smile the second I see Vaughn's face.

"Hey you," I say.

"I'm glad you two are working things out," he chuckles a bit. "What's Shaw doing?"

"Just getting naked." I flip the camera around so he can see his boyfriend stripping down to nothing but his thick erection and look of determination.

"I don't hate this view either. Sad I can't be there, though."

"Next time," Shaw says. He climbs on the bed and wraps his arms around my thighs. I hold my breath as he pulls me close and doesn't waste any time dragging his tongue over my wet slit. It's strange, seeing him in the rectangle on the phone screen, seeing his shoulders move just beyond the edges of his phone case, feeling him push his fingers inside me.

"Can you see this?" I ask Vaughn as I bite back a moan.

"I can, baby. It looks good as hell."

"Will you touch yourself for me?" I ask. Shaw groans in agreement, driving his fingers deeper into my pussy. He turns his head and gives my thigh a gentle scrape with his teeth before he turns his tongue's attention back to my clit.

"I thought you would never ask," Vaughn says. I hear the rustling of his clothes. I look at the way his glasses slip down his nose as he tries to hold on to his phone and pull out his dick.

"You have to show me," I whimper. Shaw does some magic combination of licking and stroking, and a small orgasm rolls through me. I grab his shoulder with my free hand, seeking out the anchor I need to stop myself from scurrying up my bed. When I open my eyes again, I get a screen full of Vaughn's hand stroking over his cock. The image is a little grainer than I'd like, but's clear enough for it to completely turn me on.

"Jesus Christ. Shaw, look at this." I turn the phone around so he can see. I'd smile at the look on his face, the way his eyebrows shoot up and the slow smirk that follows, but his fingers are still moving inside me and I can't think about reacting to anything other than how good this feels. I bring the phone back up so I can see what Vaughn's doing with his long fingers and so he can see what Shaw is going with his thick calloused fingers and his amazing tongue. I regret the fact that I don't have a phone stand. I also regret the fact that I didn't tell Vaughn to come down to my apartment too. Shaw and I could have talked alone and then Vaughn would have been here to enjoy the fun. Next time, I tell myself, 'cause there's definitely going to be a next time.

"Sorry, babe. I can't wait," Shaw says suddenly. He stands off the bed and grabs a condom from his pants pocket. Once he has it in place, he takes the phone from me. "I think Vaughn might like this view a little bit better." I look down as he pushes my thigh up with his free hand. I reach and help him center the tip of his cock right at my opening. My hips move on their own, pushing down to meet his gentle thrust. Shaw's dick is huge and I love how much he's filling me up.

I don't realize my eyes are closed again until I hear Vaughn's groan coming through the speaker.

"Fuck, man. You didn't tell me her pussy was this good," Shaw says.

Vaughn laughs a little as Shaw lets out a deep breath. "Yes, the hell I did, but you didn't want to believe me. Fuck." My pussy clenches hard at the hiss coming from him. God, I wish Vaughn was here.

"Well, shit. I believe you now. You gotta stop hiding this body from us, baby. This pussy, your ass. It's too good."

"I'll do my best," I groan out. I stop talking and focus my every thought to where Shaw and I are connected, the way his erection feels pumping in and out of me. How seriously fucking wet I am. I couldn't be more turned on by the fact that Vaughn is watching us, that he's touching himself while he watches us. I can't see him, but I can hear the way he's breathing hard near his phone. I can hear the way he says my name, the way he says Shaw's name. I can just picture the way he looks stroking his dick. If I didn't have the career I have or a fear of losing it in a foolishly scandalous way, I'd tell Shaw to hit that screen record. I want to relive this moment.

I feel an orgasm coming for me and I can't hold back as soon as I feel it. My pussy won't let me. She's craving this release. My hips grind down hard on Shaw's lap and I feel the tremors running through me.

"Yes, that's it, baby," he says quietly. "Vaughn, look at this beautiful girl coming."

"You look so pretty, baby," Vaughn says. "Holy shit."

I lean up on my elbow and grab Shaw's hip. He knows what I want, grinding into me deeper and harder. I come again, practically screaming his name and then again at the sound of his and Vaughn's grunts and groans. I come again and again until I feel Shaw tense above me. He curses, loud, just before I feel his cock flexing inside me as he fills the condom. I hate the way it feels when he sits back, letting his dick slip out. I feel cold when he steps into the bathroom, but he's back a moment later, climbing on the bed behind me, pulling me close.

He hands me his phone and buries his lips against my neck. Vaughn's moved, setting up his phone so we can watch him jerking off in an office chair. "Okay, Vaughn. You can come."

"Thank you," he says. There's no build up and I don't blame him. He strokes his dick twice and thick jets of cum shoot up his stomach. It's sexy as fuck to watch, the way his abs and his thighs tense. He reaches down, squeezing his balls and more cum dribbles from the tip. I push my dress up again and let my hand slip between my thighs, like I didn't just get dicked to oblivion and back. Shaw's fingers join mine. He stops me from stroking my clit, but the way our hands cup my pussy together is more than enough to get me fired up again.

"Ms. Lewis and I have more talking and fucking to do, but I'll be at your place in the morning. You should get some sleep."

"Sounds good." Vaughn reaches for his phone, bringing

it closer to his face and I let a quiet giggle slip as he pushes his glasses back up his nose.

"Goodnight, Vaughny," I say.

"Goodnight."

"Love you," Shaw says and Vaughn replies in kind before we end the call. For some reason their comfortable exchange sends an icy feeling through my chest. I think about every time I told Josh I loved him and how he was lying every time he said it back. I have no idea what it'll be like to be able to say those words again. To mean them, to trust them.

"You want more?" Shaw whispers in my ear. His fingers flex around mine, squeezing my clit against my labia. That's enough to warm me all over.

"Yes," I say, before I roll onto my back and let my legs fall open. I watch Shaw as his gaze roams over my face for a few long moments and then he's kissing me again. He guides my hand over my still soaking pussy and we make me come again, together.

It's close to midnight and the AC has finally brought the temperature in my apartment down, but I'm still covered in a nice sheen of sweat. I might be more comfortable if Shaw wasn't laying on top of me, his cheek resting on my breast. I don't want him to move though. This is something I've missed more than I'm willing to admit to anyone, the heavy weight of a man on top of me. I know he can't, but I want him to stay longer.

He's spent the whole night worshipping my cunt. I could handle more, but this quiet moment where I see if we can just exist together in the same space, this is why I wanted him to come see me alone. This is what I needed. I trail my fingers over his bare back, along the soft skin over his spine. I didn't think I'd touch a man like this again.

"Do you, by any chance, think this is a bad idea? You know, in the real world sense," I ask him. He glances up at me before he closes his eyes again.

"It's a terrible idea. Three of us clinging to each other, trying to fuck our way through the lingering remains of our trauma."

"He's a poet too, folks."

"It's a really bad idea. But that doesn't change how much I want you," he says.

"Me neither. I—I feel foolish with you two. Like, really reckless."

"Welcome to the club."

"No, I don't think you get it," I say. "I almost told Vaughn that I wanted you both to nut inside me. Like, that first day at your place. So clearly you two aren't the only ones in danger here. Not to be corny as hell, but I feel alive with you two. After feeling so numb for so long, I felt *something*, but I don't want to lose control."

"I think we all have things we're afraid of here."

"What are you afraid of?" I ask.

"That Vaughn will fall in love with you."

"Why?"

"Because I can't say no to him."

I feel myself scowling at his response. Something about

it feels off. "I don't get it. Can you clarify or—?"

"It's how we work. Vaughn shows all the emotions for both of us. I get to be blunt and rude and closed off. It's our system. Well, my system."

"So what does that mean for me and you?" I ask, ignoring the flashing red sign that has just flipped on in a corner of my mind. I thought we'd made some progress, but maybe that was just so he could get me in bed.

"It means that it's Vaughn's job to tell you how smart you are. How fine you are. How much he likes kicking it with you. How the sound of your laugh makes him smile in a way he thought he would never smile again. To tell you he could easily see himself being with you 'cause it's true *and* it's what you deserve."

"And it's your job to remind me not to fuck it up?"

"Yup. Otherwise how do I keep you a comfortable ten feet away?"

I swallow the anxious feeling in my throat, then take a chance, asking, "Is that how you stop me from breaking *your* heart?"

I know then what's really going on between me and Shaw. Or what's not. This has nothing to do with me. I could be any woman Vaughn brought back to Shaw with that sweet smile and those damn glasses that won't stay on his face. This isn't about me. Shaw's mourning Corrine. He's had time to be angry on Vaughn's behalf, but he hasn't grieved for himself. Not enough. Shaw is truly afraid he'll get hurt again.

I'm about to tell him it's okay. That I understand. That I won't push anymore because, while Vaughn and I have tried our best to process our shit, Shaw's been shoving it all down. He sees me coming and he feels backed into a corner where he'll have to face those feelings and he's not there yet. He's not ready.

My lips part and, just as I draw in the breath I need to state my case, I feel it. A change in the air. The sudden tension Shaw is carrying through his whole body. It happens so quickly, but so clearly, that I feel stupid for not noticing how close he was to the edge before. The way he's been laying on top of me, the tightness in his body, how he's trying to pull his whole spirit away, but he's losing the fight. I look down at him, just as two fat tears slip over the bridge of his nose and land on my chest.

"Shaw," I say quietly. He moves off me and sits on the edge of the bed, wiping his eyes.

"You happy now, Brook? You broke a man," he says dramatically. I chuckle and sit up. I draw my fingers over the tattoos covering his arm.

"That's not what I wanted."

"I know. You wanted honesty. Well, you got honesty. I'm still trying to figure out how to keep you the fuck away from me and how to keep Vaughn close."

"Come here," I say, but it's me who scoots closer. I lean against his perfectly sculpted back, put my head on his shoulder and let Christopher Shaw cry.

FIFTEEN

Vaughn

"How did this happen?" Shaw laughs. I look between him, my mother and the kitchen drawer that is now in three different pieces on the counter.

"Boy, I don't know. I opened the drawer and it fell apart." Shaw looks around the clean kitchen. The space is warm and inviting, slightly beat down by years of wear and tear.

"Might be time to do some remodeling," Mom says, following his gaze around the room.

"You want me and Vaughn to buy you a new house?" Shaw says.

"I mean, if you're offering."

"Shaw is welcome to buy you a house. In the meantime, I'll pitch in and get this place fixed up for you," I reply. My mom has lived in the same three-bedroom house in

Dorchester since I was twelve. Parts of the neighborhood have been bought up and flipped, but she has no plan to go anywhere. I support her decision. The least I can do is remodel her kitchen.

"I can fix this for you. You have any wood glue?" Shaw asks.

"I still have the bottle you bought out in the shed."

"I'll be right back."

"Glad he uses his handy work for good," she teases once he's out the back door.

"You and me both."

"How are you doing, baby?"

"Ya know, I'm good. Work is good. Shaw is good."

"That all sounds very good."

I smile at her. I know when she's digging. "I'm good, Mom. We're both good."

"You know it's my job as a mother. I get to ask."

"I appreciate it." My phone vibrates in my pocket. I reach for it too quickly, hoping it's Brook. I catch the way Mom's eyes spring wide in response to my quick hands.

Hope you guys are enjoying your Saturday. <3

She's added a picture of herself walking down the street as she blows a kiss to the camera. I think I do a decent job of ignoring the heat that's blooming in my chest. I quickly send her a response, trying to wipe the smile off my face as I type.

Back at you. We'll give you a shout later. <3

"Something important?" Mom asks as I slip my phone back in my pocket.

"No, just a friend."

"You're not stepping out on Shaw are you?"

"What? No." I know she's joking. She knows Shaw and I are open with our wants and needs. She knows neither of us would cheat, especially after what happened.

"You know I'm just giving you a hard time. I haven't seen a smile like that on your face in a while."

"I wasn't smiling. Was I?"

She smirks at me and pats my hand, just as I hear Shaw come back through the side door.

"I need more wood glue. I'm going to run to the store," he says. "Need anything while I'm out?"

My phone vibrates again and I feel my expression fall as my mom's eyes drop to my phone.

"You okay?" Shaw asks, glancing between me and Mom. She's doing a horrible job holding back her laughter.

"I got a text and Mom thinks my behavior's off."

"You're standing like you have a rod up your ass, so maybe she's on to something."

"He said he got a text from a friend," Mom laughs.

"Oh. Ooh!"

I let out a deep breath and Shaw nods. He knows the drill. I can't keep shit from Lynetta Coleman.

"We did meet someone," I confess.

"Oh? Who is it? Do I know them?"

"No. We, uh—I. I definitely acted alone here. Last year, I reached out to Brooklyn Lewis. She was engaged to Josh

Delinsky. The guy Corrine was with when everything happened. The man who was killed…"

My mom cringes, bracing herself for more. "Okay. So you two are seeing her now?"

"I don't know actually." I glance over at Shaw and he doesn't have any answers either.

"I just wanted to talk to her at first. And we did talk. That was over a year ago. Right after it happened."

"Okay."

"I wanted to talk to someone since Mrs. Johnson was freezing us out."

"And she was dead wrong for that. She still is." My mom is still pissed at Corrine's mom for thinking the worst of me and Shaw. She figured, like we did, that there was an opportunity for our family community to grow, not to be diminished by the fact that her daughter loved two men instead of one. That's water under the bridge for me and I need to save my brain cells for things like explaining to my mom how talking to Brooklyn isn't as bad as it sounds. I don't need to waste more time thinking about how Mrs. Johnson probably still thinks we're sexual deviants and users of women.

"Well, we talked and it was good, but she said she was still processing stuff, as were we, so we basically left things at that. She had our numbers and we made it clear that we wouldn't bother her about Corrine or the case or anything. But then—"

"But then?" Mom says.

"She reached out to Shaw a few weeks ago."

"And now you're sleeping with her?"

"Yeah."

"Do you want my opinion? My approval? What needs to happen here?"

"I'd like your opinion," Shaw says. "I had some complicated feelings about it and didn't handle the situation well at first. Of course, your son was a perfect gentleman. You raised him right."

"And what, I somehow failed you all these years?"

"No, ma'am. I have no excuse."

"What did you do?" she asks.

"I was kind of a dick to her."

"While you were sleeping with her?"

"Yeah. But I apologized. We made up last night. Everything's cool."

She frowns at Shaw and we both know if he wasn't standing across the kitchen, she'd smack him upside the head.

"I promise. I apologized."

"Uh huh. So, you've spent enough time with her that Shaw had to apologize for something. Any clue where it's heading?"

"At this moment, no," I say.

"Nope," Shaw adds.

"Well, since you two seem to have this all figured out."

"We don't at all. I think we just like her," I confess.

"My opinion is to be careful. I don't know the girl, so I don't want to say anything about her, but you better make sure you're on the same page and that you're looking at this with clear heads and not your lusty loins."

"Thanks, Mom."

"I'm serious."

"We know you are and we hear you."

"Good."

"Let me step out and get this glue," Shaw says, wanting to get the hell out of this conversation. "Miss Lynetta, when I get back, let's talk about renovations. I can vet some contractors for you."

"You're not going to do it?"

"I can build you some cabinets, but you know that's not my specialty. I definitely don't do floors and, girl, you need new floors. Also, I know jack all about building codes."

"Plus, he'll charge you triple and take three times as long," I add.

"I'd appreciate it if you didn't knock my process."

"Sure, let's talk," Mom laughs before she hands him a twenty-dollar bill. "Pick me up some milk and some of those Ferrero Rocher."

"Yes, ma'am. I'll be right back." Shaw kisses me on the cheek before he heads out the door. I notice that he's left the twenty on the edge of the counter. I grab it and hand it back to my mom. Her smile quickly fades. Now she's glaring at me, her eyebrows going up.

"I know, Mom."

"Look, I know you don't have to listen to me when it comes to romance. I haven't set the best example." My mom doesn't believe in marriage. She's had a series of boyfriends over the years, all good men, who all left when they realized she's serious about not becoming a Mrs. Anybody. My dad has his own family, grown kids with his wife, and he's still bitter that my mom wasn't *the* one. She's currently dating a high school Vice Principal named Harold. Another good man. We'll see what happens.

"I would never say that. I don't even think that. Harold is great."

"Okay, but I do want you to listen to me. You two need to be careful. Like I said, I obviously don't know the girl, but this is ten steps further than what you two had with Corrine. Her mother couldn't comprehend a healthy polyamorous relationship, fine. Whatever. Have you two considered what this means for this young woman's life?"

"I have."

"What's her name? What does she do?"

"Her name is Brooklyn. She's an A.D.A. from the Bronx."

"Vaughn."

"I know." For the second time in twenty-four hours, I regret not going with Shaw.

<hr>

"What did Miss Lynetta have to say?" Shaw asks when we're back in his car. We'd spent the rest of the afternoon helping my mom around the house and now we're heading to my place for dinner. I thought it was safer to wait to debrief him on the piece of her mind she'd given me about Brooklyn while he was out getting chocolate and wood glue.

"Just what you'd expect. The extended version of 'don't fuck around and get Brooklyn fired from her highly political job. Don't fuck around and end up with the cops wondering if the three of you planned this whole thing.'"

"Ooof," Shaw groans.

"Yeah. I mean, I don't want to think that way, 'cause it's not true and the cops are too lazy to open a closed case just to point the finger in the wrong direction, but..."

"But what?"

"For some reason, I keep thinking about Mrs. Johnson and what she would do if she found out."

"If she found out about Brook? Or if she found out about us with any woman? 'Cause I don't think she'd be too jazzed about either of those scenarios."

"You're right."

"And, to be honest, I don't give a shit what she thinks. We were good to her daughter and her daughter wanted to be with us for a while. Whatever happened, all of it involved her daughter making her own grown-ass decisions. The only person she should be pissed at is the man who took her daughter away."

"You're right."

"What's really eating you?" Shaw asks.

"Man, I don't know. That this feels—shit. It feels good to me. I want to get to know Brook better, but you know me."

"I do. And you're right. Your intuition is pretty spot on. But your mom is right too. This isn't just about us and after last night, I want to make sure neither of us forget it."

I reach over and squeeze his thigh. "I'm glad you two had that time together. Jealous as hell I couldn't be there for the fun parts, though."

"You missed the extremely rare sight of me shedding tears too."

"Babe." Shaw told me they talked and gave me a good summary of their conversation, but he hadn't said anything about breaking down, in front of Brooklyn, no less.

"It's not a big deal."

"It's not a big deal that you cried, but it's a good thing that you let it out. How did Brooklyn react?"

"She handled it well. Offered support. Let me get it out. Like I said, we had a good talk."

"That's good." I try not to make a big deal about it, but I know how rare it is for Shaw to open up like that and I know how much he'd been struggling with his feelings for Brooklyn. If he can be that raw with her, we might be onto something. It's not a bad thing for us to have Brooklyn in our lives.

Shaw pulls into the parking structure under my building and pulls into the extra space he pays for every month. He cuts off the engine, but doesn't make a move to get out of the car.

"What are you thinking?" he asks.

"I don't know. What the fuck should we do?"

"Do you want to keep seeing her?" he asks.

"Of course I do, but I know part of that is coming from a selfish place. I like talking to her. I like hanging out with her. I definitely like having sex with her."

"Yeah, I don't hate that part."

"What about you?"

"I cried in front of her."

"Okay, yeah. Well, I guess all we can do is ask her how she's feeling and play it by ear. I think she viewed the time we spent at your house as a one-time thing, but after last night…"

"Yeah, it didn't feel finished when I left her place this morning. She wanted me to stay and I didn't exactly want to leave."

"I'll text her and see when she's free."

"Sounds good. Let's order something and then I'm gonna swallow your dick."

"Sounds romantic." I step out of his SUV, chuckling to myself as he comes around the car and takes my hand.

Brooklyn

"Does this fit?" Rayna steps out of the dressing room and twirls. I tilt my head to the side and take in the wonky-ass sack dress she's wearing. It has these weird sleeves and shoulder cut outs. Her boobs seem to be fighting against the whole thing.

"Ehhhh…" Is my gut response.

"How does it feel in the shoulders?" Noa asks.

"Terrible. I actually want to go to this wedding. Why doesn't the universe want to give me the nice dress I deserve to wear to this wedding?"

"Because the universe doesn't want you to steal the bride's thunder," I say, winking at her.

She turns and checks herself in the mirror against the wall. I'm about to give her my full assessment when my phone vibrates in my bag. I pull it out and manage not to smile at the text notification from Vaughn.

Hey beautiful.
Let us know when you're free.
Shaw and I wanted to talk to you about something

"It does make my butt look good, though," Rayna says.

"I'm sure we can find another dress that makes your butt look outstanding," Noa replies. "Where's this wedding again?"

"Baltimore. I'm leaving Friday morning as soon as my uncle picks up my nana."

"It'll be nice to get a little break," I add. I'm paying attention to my friends, I swear. My mind is definitely not thinking about Shaw and Vaughn, ass naked and making a Brook sandwich.

"I need to put in more time-off requests with my cousins. I need a real break. Not just a few hours here and there to see you guys and then one weekend a year to go to a wedding. I have rights!"

"You do. You should definitely ask them. She's their grandma too. They can help out more," I say, reading the text from Vaughn again.

"When's Claudia coming to visit?" Rayna asks."

"Not for a while," Noa replies. "She and Shep are looking at houses, not on the mountain. She wants to get that squared away before she starts flying back and forth again."

"Good. Maybe we can actually visit them. I swear if any more of you bitches move..."

"Not going anywhere. I promise," I say, smiling at her before I look back down at my phone. I quickly respond to Vaughn's text.

I hope it's a good something.

We hope so too.
Shaw will be at my place through
tomorrow afternoon.
Let us know when you're free.

Out with my girls.
I'll give you a call later tonight.

Looking forward to it
<3

"Are you texting with your friiiiiend?" Rayna teases. I look up and she's still standing there in that dress, which is getting uglier by the second. I chew on my lip and look at my phone. Rayna and Noa are two of the best friends a girl could ask for.

It's taken a herculean effort to not breathe a word about how well Shaw fucked me the night before. It's even harder not to mention that he comes in the world's sexiest package deal. Just the thought of Vaughn adjusting his glasses gets me hot. I'm not ready to tell them what's happening, but it's getting harder and harder to keep it all this close to my chest. Especially when I haven't felt this good in almost two years.

"Hypothetically, how would you feel if I started dating again?"

"I would feel great about it," Rayna says.

"Yeah, you mentioned it before. I am team 'Brook starts dating again,'" Noa adds.

"Same. Ugh, let me take this off. I'm not buying it. Just come inside." The three of us crowd into the tight space as Rayna starts to change. "So, you were saying? Did you meet someone? Is this someone whoever you were just texting with that dopey smile on your face?"

"Nothing I ever do is dopey," I say, instead of answering her question.

I want to come clean, but I know it's not that simple. The opposite. This is a complicated, fucked-up situation that I know my friends and my sister wouldn't agree with.

"I—I think Josh broke me."

"No. Josh absolutely did not break you. You are amazing and whole," Rayna says.

"Thank you" I say, fighting the urge to roll my eyes. I know she's trying to help, but this is why it's hard to talk to people who are trying to be supportive. "Let me say this, 'cause you saying nice things doesn't change the way I feel."

Rayna looks hurt at the way I responded to her encouragement, but damn. Denying the way I feel with false positivity isn't gonna get me anywhere. Noa reaches over and takes my hand. "Keep going, babe. Tell us how you feel."

"Your girl is having trust issues. Especially when it

comes to men who look great on paper. Josh was fantastic on paper."

"Right," Rayna says.

"I think I want to give myself permission to just see what's out there. Not to find the perfect man immediately."

"Brookie, that's brilliant," Rayna says. "I love that idea."

"Yeah. I think testing the water just for the heck of it might be a good thing for me. But I don't know."

"What's holding you back?"

"Guilt." And knowing that I'm being a complete dumbass with two men I never should have reached out to in the first place.

"So, are you texting someone you want to test the waters with?" Noa asks.

"Can neither confirm nor deny"

"So yes?" Rayna laughs.

"Whatever."

"Well, if he turns out to be more than perfect on paper or via text, I look forward to meeting him. What advice did Liz give you?"

"I haven't really talked to her about it yet. I don't know. When I go up there, it's baby time. Not too much time to talk about much else. I don't mind. I love those chilrens so freaking much. But two small kids and a whole farm and bakery—"

"Yeah it's a lot," Noa says. "But you should tell her. I'm sure she'll want to know." I lean back and look at her 'cause she's using her delicate tone.

"Did she say something to you?"

"No, she was just saying that she misses us. The chat isn't the same."

"Oh." She's right. We all still talk, but ever since she had Palila, she's been busier. Plus, Claudia spends more than half her life in a different time zone. It's not the same when you can't meet up three or four times a week for drinks and foolery. I haven't told Liz because until this moment I wasn't sure there was anything to tell.

But as I sit here, my phone burning a hole in my purse, I know that isn't true. I have no idea what the hell I'm doing and why I think it's anything close to a good idea. But I do know that it's gonna be hard not to rush home from dinner with the girls so I can talk to Vaughn and Shaw on the phone.

"Try on the blue one," I tell Rayna. Changing the subject feels like a good idea.

SIXTEEN

Brooklyn

I pace back and forth in front of my couch. All I have to do is send a text, let Shaw and Vaughn know that I'm free to talk, but I don't know that I am. What if they want to tell me they don't want to see me anymore, don't want to speak to me anymore? Or worse, what if they do? I'd managed to keep my focus on Rayna and Noa for the rest of the evening, but as soon as Rayna was ready to go and Noa said she was also ready to turn in, I'd practically sprinted for the train.

I won't let the thought fully form, but whatever is bouncing between my head and my chest has notes of 'I can't wait to talk to them again.' I miss them. I need to know what's on their minds and I'm terrified all at the same time. There's no future here for us. I still have plans, still want to get married and maybe have a family.

I can't have that with Vaughn and Shaw. In the long run, they need a full-time kinkstress and I don't know if your girl is cut out for that kind of responsibility or cardio. But maybe I can have short-term fun with them. Fun and lots and lots of dirty sex where no one puts their long-term feelings on the line. No one gets long-term hurt. I've been hurt enough for a lifetime.

Just text them. Pull off the band-aid, I tell myself. I need to sort this shit out, whichever way it's going. I've been in this weird stasis for so long. I need to move forward. I need to stop being afraid. Well, at least, I need to stop being afraid of one phone call. I take a deep breath and send Vaughn a text.

Hey, I'm home and free to talk.

A second later, the Facetime alert starts chiming. For some reason, I panic and hit Reject. I was not expecting video chat. I cannot do video chat.

"Yeah, but you just hung up on them, dummy," I say out loud. I click back over to my recent calls and call Vaughn back via voice call.

"Hey," he answers right away.

"Hi, sorry."

"No Facetime?" he laughs. "I'm sure you look amazing."

"No, that's not it. I'm feeling a lot of feelings and if I'm going to be feeling more feelings, I'd rather you couldn't see my face."

"Fair enough. Let me put it on speaker."

"Hey Brook," Shaw says, his voice still annoyingly sexy.

If they are gonna kick me to the curb, I hope they do it quickly so I can start the process of getting over the little things I'm starting to love about them. Like. *Like.* There's no love in this equation quite yet. Like is just fine.

"Hey Shaw. So, what's going on?"

"Not much. Thinking a lot about last night."

"Oh, word?" I laugh. "Is that what you guys wanted to talk to me about?"

"Kind of," Shaw says.

"Well, by all means. Please proceed."

"Shaw and I were talking and the first thing we wanted to do was check in with you and see how you're feeling," Vaughn says.

"I feel...okay. I'm trying not to think about how I'm feeling, to be honest."

"Why's that?" Shaw asks.

"Don't wanna harsh my own vibe, I guess."

"Oh. Well, maybe we should go. Vaughn's about to harsh all over your vibe," Shaw says. I think he's joking a little, but a big-ass knot quickly ties itself in my stomach. My nerves bubble up as a strained giggle. I don't like it.

"Shaw, shut up. We do not want to harsh anything," Vaughn says. "We just wanted to have a realistic talk about where we see this going."

"Oh," I say. "To be honest, realistically, I don't see it going anywhere."

"Oh." I hate the shocked disappointment in Shaw's voice, but that doesn't change the way I feel. Still, whatever rain I've sprayed all over their parade doesn't stop Vaughn from pressing on.

"Let's talk about that though. How do you see this playing out?" he asks.

"I mean, my vision of things involves some fun for sure, but mostly both of your dicks in my face or in my hands or in my ass. And that's great. I like that idea a lot. But I don't know how long that goes on for, you know?"

"Yeah," Vaughn says.

"I want to get married. The jury is out about kids. Watching my sister go through it twice has changed my outlook on that, but still. I don't know. I mean, I guess I wish I could deprogram whatever society has drilled into my head. But that's just the vision I have for myself. I do want a husband. I do want a certain kind of stability and a unit. I want something I can call my own. What you two have is amazing, but I don't see what I have in mind meshing with what you two have in mind and it wouldn't be fair to any of us, to set ourselves up for that kind of disappointment. If it got that far, I mean. I guess I just need to be more open-eyed about how I do things for myself this time."

"Are you interested in casual dating at all? Or are you only interested in dating with marriage in mind?" Vaughn asks.

That makes me pause. I think back to the conservation I had with Noa and Rayna just hours ago. I want to be practical. I want to be smart. But I also want to give myself permission to relieve some of the pressure.

"No. Actually, I'm not. I don't have to date with marriage in mind. I probably shouldn't right now, to be honest."

"So, you want to settle down, but in the meantime you'd

be cool with getting dicked down by two dudes from Massachusetts?" Shaw says.

I laugh even though dread is still sitting comfortably in my gut. "I guess I should have just said that. My bad. I'm still trying to work a lot of things out in my mind."

"Don't apologize. We're talking it out. Expectations are important. Let's start over," Vaughn says. "Shaw and I want to keep seeing you as long as you want to keep seeing us, but we want you to be comfortable and we don't want to get in your way."

I sit on the couch and consider what I want to say next. I know this is bad and wrong, but I've tried the plan. I did everything right. I followed all the steps and look where that got me. Why can't I have fun with Shaw and Vaughn in the meantime? Why do I have to force myself to be unfucked and lonely until Mr. Right decides to materialize out of thin air? Why am I even acting like I'm ready to go looking for Mr. Right, as if I'd even trust him if he was right in front of my face? I'm definitely not looking for Mr. Wrong. Hell, I can call Deek right now if I'm that bored.

"Brook?" Shaw says.

"Yeah, I'm still here. I'm just thinking. My mind is kinda all over the place. Let's just play it by ear. How about that? We see each other when we can and if it's not working, we let each other know. For me, right now though, it is working. I don't like the idea of not seeing you two again. And Roger. I can't forget Roger."

"I think we can swing that," Shaw says. "And, no, we can't forget my man, Roger."

"Wait," I say. "What about you two? What do you want?"

"I don't want to put the pressure on myself or anyone else. I miss just having a good time," Vaughan says.

"Yes!" I say. "Sorry. Didn't mean to shout. I totally agree. I love that we are being honest with each other, but between our serious, yet necessary talks and the way my friends are handling me so delicately, I feel like I'm not allowed to just have a good time. We can do that together. Let's just hang out. No expectations. I just—when I am ready for expectations, I want to be clear with them."

"Shit, I'm down," Shaw says.

"I am too," Vaughn adds. Suddenly, I feel so much better. There is space between "forever alone" and sprinting down the aisle and I deserve to occupy that space for as long as I want, with whomever I choose.

"Okay great. How does next weekend look?" I ask. It wouldn't hurt to get something in the books.

"Next weekend works fine for me," Vaughn says.

"Me too," Shaw adds.

"Great. Saturday morning at your place, Shaw?"

"See you then."

A sudden shyness washes over me and I hate how much it feels like first-date jitters. I need to go. I need to end this call before they experience the panic attack that's rushing for me.

"Wonderful. It's on my books. Well, I need to get off this phone. I'll let you guys know if anything changes."

We say our goodbyes and I collapse back on my cushions, suddenly unable to breathe. Tears rush up to my eyes and all I can think is *not again*. Not again. I shouldn't have agreed to this. This planned meeting between the three of us feels different than before. It feels foolish this time. Dangerous, especially for me. But that doesn't mean I'm going to change my mind and cancel. I know I won't. I want to see them, and I fucking hate just how badly I want to see them. How badly I crave their touch.

I let out a few shaky breaths and pick up my phone. I dig up my last conversation with Claudia and send her an SOS.

I need an adult.

Thank god her kinky-ass husband doesn't have her tied to a chair or a tree or something because she responds right away.

I'm an adult, sort of.
What's going on?

I'm about to do
something stupid.

How stupid are we talking?

Very stupid.

Give me a minute.
And I'll call you.

A minute later my phone rings. My breathing has slowed, kinda, but odd tears are still leaking from my eyes. I hate this feeling so much. Claudia skips the pleasantries and gets right to it.

"Like stupid stupid or stupid illegal?" she says.

"Not illegal, just exponentially foolish."

"Okay. Shep's out with the dog, so I got some time. Go for it."

I tell her everything. Well, mostly everything. I don't rehash the intimate details of each time I've been with Vaughn or Shaw, together and separately.

"Okay," Claudia says. "And you called me 'cause I made my own personal trauma buddy into my husband."

"Jesus, I hadn't thought of that. I called you 'cause I knew I could tell you the truth. You—"

"I lost someone I love in a super fucked-up way."

"Yes. I was thinking of Miles." It sounds almost made up, but Claudia and her brother were hunted through a national forest by literal serial killers and her husband Shep was the one who saved her. Poor Miles wasn't so lucky. She has experience with moving on and finding love after something so extreme. It didn't even dawn on me that she found love with the one person who also survived that night, maybe 'cause I'm not looking to fall in love. I just want permission to be a little reckless. I want someone who I know will hear me. "Noa is being too nice and Rayna—"

"Isn't actually listening to you?"

"Yes!" I laugh. "I knew you were the right person to talk to."

"There were more than a few times when I'd be talking

to her and Liz about my issues with Jason." Her asshole ex that we most definitely hated. "And she would say something about him being supportive after Miles died which he actually wasn't. It was really annoying."

"Ugh, I'm sorry. I didn't know that."

"It's okay. I didn't want to cause any ripples in the group chat, so I left it alone. We're fine now, though. What about Liz? Did you tell her?"

"Uhh... no? Too close to home, maybe. I don't know."

"And you know she'd fight you 'cause you're her world and she loves you. And yeah, this might be a stupid idea."

"I mean, Silas and the girls are her world, but yes, she would definitely have something to say about it."

"Well, if you want my advice, I think you have to do it."

"You do?" I say. I'm actually shocked. "I thought your brilliant hindsight would tell me to go running in the other direction."

"That's the smart move, but my brilliant hindsight also remembers what I felt like when I showed up looking for Shep again. I remember booking my flight and not telling you guys I was flying back to the scene of the crime to ask a man I barely knew to hug me 'cause I know you would have talked me out of it."

"I would have asked to come along."

"I know you would have," Claudia laughs. "But Liz was not pleased with me at all."

"No, she was ready to fuck you up."

"Okay, how about this. In the interest of your safety, give me their info so at least one of us knows where you're going and who you'll be with and then I think you have, let say, two more weeks, and then you have to tell your sister if you think you're going to keep seeing them."

"I mean, I'm not seeing them. We're just hanging out."

"Hmm. Sure."

"Whatever, bitch," I laugh.

"You have fun with your little friends, but work up the courage to tell your sister. Even if nothing happens, she's gonna be pissed if she finds out later. And hurt."

"You're right."

"In the meantime, work your shit out. Trust me. It's part of the process. You've done the mourning. It's time to do something stupid. It's another signpost on the road to better health."

"Yeah," I say. "Let's go with that."

I spend the next six days asking myself what the fuck I'm doing. I need to take care of myself and move on, but then I have another dream about Josh and when I'm awake, Vaughn is sending me texts and Shaw is waiting until I'm home from the office to send me lewd photos. I can't think clearly, but whenever I think I've come to a decision, Claudia's words ring truer than ever. I'm going through with this for now. Of course I am. This messy-ass shit with two men is now a part of my process.

The door is already open. I've already walked through it. There is no back, only forward, toward something good or another implosion. When I wake up early Saturday morning, *not* going is not an option. My alarm goes off and

I'm in the shower. I'm gathering my things. I'm sending Claudia a text telling her I'm leaving. When I get into my car, I'm grateful that Noa has plans this weekend with her cousin, Rayna is still away at that wedding and Liz is busy with some toddler birthday business. No one will miss me. I'm free to be stupid as can be all weekend long.

I head toward the Cape, watching the scenery change from city to tree-shrouded highway to the low-grass beaches and tall pine trees that bring me to Shaw's farmhouse. Something about it calms me and terrifies me all at the same time. What would it be like to have this as a place to go week after week? What would it be like to call this place home? I imagine the calm lasting. A promise of a good time. Vaughn's gentle care. And Shaw's ability to make me want to jump him and punch him in the face, all at the same time. What would it be like to really know them, to have them to depend on? I blink hard as I pull down Shaw's street and force that thought to the realistic part of my mind. Maybe Mr. Right has all of those things rolled into one man. With the tattoos too. Definitely with the tattoos.

As I pull up to Shaw's house, he's coming out of the barn. I cut off the engine and watch as he walks over and waits. He doesn't try to open my door for me. He doesn't ask me what I'm doing just sitting behind the wheel and looking at him. We watch each other for a moment and then something clicks. He comes close and I open the door. I don't get out.

"Hey," I say, looking him up and down.

"Hey." He comes closer and I sit still, my voice caught in my throat as he reaches over my lap and gets a firm grip on my thigh. I help him as he turns me in my seat, spreading my legs. I help him hike up the light fabric of my dress. I hold still as his fingers start to explore. I do my best not to squirm as he discovers how wet he's made me in less than a minute.

"Shouldn't we take this inside?" I ask as I inch my ass closer to the edge of the seat.

"Do you want to?" he asks as he pinches my slippery clit between his fingers.

"No," I groan. "Where's Vaughn?"

"On a call."

"Oh. Well, then we shouldn't disturb him."

He shakes his head. "Nah, we shouldn't."

I grip the steering wheel with one hand and the back of the seat with the other as my hips pump forward. I'm grateful Shaw's yard is surrounded by trees. I'm glad his prim and proper Polo-clad neighbors can't see Shaw push three fingers inside of me. That they won't catch my hips arch off the seat. The way I start fucking myself on his hand, my pussy starting to straight-up leak onto his driveway.

My cunt starts to squirt when he finds that perfect spot and we both hit that perfect rhythm, shooting my juices all over his tattooed wrist. They can't see the way he's looking at me or notice how fucking turned on I am by the dark spots I make on his nice clean shirt. They might hear me when I come, when I cry out, whimpering Shaw's name. They might hear me, but I can't bring myself to care.

SEVENTEEN

Vaughn

Shaw is still standing at the sink where I found him washing his hands after he apparently fingerfucked Brooklyn in the driveway. I get it. I've been waiting almost three weeks to see her and touch her again, but damn. He couldn't even let me say hi. I could smell her on him as he explained that she was upstairs getting changed. When she comes back down, she at least knows she'd been caught leaving me out in the cold again. I hadn't said anything, just sat back down at the table.

"Don't be mad." Brooklyn looks down at me as she lets out this throaty laugh right before she hugs my head. I fix my glasses, jostled by her arms, but I don't pull away. Her arms feel good around me. She feels good in my lap.

"Who said I was mad?"

"Your face," Shaw says from the kitchen.

Brooklyn collapses in my lap and covers my face with kisses, trying to make me smile. I won't budge. They will suffer my wrath for another twenty-something minutes.

"How can I make it up to you?" she says, kissing me again.

"You can't. You ruined it. Both of you. Weekend's over. I want a divorce. I want to go home."

"Are you two married? I never asked." Brooklyn suddenly says.

"No, it would fuck up Shaw's vibe." I'm just fucking with him and he knows it.

"Shaw, marry him and then he'll stop being pissed at me."

"I'm not pissed. Just disappointed."

"How about Shaw and I spend the rest of the weekend making it up to you? What do you want? What do you need?"

Stop fucking each other without me, I almost say. I'm fine with the fucking itself. I'm not jealous or anything like that. They needed last weekend and I'm glad they had that time together to sort their shit out, but I want to fuck too. Damn.

"I need Shaw to control himself."

"Can't, sorry," he says, staring me dead in the face. I hate when he does that 'cause he knows that his ego is part of his appeal.

Brooklyn sucks her teeth at him. "Stop."

"I want Shaw to take us out on the boat," I say.

"Oh, I'd love that, but like not too far out?" Brooklyn asks." I can swim, but I can't *swim*."

"We'll be right in the harbor. Plenty of people around. Lots of witnesses," Shaw says, winking at her.

"Well, in that case," Brooklyn says sarcastically, looking back at me. I give her thigh a gentle squeeze and she lets out a soft breath. "I think we owe you more than a boat ride. What else can we do for you, Vaughny? How can we make this up to you?"

"I'll think on it. Let's head out. We can get lunch on the way."

"Sounds like a plan," Shaw says. "Brook, why don't you help Vaughn get ready? Wink, wink."

"I'm gonna fuck you up one day," I say to Shaw as I ease Brooklyn off my lap. She stands beside me and takes my hand.

"Come on. I need to change into my bathing suit. Help me."

I glare at Shaw as Brooklyn pulls me out of the kitchen and up to her guest room. I step into the room, taking in the unused space and Brooklyn's things on the foot of the bed. I turn back to her just as she closes the door. I don't miss the look on her face as she crosses the room. Maybe I shouldn't be pissed at Shaw. I don't know what kind of mood she was in when she arrived, but she's turned on now and it would stupid of me to not to lean into that. She steps close to me, putting both of her hands on my chest. She has to crane her neck to look up at me, giving me a damn good view of her beautiful face.

"I'm sorry," she says. "He caught me off guard."

I reach up and stroke her cheek. "You don't have to

apologize for getting off. I understand the difficulty in resisting Shaw."

"Come here." She nudges me back toward the bed, going for my belt, but I stop her.

"Hold on a sec."

"You sure? My head game is next level."

"I know. I remember the last time I nutted in your mouth."

"Good, 'cause I definitely didn't forget."

"It's not what I want."

"Well, tell me what you want," she whispers. I gaze at her lips and think about the way I feel when she responds to my texts. How the silly selfies she sends me from her office are becoming the highlight of my day. Yeah, I've been waiting over two weeks to be inside Brooklyn again, but what I really want is to hold her and kiss her. My hands slide up the side of her neck and I lean down, pressing my lips to hers. I feel it in my chest when she sighs against my mouth.

"You are such a good kisser," she says.

"Yeah?"

"Yeah," she smiles. There's something on the tip of her tongue, but she's doing that thing again, holding back.

"What is it?"

"Tell me something bad. Give me one little thing to hate about you."

"Why?" She's said this before. She was joking then, but now I think she's actually searching bad shit out.

"'Cause I don't want to fall for you, Vaughn. Make it easy on me. Please."

"I hate doing dishes."

"Yeah, but you're a great cook and that kinda makes up for that. Try harder. Dig deeper. Give me something truly awful. Tell me you bite your toenails."

"That's nasty as fuck."

She laughs as she gently nudges my stomach.

"What would be so bad about falling for me?"

"Well, for one, I'd have to put up with that asshole downstairs," she says with a sexy smile.

"Yeah, he sucks wicked bad. But besides that shiftless bum?"

"I'm not ready and you, Vaughn Coleman, deserve someone who's ready. I mean, besides Shaw. If that's what you want."

"Fucking Shaw." I lean down and kiss her again, slow and deep. I soak in the way she sags against me, her arms wrapping around me. I need to let go of this desire to keep Brooklyn with us. It's gonna fuck me up in the process, but I have to. I believe her when she says she's not ready and she's right. I want to move forward with people who want to move forward with me. I break our connection and focus on the weekend we've agreed to spend together. That's good enough for now. It has to be. "I'll give you one thing."

"Oh! Please tell me."

"I hate Christmas."

"Vaughn, what the fuck!" she laughs.

"My cousins used Gremlins and Home Alone to play fucked-up mind games with me when I was a kid and I was convinced that some horrible shit was always going to happen on Christmas."

"I forgot about Gremlins. That *is* technically a Christmas movie."

"With a whole story about a dad getting stuck in a chimney and dying 'cause he thought he could play Santa Claus. People tried so hard to convince me it was safe, but it just made me hate the whole concept of the season."

"Aww, poor Baby Jesus. So, do you just not celebrate?"

"No, I celebrate. Shaw loves Christmas. It's the only time of year he's outwardly pleasant. I just look like this the whole time." I give her my best gritted teeth grin, smiling at her for real when she fails to cover a loud snort.

"You're saying I need to stick around at least til Christmas so I can see that face again?"

"It could help take some of the pressure off me. Especially if you like Christmas music. You and Shaw could sing your hearts out while I hide in a corner somewhere."

"Okay, fair. That's a little, well, not odd. Plenty of people don't like or celebrate Christmas for obvious reasons. I'll just accept that you're perfect and I'll spend time alone wondering why we couldn't have met under different circumstances."

"Sounds like a bad plan, but I'll accept it for now."

"Thank you." She steps away from me and goes over to her weekend bag. "Why don't you head down while I get changed, 'cause I don't think we'll make it to the boat if I take off my clothes in front of you."

"You're right. I'd be all over that."

She rolls her eyes before she shoos me away. I go down to my room, change into my swim trunks and grab the rest of my stuff, then head to the kitchen where Shaw is waiting with Roger.

"All good?" he asks as he looks up from his phone.

"All good. She's getting changed. We managed not to touch each other's genitals."

"I didn't mean to make you feel like that," he says instead of cracking another joke.

I squat down and Roger comes right to me. I give his head and neck a rough scratch. "I know."

"I just—"

"I know."

"I mean, look at her."

"I know," I say, chuckling. "Makes me feel a little better when she has us both a little fucked up."

"Do you want to get married?" he says suddenly.

"Do you?" I ask, shocked.

"You may not believe it, but Brook is teaching me some things. I know we talked about the idea of it before, but that was before...before Corrine."

I look back at him, blinking. Shaw is who he is and I've always loved him for it. I know he's being serious right now. I know that he's trying. He just caught me way the fuck off guard. I stand and cross the kitchen to him. He watches me, carefully. He's expended all of his emotional bandwidth for the day just by asking me that question, and he's warning me with this hesitant expression, so I know not to push him for more. I take his cheeks in my hands and squeeze his face. He scowls at me, his lips puffed out but he doesn't move.

It's not a question of if I want to marry Shaw, but if *he* wants to marry me. I know I'm a lot for him. Most people are. It's why he likes to live alone in this giant house. I'm sure a therapist would have something to say about the way he keeps people at arm's length. I know it has a lot to do with his parents and his fear of abandonment, and the way everything went down with Corrine didn't help those issues one bit. Still, I know how he feels about me and I know what's trying to say. He doesn't want to lose me and if marriage is what I want, he'll give it to me. That's a bigger conversation for another day. And it still does change my desire to add more, permanent partners to our relationship in the future.

"I love you." I tell him.

"I love you, too." he mumbles back, his lips still squished together. I kiss him and step away, giving him the moment he needs to slide his hard shell back into place.

A few moments later, Brooklyn steps into the kitchen and makes a dramatic show of putting on her large-frame sunglasses. "Come, gentleman. Let's go yachting."

***

Shaw finds a place on the water for us to chill. I help Brooklyn apply sunscreen to her back, she helps me and then we both help Shaw before he goes back to his Captain duties while Roger makes himself comfortable on the other side of the deck. It's a beautiful sunny day on Cape Cod Bay, but I can't keep my eyes or my hands off Brook's ass. She is lying on top of her towel on the deck of the Dirty Diana, her floral two-piece bathing suit leaving absolutely nothing to the imagination. I'm on my towel beside her, gently caressing and lightly smacking her ass. Her giggles and sighs let me know she approves.

Shaw was right. It's a busy Saturday on the coast. Everyone's keeping their boat at a safe distance, but there's definitely too many people out for me to casually start eating Brooklyn's ass without anyone seeing. *Still tempting though*, I think as I slip two fingers under the fabric of her bikini. She squirms a little, spreading her thighs an obvious degree, but I resist the urge to stroke her pussy from behind. For now.

"I see why you put up with him now. This is like a porno." I follow her eyes and see Shaw securing the main sail. The sun is glistening off his skin and he's wearing the Ray-Bans I got him for his birthday. It's not a bad view at all. He's calmer out here, quieter. Happier. I love the ocean, but not like Shaw does. He comes over to join us, easing onto the towel beside Brooklyn. I move as she rolls over and puts her head on his thigh. I still have access to her perfect ass.

"Hey, you guys wanna play a game?"

"You wanna see a dead body?" Shaw drones. Brooklyn playfully smacks his foot.

"I'm serious."

I sit up and slip my glasses back on my face. "Sure, what's your game?"

"It's a classic I like to call 'Never Have I Ever: The Brooklyn Edition.'"

"Whatever the rules are, I'm gonna cheat," Shaw says.

"I wouldn't expect anything less there, you punk," Brooklyn laughs. "Okay, so I say something like 'never have

I ever shoplifted from a dollar store' and if you have, then you have to pick someone to kiss, on any part of their body."

"So, if you say some shit like 'never have I ever played basketball,' I have to come over there and swallow Vaughn's dick?" Shaw says.

"I mean, if you want to give that elderly couple over there a show, go for it." I look where Brooklyn is nodding and, sure enough, there are *two* old white couples hanging out on the deck of a nearby boat.

"If Shaw and I kiss on the mouth, that might be enough to give one of them a heart attack," I say.

"I'm willing to risk it. I'll go first. Never have I ever...done something stupid that landed me in the ER," she says.

"I'm interested to see how playing this with an A.D.A. goes. I'm pretty sure your answers are going to be pretty tame," I say, giving her a hard time.

"Phsssst, whatever. I might be a public servant, duty bound to protect the innocent, but I can get pretty wild. I'm on a boat with two dudes I'm definitely gonna bone later. Plus, my sister used to use me as a crash test dummy. I've been to the ER. Just answer the question."

"False. Okay, Vaughn. Truth or dare?" Shaw says.

"No, wrong game," Brooklyn laughs. "Try again."

"Okay. Uhh—" Suddenly I don't like the way he's looking at me. "Never have I ever had three girls try to share me at prom."

"They didn't try to share me. We went as a group."

"Oh, so is that where this plural-love thing started," Brooklyn teases.

"Three girls asked me to prom my senior year on the same day. I felt bad, so we all went together."

"That's amazing. What about you Shaw?"

He shrugs and tugs at the edge of his shorts. "I didn't go to my prom. But during my modeling days, I did have an orgy with that photographer Corbin Wills and three Victoria Secret models at an after party. I imagine that's better than prom."

"Geez. I just went with this boy in my history class. Most action I got was a kiss on the side of my ear at the end of the night."

"Sounds romantic to me," I say.

"Vaughn, you lost," Shaw announces.

Brooklyn laughs again, "Vaughn didn't lose and you both ignored my question." She rolls to her side and kisses me on my forearm. "I let my sister push me down the street in a shopping cart once and broke two fingers and a toe."

"Glad you survived that brush with death," Shaw says before he leans over and kisses her on the mouth. "I used to street race for a while. Crashed my buddy's car and broke my arm."

"I feel like Shaw's going to have James Bond level answers to every question."

"I lived a crazy life, what can I say."

I roll my eyes. "Okay, I'll go. Never have I ever spent a fucking grip on Celtics playoff tickets only to get booted out of the Garden during the National Anthem."

"What?!" Brooklyn says with a screech of laughter as she looks between Shaw and I. Shaw sits forward suddenly, rolling Brook toward me with a casual "Excuse me," before he stands. He throws me his phone, which he's lucky I catch, and does a backflip into the ocean. Of course, Roger thinks it's play time and goes leaping into the water after him.

"Is he serious?" Brooklyn says before rushing to the edge to make sure neither of them have drowned. I shake my head as I stand and make my way over to the ladder. Shaw takes his sweet-ass time, but eventually he and Roger swim over to that side of the boat. Shaw hoists Roger up to me and I help the dog back to the deck. I turn my head to avoid the splash zone as Roger gives his body a shake, spraying sea water everywhere. Shaw follows and does the exact same thing, splashing water all over me. It would be annoying if it wasn't for the sound of Brooklyn's laughter.

"Clearly it's true or were you suddenly drawn to the ocean?" she says as she throws his towel in his face. I take my seat, my skin warming again when Brooklyn settles back down with her head in my lap. Shaw comes over to us and carefully gets into a push-up position over her body. I watch, my dick getting a little hard as he lowers himself down just enough to kiss her beautiful lips. He carefully straddles her then, knees on either side of her soft stomach before he leans up and kisses me. He gives my nipple a hard squeeze for old times sake.

"Yes, I paid many Gs to see the Celtics in the finals, but when I got to my seat, this fool was harassing two young girls before the game started. He wouldn't stop, so I smacked the shit out of him."

"Shaw, oh my god," Brooklyn says.

"Got us both kicked out, but it was worth it. One of the

girls' parents tracked me down on Twitter and it turns out it was her fifteenth-birthday present and her first big outing without her parents. I missed the game, but at least I did a good deed."

"I guess that's not so bad. Sorry you missed the game."

"It worked out for Vaughn too. I used my one phone call to get him out of a work function."

"Yeah, it was fun making sure you didn't have to spend the night in jail."

"It was a blast, what are you talking about." He looks at me with a blank stare for a moment before his gaze drops to Brooklyn. "You ticklish?"

"I am and don't you even think about it."

"Don't even think about what?" Shaw lightly pokes her side and she jerks, the cutest fucking giggle bursting out of her.

"Don't Shaw. I'll push you right off the boat and leave you here."

"Don't what? I can't hear you over the sound of the ocean. Never have I ever tickled a woman until she came."

Brooklyn freezes, then glances up at me before she looks back at Shaw. "Wait, is that possible?"

"Let's find out." Shaw leans down and buries his face in Brooklyn's neck as he tickles the hell out of her.

I just watch, smiling to myself. Happy to be a cushion between Brooklyn and the hard deck of the boat as her loud laugh fills the sea air above us. I don't tell them how perfect this moment feels. I don't tell either of them that I haven't been this happy in a long time.

EIGHTEEN

Brooklyn

A nap was in order when we came back to land. When I woke up, Vaughn had already fired up the grill for dinner and Shaw was piling wood on the stone fire circle so we could make s'mores for dessert. I had to admit it was a pretty perfect summer day rolling into an even better summer night. I'm still turned on from our time on the boat. Lots of kissing and touching, but somehow all three of us managed to keep it in our pants. I know at some point we'll probably move things to Shaw's Room of Pain and Sexytime Pleasure. I need to get fucked by Vaughn and Shaw, and *bad*, but I'm enjoying myself just hanging out with them in Shaw's expansive yard.

After a quick trip to the restroom, I step back into the backyard, giving Roger's head a scratch as he trots over to greet me. Vaughn is still sitting in one of the oversized

Adirondack chairs Shaw built, but the master craftsman himself is nowhere in sight. It's not exactly cold out, but the temperature has dropped a lot in the tree-shrouded clearing. I wrap my sweater tighter around myself and scoot the edge of my chair so I'm closer to the fire pit.

"Where's Captain Christopher?" I ask, making myself shiver a bit at the thought of Shaw sailing that boat. He drives me crazy, but he sure is sexy and skilled.

"He just went inside to grab some things. He'll be back in a second."

"Oh, alright. Are you enjoying yourself, Vaughny?" He's been sweet as fuck all day. A little quieter than usual, but in good spirits. It's been nice just spending time with him. Stealing kisses from him hasn't hurt either. I should have taken a seat in his lap instead of on the other side of the fire. I watch him through it, his handsome face lit a lovely deep brown as he pushes his glasses up his nose.

"I am enjoying myself. Thank you."

"Baby, why don't you get some new frames or adjust those? They are driving you crazy," I say.

"I've been meaning to, but I always put it off."

"Here." I pull out my phone and send him a link that it takes me two seconds to find. "One of our newborn A.D.A.'s has like four hundred pairs of glasses and she's always going on about this site." I watch him in silence, smiling to myself as he starts to scroll through the online store.

"Thanks. I'll set a reminder for Monday night and actually make time for this."

"Happy to help," I say as Shaw steps back outside. I look

over and see that he's carrying a small, clear plastic tub in his hands. "Whatcha got there, friend?"

"Tools of the trade. I fleeted and got all cleaned up for this little party. It's fucking time."

"Oh, we're doing this outside?"

"Yup. Can't waste a perfectly good fire. We're not doing anything with the fire. Just—"

"I get it," I laugh. "I'll trust your process."

"Good. I'm ready to get fucked and do some fucking." He sets the tub on a decorative tree stump that serves as a table. "Hey Brook."

"Hey Shaw."

"Come over here for a minute."

"Are we starting now?" I ask as I come around the side of the fire pit. Shaw doesn't respond right away. He just takes my hand and pulls me closer. I watch his dark eyes as his hand slides around my waist. His other hand cups the side of my neck. He kisses me, slow and deep. It goes on and on until I'm not sure I know how to breathe anymore.

This is Shaw's superpower, I realize. Capable of bringing you from zero to sixty with a single kiss, touch or look. Of course, he ruins it the moment he opens his mouth, but the way he's kissing me now makes up for it. It's hard for me to picture not wanting him. When he leans back just enough so our lips are no longer touching, I'm under his spell. It happens that quickly and completely.

"Yeah, I think we're starting now," he says as he eases his thumb over my bottom lip. "Vaughn, you want to start now?"

I can't see Vaughn from where I'm standing without

turning around and looking away from Shaw's deep brown eyes, I hear the thickness that's filled his voice when he responds.

"Yes, sir. Where do you want me?"

"Right there is fine." Shaw reaches over and grabs a pair of padded leather cuffs from the container. "Turn around there, little bird, and give me your hands." I do what he asks, turning and putting my hands behind my back. He's gentle as he buckles each cuff around my wrists. They are surprisingly comfortable and the chain links between them don't put a strain on my shoulders. I could be restrained like this for a while. Too bad I still have all of my clothes on, including this big sweater. Before I can ask Shaw to do me a friendly favor and take off my leggings for me, his lips are next to my ear.

"Here's what you're going to do for me," he says loud enough for Vaughn to hear. "You're going to go over to our friend there and you're going to make yourself come on his leg." Vaughn sits at attention like he's been given the command and slides to the edge of his seat.

"With my clothes on?" I haven't had a good dry hump in a while, but I want to make sure I have his instructions right.

"Yes, baby. With your clothes on. I think you can do it. What do you think, Vaughn?"

"I have faith in her. She can definitely do it."

Shaw lightly pats me on the ass. "Don't be shy. Get in there."

I let out a shaky breath, the feeling of Shaw's breath still on my cheek. Vaughn opens his hands for me, then guides me onto his lap. A small voice in the back of my head is a little worried the weight of all my juicy curves might be too much for Vaughn's slender thigh, but when his hands come to my waist, I'm instantly reminded of how strong he is. I think about how tall and slim he looks at a distance, but how underneath it all is pure muscle. He gently settles me over his left thigh, pressing my soaked already lips and my clit against the fabric of my underwear.

I squirm a little, trying to find the perfect position, the perfect angle, just as I feel Shaw step behind me. His hands come over my shoulders, his body pushing me closer to Vaughn as he leans over and grabs the hem of my cotton shirt. Shaw pulls it up to my chin and slips one hand into my bra, exposing my right breast and then the left. My nipples are hard now, aching.

Vaughn looks down, his throat working to swallow just before his lips part like he's about to dive into the most delicious buffet. My body moves on its own, offering my nipples to him 'cause the only thing that would make this heat between my legs even better would be his mouth on me.

"Those aren't for you," Shaw says. I almost laugh at the way Vaughn's expression drops. He adjusts his glasses and looks up at Shaw.

"Yes, sir."

"You can kiss her, but leave her tits alone. Those are mine tonight. Brook, I don't know what you're waiting for," he says to me as he walks around the side of the chair. He stops and stands right at Vaughn's shoulder. "I know you don't want to rush, but I can already tell how hard our poor

Vaughn is and he doesn't get to fuck me until you come. It would be kinda fucked up to make him wait all night."

I glance up at him and then back at Vaughn. I can't read his expression, but I feel the way the tension in his body matches the tension in mine. I want to come. I also want to watch him fuck Shaw.

"I guess I should help the both of us out, huh," I manage to say.

"No pressure, but I'd appreciate it." Vaughn's nice way of saying his dick is about to rip a hole in his jeans. I start to move my hips and Vaughn helps me, scooting me higher up his lap, wedging my thigh next to his hard bulge. I start to ride him, grinding my pussy nice and slow against his body, chasing the friction from the layers of our clothes. It's the best and the worst kind of torture. My pussy is already so wet, my clit so swollen. I know I can get off this way, but Shaw knows it won't be enough.

He knows that even if I come, screaming until my voice is hoarse, I'll still want more. A mouth on my pussy or a dick inside it. Or both. I'd settle for some competent fingers. Whatever it is, he knows I'll want it enough to beg for it and I think that's what he's wanted from me this whole time. It's what he gets from Vaughn with such ease that he doesn't even have to pretend to ask for it. We're still new to this, he and I, and he wants to know that when we're together as Sir and his new submissive and our Vaughny, I won't pretend I don't want them both as badly as I do.

I turn my eyes back to Shaw and take in the intense expression on his face. The way his eyes move from my tits back to my lips again. My mouth parts a bit, his tongue darts out like he's thinking about filling it, and I grind away.

"Put your dick in my mouth, sir. Please." I whisper. He reaches down, covering my breast with his whole palm and massaging it roughly. My eyes squeeze shut as the sensation goes right to my clit. I settle into my hips, pushing my cunt in a hard, slow circle against Vaughn's lap. Shaw gives my nipple a hard squeeze, holding it in a tight pinch until I moan. He releases it and goes back to massaging my tit again. I think of the gentle, then hard, way he tickled me on the boat deck that afternoon. How if there hadn't been all kinds of boats coming and going around us and the occasional sea plane overhead, I would have begged them both to fuck me right there and then, under the bright sun and in the salty ocean air. I didn't come from being tickled because I was holding back, but I'd like to see him try again.

"My dick's not for you tonight. Not yet," Shaw says. "But since you want something in your mouth so badly, I thought Vaughn should use his tongue."

My gaze drops back to Vaughn's just in time to catch the way he looks at my lips before he closes the small distance between us. He kisses me in that perfect fucking way, that way that makes me wish he was mine forever. Not just for tonight. I kiss him back and, after a moment, I feel his arms loop between mine. He pulls me as close as he can, my pussy pressing even harder against the apex of his hip and thigh and the hardened bulge of his cock. My exposed breasts press against the fabric of his shirt. Behind my back, he laces his fingers with my bound hands. Shaw's hand comes up the back of my neck, reminding me that he's there and he's watching Vaughn and I meld to one another.

I lose myself at some point, my remaining brain cells split between kissing Vaughn and finding the exact pressure my pussy needs. I find it, repeating the same rocking motion again and again, harder and harder, until I can't do both. I can't kiss Vaughn and chase the orgasm. My lips break away and I gasp for air. I'm so close, so fucking close. I don't stop until it happens, a shattering orgasm rocks through me. Part of me worries I might be hurting Vaughn, the way I'm fucking myself against him, but he's holding me close, telling me to come, egging me on. I say his name, the sound of it mixing with the crackling of the fire at my back. I don't know how long it is before my eyes blink open, but they do, Vaughn is smiling at me.

"Did you come, little kitten?" Shaw asks, his voice thick with arousal. He knows the answer, but he still wants to hear me say it.

I nod before I can find enough air in my lungs to speak. "Yes, sir. I did. I came."

"Good girl. Stay right there for a minute and don't come again unless I give you the go-ahead." Shaw draws down the zipper on his jeans and pulls out his swollen dick. With his other hand, he turns Vaughn's head and pushes his dick into his mouth. Vaughn is happy for the treat and wastes no time bobbing his head back and forth even though the angle is a little awkward. He uses me for leverage, one arm still wrapped around my waist as he coats Shaw's dick with his saliva. The look on Shaw's face in the firelight as he pumps in and out of Vaughn's mouth might be the sexiest thing I've ever seen in my life.

Somehow caught up in the rhythm of it all, my hips start slowly rolling again, pussy suddenly ready for rounds two and hopefully three. Though he's better at this whole submission thing than me, Vaughn's hand goes to my ass and gives it a good squeezing, making my hips rock a little harder.

Shaw suddenly takes hold of my chin, holding me still while keeping his eyes on the magical work Vaughn's mouth is doing. "What did I say, baby? You can't come again. Stop moving."

I want to argue, but I keep my mouth shut and do my best to keep from squirming as Vaughn releases my ass. He sucks Shaw's dick for so long that I'm surprised Shaw is showing absolutely no signs of coming. Not that I mind. I'm enjoying the show and so is my throbbing cunt and my aching nipples that are still exposed to the warm air between me and Vaughn.

At one point, Shaw lightly squeezes Vaughn's shoulder and he stops. I don't stop my whimper at the sight of Shaw's wet dick slipping out of his mouth. Shaw takes a step back and takes me by my elbow.

"Come on, princess." He helps me off Vaughn's lap. Even in the dark, I can see the dark spot I've left on his jeans. Shaw moves me so I'm facing Vaughn, standing a little to the right of the chair. My hands are still bound behind my back. He goes back over to the plastic tub and grabs some lube and a condom. I stand by quietly, waiting, watching as he returns to Vaughn and takes his poor engorged erection out of his pants. He hands both to Vaughn and waits while Vaughn rolls the condom on and slathers himself with lube.

"I'm ready, sir."

"Perfect. So am I," Shaw turns, eyes focused on me as he pulls his jeans down to mid-thigh and lowers himself onto Vaughn's waiting cock, holding onto the armrests of the chair for balance. It's not graceful, the way he inches up and down, trying to hold his weight off of Vaughn, but I don't care. It hot as fuck, the best fireside show I've ever seen. The two of them find their rhythm, Shaw bouncing and Vaughn pumping his hips up and down off the wooden seat.

Vaughn glances at me at time or two, but mostly just stares down at where his cock is fucking Shaw's amazing ass. I stand there for a long time, letting one side of my body grow hot by the fire that's going to need more wood if we carry on into the night. My other side is cool to the night air, grateful for the bug repellent candles still flickering nearby. My arms are getting tired, but I know I can wait, and I know an amazing shoulder massage from Vaughn is a reward for my patience. One of many, I hope.

I continue to watch them, storing every detail away in my memory.

"What do you want, Brook? Tell me," Shaw groans suddenly.

"Me?" Of course, me. I was so busy thinking about how it must feel to take Vaughn in the ass that I hadn't expected questions. "I—"

"I know you want more. Tell me what it is."

So many things run through my mind. I want to tell the truth. The dirty, nasty truth, but I'm starting to know Shaw and some of the fearless ways he operates. He gives the orders. He also makes the fantasies come true. I swallow and take a chance, drawing strength from the straining look of pleasure on Vaughn's face. He's not afraid. He's open to it all.

"I want you to take it."

"Take what?" Shaw asks.

"Me."

"Oh, you want me to take that pussy."

"Yes," I moan. "And I want you to come inside me."

"You have a little breeding fetish you didn't mention?" he teases through gritted teeth. Vaughn hasn't let up during our conversation. He's still gripping Shaw's hips, giving him every inch he can get.

"No, I just—I just like it," I admit. "I like to feel full."

He closes his eyes again, his hands gripping the arms of the chair and I think that maybe the thought of fucking me, nutting in me, while he's being fucked by his man is enough to take him over the edge, but he keeps riding Vaughn, not a drop of jizz in sight, just precum leaking from the tip. The man is a machine. The both of them are. I've almost come twice quietly in my own pants just from watching them. He opens his eyes again and leans back more, brushing his lips against Vaughn's face.

"Come, baby," I hear him say. No one needs to tell Vaughn twice. His fingers dig into Shaw's hips and three hard pumps is all it takes before he's groaning with his head pressed against Shaw's shoulder. They both settle for a moment, just breathing. I'm focused on Shaw's hard dick bobbing against his t-shirt. I stumble off to the side as Shaw suddenly springs to his feet. He pulls up his pants just enough to cover his ass. He catches my elbow and starts pushing me back toward the door.

"Where are we going?" I ask, panicked for so many reasons, like the fire's still going and poor Vaughn just jizzed himself to death in that chair. We can't just leave him or the fire going. "What about Vaughn?" I ask.

"Come on, Vaughn," he calls out. "Brook wants you to watch while I take her." I don't hear Vaughn behind us, but I'm more focused on not tripping over my own feet as he marches me through the house to the big bed in the addition. He tosses me face first in the covers and, as I try to wiggle my way to a comfortable position, he walks to the side of the bed so I can see him slide a fresh condom into place. Then he steps behind me again and I feel his hands at my waist yanking my leggings and panties down my thighs. A few moments later, he's pushing my thighs apart just enough to get at my throbbing pussy from behind. I arch my back to help him out.

He isn't gentle as he slams inside me and even though I cry out, whimpering his name, it's exactly what I wanted, for him to take me brutal and fast. He's fucking me like it's been years since he ever had it this good. When I feel the bed dip beside me, I open my eyes. There's Vaughn, still a little bleary eyed from his own orgasm, but ready and eager for more.

"Okay, baby?" he asks me.

"Yes," I whimper as Shaw pumps into me again and

again. I'm coming. I can't wait. I can't stop myself. Shaw is hitting my g-spot just right and the thought of Vaughn watching us, the way I watched them is too fucking much. It's way too fucking much again when Vaughn slides his hand under me and finds my clit. I groan out a loud "Fuck!" as he gives it a perfectly painful squeeze. I come all over Shaw's dick again and I think I hear him say something close to, "Brook! Fuck!" before I black out.

When my senses come back to me, Shaw is still in my pussy, but he's stopped moving.

"Did I kill her?" I hear him ask Vaughn. I crack my eyes open and look at him. Vaughn smiles back at me, his glasses low on his nose again. He winks at me before he strokes my cheek.

"She's fine, but maybe get off her and let's take those cuffs off."

"Thank you," I groan. Shaw is still balls deep inside me when he takes the cuffs off. I ease my arms to the side, get up on all fours and push back on him two more times before he wraps his arms around me and pulls me upright. He pulls out and helps me stand off the bed. Vaughn pulls up my pants and helps me fix myself while Shaw gets rid of the condom in the bathroom. I let Vaughn rub my shoulders. He turns me, still rubbing me down as I face Shaw, who cups my chin and kisses me on my lips.

"I can't come inside you right now. We gotta talk about BC and other general safety shit, but soon. We'll talk about how to do it the way you want it."

"'Kay." I don't know whether to cry or come. The

considerate way he's talking is equal parts sensual and sweet.

"Good girl. Now put your titties away, or don't, but Vaughn is going to help you get ready for bed and then we're going to watch the best movie ever made."

"Which is?" I say, tucking my boobs back into my bra.

"Haven't decided yet. Let me go put out the fire before I piss off the historical society and burn this place down." He leans over my shoulder and kisses Vaughn. "You good?"

"Yes, sir."

"Good. Be right back." He literally skips out of the room and then jumps up the stairs back into the main part of the house.

I can't but help chuckle as I turn back to Vaughn.

"Let's get some water and then take a shower. Sound good?"

"That sounds perfect."

"Come on." I let Vaughn take my hand and lead me into the kitchen where Roger is now dead asleep under the dining room table, clearly over our human bullshit. Vaughn hands me an ice-cold glass of water as Shaw comes stomping back into the kitchen singing "American" from West Side Story. Our weekend isn't close to over, but I'm already scrolling through my mental calendar putting another trip to the Cape on the schedule.

NINETEEN

Brooklyn

I need to get back to the city, but first, brunch. I know it's silly. I could drive through a Dunkin' Donuts, caffeinate and feed myself, and be back at my apartment with plenty of time to do some relaxing shit like wash my hair or something else that'll help me turn my vagina off before I have to be back to work in the morning. A couple of hours after our fireside sexcapades, I somehow ended up having sex with Vaughn while a sleepy Shaw watched us and jacked his dick. Later, in the middle of the night when I came back from getting more water, Shaw fingerbanged me back to sleep. This is going to be a problem.

I went from sad, tortured spinster-in-training to insatiable sex fiend in a matter of weeks. Being around Shaw and Vaughn isn't addictive, exactly. I just wake up the next morning with the clear sense that I haven't been this happy in a long time. I know it's not a perfect scenario, but now that Shaw and I have sorted things out, I really feel like I can enjoy being with them both. And what's more, I feel like they genuinely enjoy being with me, which I didn't think I'd trust at least for another decade or so.

I grab my purse and head to the driveway, where Vaughn is sitting in the front seat of his Escalade, one leg hanging out as he blasts some Beenie Man song I haven't heard in ages. I stop halfway down the brick path and start rolling my hips.

"Okay, girl," Vaughn laughs.

"This my shit. Where's Shaw?"

"He's doing something in his workshop real quick."

"Can I go in there?"

"Yeah, of course."

"Cool." I cross the driveway and make my way over to the barn. The side door is cracked open and I find Shaw inside. He looks fine as hell, as usual, but I'm overwhelmed by the smell of saw dust and the sheer size of the workshop. There are several workbenches around the perimeter. Tons of tools. Racks of wood and what looks like a halfway-completed canoe mounted in the middle of the room. He turns when he hears me walk in.

"Hey. I got a request for a quick project. I just need to check the ol' supplies for something."

"Take your time. Vaughn's outside reliving his dance-hall days."

"You haven't seen him dance yet, have you?"

"No, why?"

"Three prom dates. That's all I'm saying."

"Okay," I laugh.

I cross the room and join him at his computer. His desk is filthy. Sawdust and wood chips everywhere. Supply catalogs with water-wrinkled pages. He writes something in a notebook that looks like it's been around since the early 90's, then turns and looks at me.

"I thought I had a few pieces of white birch. But I don't, 'cause I fucking hate white birch."

"Why?" I chuckle again. I know nothing about wood. The forest kind, at least.

"It's cheap and it looks cheap, but some people like it."

"You could use the scraps to finally teach me how to whittle."

"You don't want to whittle with birch."

I roll my eyes and nudge him in the stomach. He grabs my hand and pulls me closer, settling his ass against his high desk.

"So, I was thinking," he says.

"Ooh. Don't hurt yourself."

"See," he sucks his teeth. "I'm trying here and you're just throwing it in my face."

"No, no. I'm kidding," I say, wrapping my arms around his waist. "Tell me. What were you thinking?"

He reaches up and strokes my cheek with his thumb. "I was thinking about what you said last night and I see that you're holding back. I understand why, but I don't think you want to."

I stand back just a little, so I can look him in the eye without craning my neck. I drop my hands from his waist and grab his fingers instead. "I mean, it is nice to just tell you what I want and to have you actually listen. You *and* Vaughn. It's pathetic that most of my experiences with men haven't been like that."

"Say more."

"If I said to, I don't know, just lick my pussy a little slower or fuck me harder, but not necessarily faster, it's like the message didn't make it all the way to their brain. Josh was...better than most, I guess. Probably part of the reason why I wanted to marry him, but—"

"You said you felt like he was rushing you."

"Yeah."

"No rush, but think about what you want your submission to me to look like. I want to get to know your desires better, so I can anticipate your needs and you can anticipate mine."

"I think I can work on that."

"Good. You're not coming back next weekend, right?"

"No. It's the Fourth. I'll be spending a few days with my sister and my family. But maybe the week after?"

"I'll be here."

"'Kay. I'll let you finish up in here. I don't want Vaughn to think we're fucking without him again. Poor guy."

"Yeah, I woke up in the middle of the night to you pogo-sticking on his dick. Poor, poor, Vaughn."

"Bye, Shaw!" I leave him to his inventory and join Vaughn in the Escalade. Shaw is only a few seconds behind me. We wait for him to lock up the barn and house, then we drive into town to a breakfast spot called the Salty Dog. It's a beautiful summer morning, so we grab a table outside. I make myself comfortable next to Vaughn while Shaw sits across from us. A nice, white girl hands us our menus and tells us she'll be back with waters and the gallon of orange juice Shaw has preemptively ordered.

"Okay, what's good here?" I ask.

"They have cinnamon roll pancakes you might enjoy," Vaughn says, pointing them out on the menu for me. He's sitting with his other arm around me. I know I'm going to miss this closeness with him, with the both of them, as soon as I get back on the road. Our server comes back and I order the cinnamon pancakes and some eggs, while Vaughn and Shaw order the rest of the menu between the two of them. It takes a lot to feed that much man.

"Shaw, what's on the agenda for this week, besides your hatred of all things birch?" I ask.

"I have—Jesus Christ." I turn and follow his gaze over my head, just as some man brushes by me. Detective Jansen pulls out the open chair beside Shaw and takes a seat. "Man, what the fuck."

"I have to say, I thought I was seeing things, but I'm not," he says, attempting to keep his voice down. "It really is Bronx Assistant District Attorney, Brooklyn Lewis, sitting here cozy as can be with Corrine Johnson's former lovers. Both of them."

"You can leave now," Vaughn says.

"What the fuck are you doing here?" Shaw says.

"Detective Jansen. How are you? What brings you to the Cape?" I say calmly. He and his partner were good to me during the whole ordeal, once they cleared me. Comforting and kind. They did their best to keep me in the loop. Still, I am less than happy to see him.

"Just visiting family, quick stop before we get back on the road." He nods toward the window. I peer through the glass and there's a table of eight or so white people watching us. Great. "What are you doing here, Ms. Lewis? I actually spoke with the Delinskys last week."

"Good. How are they?"

"Good as can be expected. Still dealing with the grief, of course."

"Look man," Shaw starts, but Detective Jansen just keeps his eyes focused on me.

I feel my own face heating. I'm pissed, mostly, because how fucking dare, but my A.D.A. brain has already kicked in.

"Detective, is there anything in particular you would like to discuss? If not, I would really appreciate it if you let us enjoy our breakfast. And I'm sure your family would be happy to see you back inside."

"I'm just wondering how this all came together. Your cheating fiancé dies with their cheating partner and then, bam, the three of you out enjoying yourselves miles and miles away from the comforts of New York City. I mean, this doesn't look like a casual run-in. This looks like a weekend getaway. But you live closeby don't you, Mr. Shaw? Did you invite Ms. Lewis out here to partake in the less than savory activities Mrs. Johnson mention to me?"

I glance over at Shaw and see that he's doing his best not to punch the man in the side of the head. I can feel Vaughn practically vibrating beside me. I stand and nod down the street. "Let's go."

Detective Jansen raps his knuckles on the table, a nice

fuck you to the guys, and then follows me down the street. A few people are watching us as I try not to hurry. I step into the alcove of a closed jewelry store and turn around.

"Do you really think that was the best way to approach us?" I ask him.

"Do you think spending time with them is a good idea? What the hell are you doing?"

I take another deep breath and think about the detectives I work with every day and what they would say, what *I* would say if we found out the significant others of two murder victims were suddenly hanging out together. Trauma does weird things. Victims and survivors turn to the most unexpected people for all kinds of comfort after a tragedy. But I'm sure he never expected me to turn to Vaughn and Shaw. Not that it's any of his business. Not anymore.

"Do I need to reopen this?" he says, trying to put some bass in his tone.

"What? Of course not. Vaughn introduced himself to me *after* Josh's funeral because he was trying to get some closure. He didn't even know Josh's name until you and your partner spoke to him. *After* Corrine Johnson's funeral. I don't know about you, but I haven't mastered time travel enough to plan a double-murder homicide of the man I didn't even know was cheating on me."

Detective Jansen sighs and scrubs a hand down his face. He knows I'm right. I talked to him and his partner for hours. Shared every detail of my life with Josh. They both sat with me while my emotions caused me to vomit more than once. I know how this looks now, but I sure as fuck

—*we*—did not plan Josh and Corrine's deaths. That was all Ryan Morgan and Ryan Morgan alone.

"Fine. Okay. But are you shacking up with them?"

"I really want you to rethink that question. And I don't appreciate you speaking like that to Christopher or Vaughn. They lost someone too, no matter how you personally feel about them."

"All I'm saying is Miss Johnson's family had nothing good to say about these two and, considering the circumstances, I'm thinking about how this looks for one second. I get reaching out, but Sunday breakfast on the Cape isn't reaching out. What would you do if this fell in your lap? Would you just let this slide without asking a single question?"

I swallow and look past his shoulder. Vaughn is watching us. I can only glimpse the back of Shaw's head. I'm sure he's trying to grind his teeth right out of his jaw. It's taking everything in my power not to start explaining. It really is none of his business and the more I say, the more it'll sound like I'm trying to rationalize what I know is a bad idea. Like I've committed a crime, which I haven't.

"If you have questions that you truly think are pertinent to your case, then go through the proper channels to ask them. But what you want is to satisfy your personal curiosity."

"Look. I remember the look on your face when we first came to talk to you. I remember how discovering the layers to Josh's murder destroyed you and I cared. I still do. We all, my partner and I, we felt bad for Josh's family and we were really worried about *you*. I'm just shocked to see that this is how you're moving on."

"Your concern was and is appreciated, but you can't approach us like suspects because you are surprised to see us hanging out together."

"I'm not kidding about Corrine's family. They hate those men. What do your people think about this?" That's the question that sends my stomach down to my feet. When I don't respond, that's answer enough for him.

"Oh, so they don't like them either."

"That's not what I said."

"They don't know." I hate this, being on this end of an interrogation that shouldn't even be happening. "Listen, I won't tell you what to do, but maybe think about why your family doesn't know. The two of them were a problem for Corrine Johnson before she was murdered. Drove a huge wedge between her and her mother. If everything's all good here, then there's no reason to keep it a secret. And I would think you wouldn't be interested in getting caught up in something that might hurt you again. Enjoy your brunch."

"Detective—" I'm genuinely torn between cussing him out and trying again to convince him there's nothing to worry about, but nothing else comes out of my mouth.

"Have a good one." He heads back into the cafe without giving Vaughn or Shaw a second look.

I return to the table, just as our server brings out my pancake. "Thank you so much, but we actually have to go." I reach into my wallet and pull out all the cash I have on me, more than enough to cover our meal and her tips for the rest of the day.

"Oh, thank you. So sorry you have to rush off. You guys have a nice day."

"Thanks."

Shaw sighs and stands, motioning for me to lead the way back to the car. I know Vaughn follows.

"I have to head back," I say when we get back to the Escalade.

"What did he say to you?" Vaughn asks.

"Some things he shouldn't have and some things he wasn't entirely wrong about."

"What the—"

"Shaw." I put up my hand to stop him and he goes on. He hears the A.D.A. tone I haven't shaken from my voice yet. I'm going over every angle of this, trying to think if it will be worth it for Detective Jansen to bring this up as evidence in an integrity review. The case against Ryan Morgan is closed, but if they feel strongly enough to start looking around, they can and none of us need that right now. "Let's just go and I'll explain on the way."

And I do, leaving out as much emotion as I can, trying to make them both see how Detective Jansen can approach this nice and legally. They aren't psyched about it, but both of them understand how serious this is, how serious it can be. When Shaw lets me into the house, I go right to the spare room and grab my things. They are still standing in the driveway when I come back down. Roger has joined them.

"Listen, I know how the system works and I know how all of this feels and sounds, but there is a chance they might want to talk to you two again. I know you want to fight

Jansen right now. Like, really fuck him up. So do I. But please. Just cooperate, please. I will do everything I can on my end."

"We didn't fucking do anything," Shaw says.

"I know we didn't, but it's kind of out of our hands now. I take the blame for this. I knew better and I...anyway." I sigh and smile at them both. It's a sad, pathetic smile, but it's all I got. "I had an amazing time." They both step closer and I stand up on my tiptoes and kiss them both on the cheek. There's nothing left to say. Once I get in my car, we all know I won't be coming back.

TWENTY

Vaughn

I'm about to leave my office when I get a text from Shaw.

No traffic. I'm here.

Leaving now.

It's been a long week. I've done my best not to reach out to Brooklyn. I want to check and see if she's okay. I want to know if Detective Jansen or anyone from his department has contacted her, but I can't, not with the way she left things. She's done with us. That much was clear from the eerily calm way she got the hell out of town. What we did wasn't smart. Were we free to do it? Yeah. Still, I think all three of us knew we were playing with a certain kind of fire. I'd happily punch Detective Jansen in his smug face for the way he ambushed us like that, but after Brooklyn explained more about how he's actually free to submit a review of evidence if he has any suspicion that the three of us had something to do with what Ryan Morgan did to Josh and Corrine, I really saw the weight of what we've done.

It wasn't farfetched in theory. Scorned lovers have killed for less. I know we did nothing wrong and that we have nothing to hide, but I understand how it looks. I also know how cops work. Jansen could just want to see us locked up for the hell of it. So, Brooklyn pretty much made it clear she was done with us. It's the right decision, but the pain that's been following me around all week makes me realize that I was starting to fall for Brooklyn Lewis. Now seems like a great time to start getting over her and I'm glad I don't have to do it alone.

Shaw and I had already planned to spend the long weekend with my mom and her boyfriend. Take in some fireworks and eat our weight in barbecue. Try not to think too much about the bullshit legal trouble we might find ourselves caught up in.

"Yo." I call out.

"In the kitchen," Shaw says. I take off my shoes and set them in the shoe rack in my entry closet, then head through my apartment to the kitchen. Shaw is busy looking through the fridge. I walk up behind him and he turns his head just enough for me to kiss him. "Hey. You want a beer?" he asks.

"Yeah, thanks." He grabs two cold ones and uncaps them with the bottle opener on his keychain before he hands one to me.

"Roger all good?" I ask before I take a seat at the island and chug half the bottle before coming back up for air.

"Yeah, I dropped him off with the boarding spot this morning. They're gonna play music for the dogs during the fireworks."

"I'm sure he'll like that," I say, smiling at the thought of Roger vibing out to some calming tunes.

I watch Shaw take a sip of his beer before he sets it down. He leans against the counter and scrubs his beard.

"How are you doing?" I ask him.

"You know. Have you heard from her?"

I shake my head. "I would have told you if I had."

"Do you feel like you're wasting your time with me?" Shaw says suddenly. I carefully set my beer down and stare at him.

"No. I don't feel that way at all. I love the hell out of you."

"We've been doing this a while and I didn't know if you were sick of waiting for me to, like, commit and shit."

"You're not committed to me?" I ask, my eyebrows going up. "That's news to me."

"I am. I love you, too. I know I give you shit about wanting to get married, but I know you want certain shit and I want to be the one to give those things to you. I just—" He scrubs his hand down his whole face this time. I think I know what he's trying to say and I know why it's so hard for him to say it. "It's not you."

"I know it's not." I chuckle a bit, but I know he's serious. "I know what kind of partner I've been. It would be pretty fucked up if you had some theory that I've done you wrong."

"I know, I know. You've been patient as hell with me. I haven't done the work yet and I didn't think I would have to. I didn't think I'd ever meet someone worthy of doing the work for. Of dredging all that shit up and trying to fix it. I'm sorry I didn't see that I need to do the work until now."

"I appreciate you saying that, but that's how life works and I don't want you to apologize for developing some issues after your own parents—shit, most of your family—turned their backs on you. But we don't have to get married if you're not ready. I want you to be in a good place for *you*. If you're ready to start talking to someone about how commitment makes you want to run, I think you should."

"I am—I'm ready."

"That's great. And if you get to a place where marriage is something you want, then let's do it. If not, that's okay too. I don't feel like I'm settling for you, Shaw. I know I'm not. I'm still figuring this out too, but the constant thing I see here is how much I want to be with you. And I don't see that changing. What's making you say all this?"

Shaw shrugs and takes another sip of his beer before he goes on. "After Cor I felt—you pulled away."

"Because I was sad. And I was lonely here without her. I still am. And that doesn't mean I want you to give up your place and move here, but—"

"You want more."

"It's not more. It's a community, I want. A Unit. So I don't have to put all of my needs on just one person."

"But you still want me?"

"Always."

"'Kay, cause I do love you and shit, and I want you to have as many healthy relationships as you need to get right."

It's actually a relief to hear Shaw say that. I know it's possible to make a polyamorous relationship work. But like any other relationship, for it to be good, it requires the right place, right time, right combination of people with the right amount of give and take. That's lightning in a bottle and, as I creep closer to forty, I think I know it might be harder for me to find that special mix of people, but knowing that Shaw will still be there for me, makes it more bearable. Corrine is gone and Brooklyn can't be a part of this situation anymore. I know I need more time to heal, but hopefully someday soon, we'll meet the person or persons who make this all right.

"Were you thinking about this the whole drive here? That you might not be enough?" I ask Shaw.

"I've been thinking about this since you left Sunday night. I saw how happy Brook made you and, I guess, I thought she was aight."

"Just aight?" I laugh.

"I'm not copping to anything else."

"Okay. Go on."

"I just want to make sure you're happy with me."

"Look, I miss Brooklyn. Part of me still misses Corrine. I've even thought about moving to a new place. Some place she and I didn't share together. You and I have been pretty open with each other, but we haven't had real conversations about our future. If you want a future with me, that's what I want with you, and I think it's just the human experience to figure the rest of this shit out as we go along. Does that work for you?"

"Yeah," he says. "I think I might call my pops."

Another bit of shocking news. "To say what?"

"Not sure. I might just cuss his ass out. I'll figure it out."

"Well, I'm here if you want to work out a script beforehand. I'd love to cuss out your dad."

He looks at the floor and just nods. He's done with this conversation, which is fine. I think we're on the same page. I need a little time to get Brooklyn out of my system and I just have to accept the weird rolling trauma that still pops up when it comes to Corrine. That doesn't change the fact that we still have each other and a whole weekend to spend together.

"You want to order dinner or walk somewhere?" I ask him.

"There's fucking tourists everywhere. Let's order."

"Okay, let me just change." Just then, my cellphone rings in my pocket. I pull it out and a nerve in my neck pinches on itself when I see the name on the screen. "It's Brooklyn," I say.

Shaw sighs. "Answer it."

I hit accept and put it on speaker phone. "Ms. Lewis."

"Hi Vaughn." Her voice sounds strange and overly cautious.

"I'm here with Shaw. You're on speaker."

"Oh, hi Shaw."

"Hey Brook." He's looking at the floor.

"I won't keep you guys. I know you're probably ready to get your Fourth of July weekend started, but I just talked to

Detective Jansen. I don't think he planned on calling you guys, so I thought I should."

"What did he have to say?"

"They aren't going to open the case up for review."

"Work your D.A. magic?" Shaw says. Brooklyn lets out a nervous laugh.

"Not quite. He did come down and interview me again, but I reminded him that they'd already reviewed all of my phone records and stuff the first time around. The fiancée is always a suspect and they had cleared me. And, I reminded him that Vaughn never would have found me without the information he and his partner gave him."

"That is true," I say.

"In any event, it's over. They won't be bothering you. I just wanted to let you know so you weren't walking around looking over your shoulder for however long."

"We appreciate that."

There's silence on the other end. I know there are things I want to tell her, but I don't get a chance.

"You two have a good weekend," she says.

"You too," I say. And she ends the call.

Brooklyn

"Everything still in the linen closet?" I whisper as I follow Liz up the stairs. I'd planned to come up to see her on Friday morning and stay until Sunday, but as soon as I got off the phone with Vaughn and Shaw, I felt like I was climbing out of my skin. I called my sister and told her I was coming up early and then I got on the road. Not that I can escape my thoughts, but it will be harder to have a full-on mental breakdown, complete with screaming and crying, when there are two small children down the hall.

"I'll get it."

"No," I say, playfully nudging her out of the way. "I'm the one who came early."

"Whatever. Come on." I follow my sister to the closet where she keeps the spare sheets and blankets, then head down to the guest room furthest from the girls' rooms. It's not super late, but the babies have been asleep for a few hours. Definitely no need to wake them up with any loud talking. I set down my bag and start to help my sister make the bed.

"How was traffic on the way up?"

"Not too bad. I think I made decent time."

"This way, you can sleep in in the morning."

"Oh, you think Iona is going to let me sleep in?"

"Well, no. And if she doesn't wake you up, I'm sure one of the dogs will."

"Charge it to the game, I guess."

Liz shakes her head and smiles as she grabs a fresh pillowcase.

I grab the top sheet like it'll give me the courage to finally come clean. "I have something to tell you and before I do, I think I should also tell you that I already told Claudia because I needed to talk to someone and I didn't know how to tell you."

"I think I know what you just said, but go ahead and tell me the thing. I'll try not to be offended that you told my best friend first."

"Whatever. Claudia is the group's best friend. She's the prettiest and the smartest and the best dressed."

"Ugh, please don't remind me. I never want to see another stiletto for as long as I live, but I do miss a good Fall cape. No appreciates a Prada cape around these parts."

"You look amazing in capes," I say, before I take a deep breath and tell her everything. Well, kinda. I leave out the details of the sex, but that I was fucking two guys at once is enough to drive the point home. I power through, watching her face as her expression goes from wide-eyed shock to straight-up cringing. We're not even making the bed anymore, she's just standing there with the other pillowcase in her hand, staring at me. When I get to the part where we were confronted by Detective Jansen before our breakfast had arrived, I think she might kill me.

Her mouth drops open and she turns into my mother right before my eyes. Hands on hips, 'I'm gonna fuck you up' glare and everything. "Brooklyn Rosemary Lewis."

I grab the sheet and fluff it out over the bed. "This is why I didn't tell you. I don't need a lecture. I know I fucked up. I know how stupid I look right now."

"I don't think you look stupid. I think you sound so dick drunk, you left all of your sense at home. How am I supposed to react to this? Like, for real. Put yourself in my shoes. You know exactly how far you'd drag me and for how long."

I sigh and bite the inside of my lip.

"Okay." She sits and holds out her hand. "Come here, Brookie. Come sit with me."

"No. I hate you," I whine as I come around to her side of the bed. I sit beside her and let out a shuddering breath.

"How can I be more supportive?"

"You're not being unsupportive. I just—" The tears are welling up in my eyes. I quickly dash them away. "Ugh, I fucking hate this."

"Why are you crying? Are you crying 'cause you're a sloppy bitch who got caught being messy as hell with two dudes? God, you slut," she teases.

"No. That's not it. Not exactly."

"Are you crying for Josh? Are you crying because of Vaughn and…"

"Shaw. Chris is his name, but he goes by Shaw."

"Because of Vaughn and Shaw."

"I don't know. I think it's all of it. I want to be over Josh. I hate thinking about him. I hate that there's, like, a specter of him behind every decision I make. I hate how every relationship I have from now until forever, I'll be thinking about what if, what if, what if with Josh. I've stopped blaming myself for what happened, but I still think about him way more than I'd like to."

"And now there's two more men."

"Two. More. Men. And they are actually here. Shaw is, oh my god. You'd want to fight him. He's like Silas and Maya mashed into one person, turned up to eleven. Grouchy and sarcastic." Liz looks at the wall and I think she's trying to picture her gruff husband crossed with her hilarious best friend on the farm and coworker in the bakery. "Yeah, I don't know. That's a lot."

"He's amazing in bed, though," I sniffle. "Just the bees knees."

"Okay," she laughs. "And what about Vaughn?"

"He's—Vaughn's just the best. Liz, he's like the nicest man I've ever met. Sweet, tall, slim. He wears these wire-rim glasses that are always slipping down his nose. It's cute as fuck. And he really, really wanted to take care of me. He's so thoughtful."

"Oh, you know I love a tall-slim. Remember Karick?"

"Yes," I manage to laugh. Liz's tall, skinny boyfriend from high school was a lanky, goofy fool who ran into the night with Liz's virginity and her heart. She probably would have married him if his family hadn't moved away. "Vaughn reminds of him, a little, but he's sweeter, if you can believe it. He's an attorney, too. So, we have that in common. Kinda."

"Okay. So, a sarcastic ass, which is truly what you deserve, a little taste of your own medicine. And a complete sweetheart who passed the bar."

"Yup."

"Okay. It seems like the cops are going to leave you alone. If this wasn't the messiest of messy situations, would you want to get back together with them?"

"I think that's the problem. We were all pretending it was just sex. I didn't let myself think it could be something more."

"Well, if it could?"

"I'd want to keep them both, like forever, but I don't

know how to do that. People can say they are so open minded, but I don't want to lose my job 'cause I have two boyfriends. I feel like if I tell them how I feel, I'd just be fucking up all of our lives. Well, mine and Vaughn's. Shaw's perfectly fine with his isolationist woodworking."

"Right, I forgot you actually enjoy your job," Liz says. She had no problem leaving corporate law to become a baker and marry her farmer man. She'd hated her job and her firm. "Here's how I see it. If you really have feelings for them, you should tell them and the three of you should give this a real shot. If they aren't into it, then you have your answer and you can step back. When you're ready, we'll help you find someone great. I mean, I never liked Josh."

"Bitch," I whisper harshly. "Yes, you did. You loved Josh."

"Okay, fine. Whatever. I liked Josh. I mean, I really liked Josh's dad. He still comments on all of our posts."

"He's a good dude."

"But yeah, if this has a chance of being anything, don't, like, slink around with them on the Cape. Not that you were slinking, but you know. Bring them around. Let us get to know them. Let the girls get to know them. Let us dig around in their social media accounts and quietly judge them behind their backs. Let the woodworking one arm wrestle Silas for our entertainment."

"I wouldn't hate that."

"If you guys work, if they fit in your life, then we can worry about you losing your job later. Also, you don't have to tell your boss that you're dating both of them. I mean, do you know about the personal lives of everyone in your office?"

"No," I admit. "One of our A.D.A.s never tells us what he even had for lunch, let alone what and who he's doing outside of the office. And Shaw and Vaughn don't even live together right now."

"Psssht. See? Let's worry about one thing at a time. If you want a real relationship with them, then you have to try in a real way. You'll sort out the rest. If you just want to sneak around and bang them, sneak around and bang someone closer to home. Like, I wouldn't go any further than Yonkers. You're just wasting gas at this point."

Okay, so that makes me laugh. "You're right. But I doubt they want anything to do with me now. I kept waffling, going back and forth. I'm sure they are sick of my shit."

"Maybe they like waffles," she says, nudging my shoulder.

"Wow. That was fucking terrible. Just, wow."

"Whatever. I spend all day with young children. My sense of humor is now catered toward the Sesame Street crowd."

"I'm sure they get your best material."

"Hey, I love you and I want you to be happy. Maybe it takes two men to make that happen. Big Boobie Brook is a whole lotta woman."

"That is true." I look down at my cleavage and give it a shake.

"Come on. Let's finish up this bed and then I have some berry tarts waiting in the kitchen. Then I can break the real tricky news to you."

"What's that?"

"When you do start something new, I think you should tell Josh's family."

"Ugh, Ebie come on," I groan, using her childhood nickname. "I know you're right, but come on."

"Brook."

"I know."

"He was a piece of crap. I will never make excuses for him, but his family really welcomed us. Especially when they found out about Mom and Dad. Those white people were ready to take us Lewis girls in. I don't think you *owe them*, owe them, but tell them. Let them know you've found love. I think they want you to be happy too."

"With two dudes."

"Listen, Mr. Delinsky is a fucking hippie. He might be into that shit."

"You're right. I'll tell them if Vaughn and Shaw take me back. Or take me for real in the first place."

"One step at the time," Liz says with a wink. We finish making the bed and I get into my pajamas before we head back to the kitchen and stuff ourselves with berry tarts and fresh lemonade. Whatever happens down the road, I am grateful for my sister and her baking ass. Spending the weekend with her, Silas and the girls is exactly what I need. It'll give me time to decide if I want to take the biggest risk of my life and really chase after love.

TWENTY-ONE

Shaw

We stop at a light. First light I've seen in this tiny-ass town. I have no idea how the hell Brook's sister is from the Bronx and is now living way the hell out here. I thought Barnstable was rural.

I look over at Vaughn and he just smiles and shakes his head.

"What?"

"Nothing."

"Look, I might be driving, but I didn't make this decision by myself. She called and we both jumped at the chance to see her."

"I know. I think we're both pathetic. We didn't even make it the whole weekend." Brooklyn called us back Friday afternoon. She was close to tears and extremely apologetic, but she'd managed to keep it together while she spoke. She had more to tell us. She wanted to see us again. She wanted to talk. Just to talk, though. No sex, just talking. After a quick look at the map, we saw it actually made more sense for us to go to her sister's farm in Ghent, New York, instead of waiting until the following weekend for her to drive all the way out to my place. It was closer and if Vaughn and I weren't bullshitting, we didn't want to wait to see her either. If she was in Ghent, that's where we were going first thing Sunday morning.

I follow the GPS route through a town center that looks like some shit out of a movie and we keep going, past a rundown gas station and on into this area that looks like it's all farms. Just apple farm after apple farm. Finally, we reach our destination, McInroy Farm.

We follow Brook's additional directions and drive past the big apple sign and the cafe, and head a couple hundred yards to a private, unmarked driveway. We continue down the long dirt road and, soon enough, we see a little pond with some trees and a picnic table. We see the big white farmhouse she'd mentioned further down the road, but Brook is sitting on the picnic table in the shade. Waiting for us. There are two dogs sniffing through the grass around her.

Brook perks up as we get closer. She's wearing her hair in this long, silky style that goes down her back and a pink sundress that is doing nothing to contain her amazing tits. I try to push down the way I feel about seeing her again. I'll get excited if this turns out to not be another conversation that leaves me or Vaughn looking like assholes. I park the car in a little clearing and cut the ignition.

"You ready?" I ask.

"Yeah."

"Let's get this over with. I can get home to get some FIFA action."

"Shut up," Vaughn laughs. He knows I'm not rushing out of here. We climb out of the car and one of the dogs, a white pit bull, comes rushing over to us. Before I have to dropkick it, though, it stops short and cocks its head before running back to Brook.

"That's Morty. He's harmless. The golden is Dirt."

"Who named that dog Dirt?" I ask.

"My niece, when she was four. Her dad thinks it's hilarious. So, he's still Dirt." She climbs off the picnic table and walks closer to us, but stops herself before she gets too close. "Glad you guys could make it. Welcome to the farm."

"It's nice out here."

"Yeah, it takes a little getting used to. It's kinda like the Cape but no ocean right outside your door. It's nice to get away up here. But please, step into my office." She motions toward the picnic table. We all take a seat under the shade of a seven-hundred-year-old tree, Brook across from the two of us. It's hot out, but not so hot I can't handle it.

"So," Brook folds her hands on the table all formal and shit, then smiles. "Thank you both for joining me today. I know you're very busy. It means a lot to me that you came all this way."

"It is easier for the three of us to talk face to face," I say.

"It is. That's why I asked you to come."

Vaughn feels bad. I can tell by the way he reaches out and squeezes Brook's trembling hands. "Go ahead."

She takes a breath and then smiles again. "I have a proposal for the two of you. It can best be summed up by the lyrics to "Baby, Baby" by the incomparable, God-fearing Amy Grant."

"I don't know that song," I say.

"He's lying," Vaughn says. "I know he knows that song. My mom loves that song and he's sung that song with her more than once."

The smile that touches her lips is more genuine now. "Well, I think the next best thing are my own words. I was thinking about all the conversations we've had and how we've talked so much about the different ways, well, we want Shaw to fuck us. And that was great. Swell even. Shaw, you're a good lay," she says.

"I'll add that to my resume."

"You should. Vaughn, You're not too shabby either."

"Thank you."

"I don't think it's really helpful to talk too much about before we met because everything's different now. Things were really different last week. So, considering how I feel *now*, here's what I propose. The three of us, if you'll have me that is. I'd like there to be a three of us, together. I'd like to give that a real try."

"Is that all?" I ask.

I know she wants to punch me, but she's letting it slide. For now. She nods instead. "Yup, Shaw." Her eyes narrow. "We all know *you* have issues." Her expression softens before she turns to Vaughn. "And Vaughny, I mean, we talked."

"Yeah," he says, like he knows he's been caught.

"I was afraid to tell either of you what I really needed because I'm still dealing with some Josh-related hang-ups. I wish those weren't an issue, but they are. But, that doesn't change the fact that what I really want, beyond you two giving it to me in both holes, is love and support. I want people to be there for me. A lot of this has been so hard because my sister has her own family now. She's there for me like always, but seeing her so happy, it made me realize how badly I want that for myself. When I told her about you guys, she also made me realize that if I wasn't afraid to give it a chance, I might be able to be really happy with you two. And then I thought about it some more and I *knew* I could be happy with you two."

"Excuse us." I stand and tap Vaughn's shoulder then nod to the car.

He rolls his eyes. "We'll be right back."

We walk through the grass to my car and I glance back at Brook as she tries to turn her attention to that dog named Dirt while we sidebar.

"What do you think?" I ask Vaughn.

"I think you're being immature as fuck right now, that's what I think."

"Man, whatever."

"Do you want to go?" he asks me. "I know why we're here. I still feel how I feel about her, but give me some time and I can get over that if you're not into it."

"No. I mean. I'm into. Shit, look at her. How could I not be into it? She makes you smile and she isn't emotionally stunted like me. Fuck, like Corrine was. Real talk, she's exactly what we both want and need. Plus we already know what we're getting into here. We got the same baggage."

"Okay, let's go tell her that."

"Wait. Let's make it look like we have more deliberating to do. She expects us to haggle a bit. Whatever you do in the courtroom."

"Man, if you don't come the hell on" Vaughn nudges me back toward the table.

"We're interested in your proposal," I say when we sit back down. "But I think you should know, I have commitment and abandonment issues that I'm thinking about seeing a therapist for."

"That's great. Not the issues, but that you've identified the issues and want to work on them."

"I think so. Vaughn and I have talked about it and it might help me be less of a dick if I know I'm working toward something stable. So, something secure, like maybe the all together-type situation you mentioned. That might could work for me."

She playfully rolls her eyes and turns to Vaughn. "And what about you?"

He clears his throat and I know what's coming. She's giving him the green light to feel his feelings. He's about to feel those big-ass feelings and I, for one, am happy for him. I know he opens up to me, but I know Brook makes it easier.

"I've been half in love with you for weeks already. I think you might be onto something. I was scared to put a name to what I want, because I wanted something more and I didn't think we could have more after—you know."

"Yeah," she smiles, tears welling in her eyes.

"We have a lot of details to work out, but I would like to give a try."

"Shaw?" she asks.

"Fuck it. Let's do it."

"Yeah?"

"Yeah. I was hoping to find a nice couple to adopt me, but I think this will work."

"Jesus," she laughs. "Well, since you're here, I would really like you to meet my sister."

"Now?" Vaughn asks.

"Yeah. If that's okay."

My first instinct is to say hell no. I remember the last time I met a mother. How Mrs. Johnson was this close to calling the cops on us. But I also remember what it was like to meet Lynetta and how she's welcomed me into her home every day since I met her son. Maybe Brook's sister is more like Lynetta.

"Sure, let's do it." We pile back in my car and drive what would have been a long-ass walk to that farmhouse off in the distance. When we get out, more dogs come out to greet us. The barking works as a perfect alarm. We don't get to the porch steps before a tall Black woman I can only assume is Brook's sister steps out on the porch. She smiles this big-ass grin and shades her eyes from the sun.

"Hey. It's hot as fuck out here. Come on in." We follow her in, past a TV room cluttered with kids' toys, back to a nice, remodeled kitchen. A swole-ass looking Brown dude with long hair and a McInroy's Farm t-shirt stands from the kitchen table and nods at us.

"Hello," he says.

"Vaughn, Shaw, this is my sister, Liz, and her husband, Silas."

We all shake hands and then take Liz's offer to have a seat. "Can I get you guys something to drink?"

"Here. Let me help with that." Her husband's a little tense in this strange way, but that doesn't stop him from grabbing the glasses that are already out on the counter.

"We have plenty to eat too, if you guys are hungry. I've been baking all morning."

We both take some of the homemade blueberry lemonade Liz offers and I help myself to two of the huge cookies that she sets down on a platter in the middle of the table. We sit and we talk. Liz is nice. And funny, like Brook. They look a lot alike, but Liz is taller. Still thick as hell, but like a stretched-out version of Brook and she wears her hair natural. She's warm and welcoming. Silas doesn't seem to have much to say, but some of the tension melts off of him after a while and it seems like he's just quiet. Still, it's clear he cares about Brook and he wants to get to know us too.

An hour later, as the conversation is still going, I glance over at Vaughn. He doesn't look back at me, but his arm comes around the back of my chair and he squeezes my shoulder. I look back at Brook and she winks at me. I don't know what to call this thing I'm feeling when I look at the two of them, but yeah, I think this thing with the three of us might work.

EPILOGUE

SIXTEEN MONTHS LATER

Brooklyn

"You okay?" I ask Shaw. He's fidgeting beside me. Liz's yard behind us is already filled with guests milling about, grabbing drinks and sampling tiny berry desserts before everything gets started. We'd wanted to keep things somewhat lowkey, since our commitment unfortunately won't be recognized by any governing body. To our surprise, almost everyone we've invited has RSVP'd yes, plus one, plus two or three. They're all here.

I turn to face him and place my hands on his chest, over the lapels of his suit. We'd had conversations about tuxedos, but he and Vaughn settled on grey and navy suits, respectively. There were jokes about how I should be wearing a medium to dark beige, after all the freaky shit we've spent the last year doing, but I couldn't be happier with the shade of white trailing behind me. This wedding dress suits me better than the one I had hanging in my closet all those months ago. I'm so happy to wear this one.

"Yeah, I'm good," Shaw says.

"Not getting cold feet on me, are you?"

He looks at me and smooths the lace cap of my sleeve down my shoulder. "Girl, if I had cold feet, I'd be halfway to Vegas by now. I'm here. Someone else is coming."

I turn around and see a red sedan driving up the road to Liz and Silas's house. We're waiting on a few more people, but most of my side of the guest list are here, including George and Kelsey Delinksy. It took some time, but when we decided to make things as official as possible, I reached out to Josh's family. Josh's mom Pattie couldn't get onboard and neither could his sister, Meredith, but Mr. Delinsky called me a week later and we talked. We talked for a long time. He's still broken up over his son. He'll never get over that, but he's happy for me and he wanted to meet my guys.

And when he'd offered to stand in for my own Dad if things were to ever get serious with the boys, I thought about the real power of love and of family and how big of a thing it is to make the choice to show up for people. I glance over and he's still talking Shep's face off. Poor man came down from the California mountains to be at Claudia's side and support me. And now he's listening to Mr. Delinksy talk about what he'd do to see Steely Dan live one more time.

The sight of Vaughn running down the front steps grabs my attention. He excuses himself as he eases around my sister, who's standing by the porch with my nieces, talking to Claudia and Rayna. Noa's over by the tire swing chatting it up with one of Vaughn's associates from his firm. Vaughn fixes his tie and smooths down the front of his shirt as he takes his long stride across the yard back to us. He takes my hand again as he squeezes Shaw's shoulder.

I admire Vaughn's restraint. He'd waited six months before he asked me to move in with him. It was hard for me to leave the borough of my heart, but moving to Boston made the most sense. Shaw was keeping his place on the Cape and it was too far for either of us to drive every weekend. After some soul searching, and then some job searching because the Boston D.A. and I don't see eye to eye on literally anything, I find a consulting gig that pays more and makes me much happier. Vaughn and I found a new apartment, a fresh start for us to share in the Back Bay. The therapist I finally start talking to thinks I'm making very healthy progress.

I had a feeling I'd enjoy living with him, but I didn't expect to fall more and more in love with him every day. I love coming home to Vaughn at night and waking up to him every morning. I love our calls with Shaw during the week and our drives to Shaw's place every weekend. Shaw refuses to move in with us and I respect his choice. He needs work space and, while therapy has done wonders for his fears that we'll leave him, it hasn't changed his ornery-ass personality. Shaw needs his own space. I love him for it. What he also needs from us is to know we'll be there, and we will. That's enough for him to agree to this special day, rings and all.

"Okay, sorry." Vaughn says, breathing hard. He goes to adjust his glasses, but the frames I finally helped him pick out are sitting perfectly on the bridge of his nose. "I drank, like, a gallon of coffee at the cafe with Silas this morning."

"You gonna be okay?" I laugh.

"Yeah, I'm good. Ready to do this."

"Shit," Shaw says suddenly. "It's my sister."

I grip his hand a little tighter as the red sedan joins the row of cars parked just off the dirt road. We invited his whole family. When his father called, just to tell Shaw that he was still very much so dead to him, Vaughn and I had done our best to let him know that he still had us. And Lynetta, Liz and Silas. He wasn't alone.

His sister steps out of her car and cautiously walks toward us.

"Hey, Chris," she says, a sad smile touching her lips.

"Hey. Um, you know Vaughn. This is Brooklyn. This my sister, Tanya."

"Nice to meet you," Tanya says.

"Likewise. Glad you could make it."

"Mom was gonna come, but when I went to pick her up, Dad—"

"It's all good."

I turn as Lynetta makes her way over. "Is this another Shaw?"

"Hi. I'm Tanya."

"I'm Vaughn's mother, Lynetta. Come sit with me. We'll catch up."

"Okay. Chris, after—"

"Yeah. We'll talk just, ya know, hang around."

She nods and glances at me. I nod, giving her the reassurance that I'm not holding any grudges before she turns and follows Lynetta over to the bar. I squeeze Shaw's hand again. He lets out a breath. Vaughn leans over and kisses him on the forehead and he relaxes a little more.

When my cousin from Texas who missed her first flight and our party the night before finally arrives we get things started. Miss Lynetta officiates, asking for our vows, and blessing our special union, this bond between the three of us, as we stand on my sister's sprawling lawn, surrounded by a circle of family and friends.

THE END

BEARDS & BONDAGE

We've come to the end of this sort of bizarre, extremely horny romantic suspense trilogy and I would just like to thank you, the readers, for going on this journey with me. I very vividly remember the night I finished writing Haven and how overwhelmed I was by the positive reception that it received. I love these characters and their dogs, and it's been an uplifting experience to write about sex, pain, love, found family and friendship in such an intense way. For now though it's time to say goodbye to Claudia, Liz, Brook, and the large bearded men who love them.

But who knows, maybe one day we'll be back at McInroy's Farm. Until then... xoxo - Rebekah

ABOUT THE AUTHOR

Rebekah Weatherspoon is still exhausted, but optimistic. Kinda.

Be on the look out for Rebekah's next book, IF THE BOOT FITS, the second in her Cowboys of California trilogy. This Cinderella inspired contemporary Western will be out Fall 2020 from Kensington Books.

Come on by and get to know more about Rebekah on her Instagram, Facebook, Twitter, or Tumblr. You can find more stories by Rebekah at rebekahweatherspoon.com

www.rebekahweatherspoon.com
author@rebekahweatherspoon.com

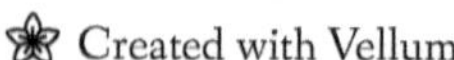 Created with Vellum

www.ingramcontent.com/pod-product-compliance
Lightning Source LLC
Chambersburg PA
CBHW021110110726
47900CB00007B/2121